Told in the East

Talbot Mundy

Contents

TOLD IN THE EAST

BY

Talbot Mundy

HOOKUM HAI

I.

A Blood-red sun rested its huge disk upon a low mud wall that crested a rise to westward, and flattened at the bottom from its own weight apparently. A dozen dried-out false-acacia-trees shivered as the faintest puff in all the world of stifling wind moved through them; and a hundred thousand tiny squirrels kept up their aimless scampering in search of food that was not there.

A coppersmith was about the only living thing that seemed to care whether the sun went down or not. He seemed in a hurry to get a job done, and his reiterated "Bong-bong-bong!"--that had never ceased since sunrise, and had driven nearly mad the few humans who were there to hear it--quickened and grew louder. At last Brown came out of a square mud house, to see about the sunset.

He was nobody but plain Bill Brown--or Sergeant William Brown, to give him his full name and entitlements--and the price of him was two rupees per day.

He stared straight at the dull red disk of the sun, and spat with eloquence. Then he wiped the sweat from his forehead, and scratched a place where the prickly heat was bothering him. Next, he buttoned up his tunic, and brushed it down neatly and precisely. There was official business to be done, and a man did that with due formality, heat or no heat.

"Guard, turn out!" he ordered.

Twelve men filed out, one behind the other, from the hut that he had left. They seemed to feel the heat more than Brown did, as they fell in line before Brown's sword. There was no flag, and no flag-pole in that nameless health-resort, so the sword, without its scabbard, was doing duty, point downward in the ground, as a totem-pole of Empire. Brown had stuck it there, like Boanerges' boots, and there it stayed from sunrise until sunset, to be displaced by whoever dared to do it, at his peril.

They had no clock. They had nothing, except the uniforms and arms of the Honorable East India Company, as issued in this year of Our Lord, 1857--a cooking-pot or two, a kettle, a little money and a butcher-knife. Their supper bleated miserably some twenty yards away, tied to a tree, and a lean. Punjabi squatted near it in readiness to buy the skin. It was a big goat, but it was mangy, so he held only two annas in his hand. The other anna (in case that Brown should prove adamant) was twisted in the folds of his pugree, but he was prepared to perjure himself a dozen times, and take the names of all his female ancestors in vain, before he produced it.

The sun flattened a little more at the bottom, and began to move quickly, as it does in India--anxious apparently to get away from the day's ill deeds.

"Shoulder umms!" commanded Brown. "General salute! Present-umms!"

The red sun slid below the sky-line, and the night was on them, as though somebody had shut the lid. Brown stepped to the sword, jerked it out of the ground and returned it to his scabbard in three motions.

"Shoulder-umms! Order-umms! Dismiss!" The men filed back into the hut again, disconsolately, without swearing and without mirth. They had put the sun to bed with proper military decency. They would have seen humor--perhaps--or an excuse for blasphemy in the omission of such a detail, but it was much too hot to swear at the execution of it.

Besides, Brown was a strange individual who detested swearing, and it was a very useful thing, and wise, to humor him. He had a way of his own, and usually got it.

Brown posted a sentry at the hut-door, and another at the crossroads which he was to guard, then went round behind the but to bargain with the goatskin-merchant. But he stopped before he reached the tree.

"Boy!" he called, and a low-caste native servant came toward him at a run.

"Is that fakir there still?"

"Ha, sahib!"

"Ha? Can't you learn to say 'yes,' like a human being?"

"Yes, sahib!"

"All right. I'm going to have a talk with him. Kill the goat, and tell the Punjabi to wait, if he wants to buy the skin."

"Ha, sahib!"

Brown spun round on his heel, and the servant wilted.

"Yes, sahib!" he corrected.

Brown left him then, with a nod that conveyed remission of cardinal sin, and a warning not to repeat the offence. As the native ran off to get the butcher-knife and sharpen it, it was noticeable that he wore a chastened look.

"Send Sidiki after me!" Brown shouted after him, and a minute later a nearly naked Beluchi struck a match and emerged from the darkness, with the light of a lantern gleaming on his skin. He followed like a snake, and only Brown's sharp, authority-conveying footfalls could be heard as he trudged sturdily--straight-backed, eyes straight in front of him--to where an age-old baobab loomed like a phantom in the night. He marched like a man in armor. Not even the terrific heat of a Central-Indian night could take the stiffening out of him.

The Beluchi ran ahead, just before they reached the tree. He stopped and held the lantern up to let its light fall on some object that was close against the tree-trunk. At a good ten-pace distance from the object Brown stopped and stared. The lamplight fell on two little dots that gleamed. Brown stepped two paces nearer. Two deadly, malicious human eyes blinked once, and then stared back at him.

"Does he never sleep?" asked Brown.

The Beluchi said something or other in a language that was full of harsh hard gutturals, and the owner of the eyes chuckled. His voice seemed to be coming from the tree itself, and there was nothing of him visible except the cruel keen eyes that had not blinked once since Brown drew nearer.

"Well?"

"Sahib, he does not answer."

"Tell him I'm tired of his not answering. Tell him that if he can't learn to give a civil answer to a civilly put question I'll exercise my authority on him!"

The Beluchi translated, or pretended to. Brown was not sure which, for he was rewarded with nothing but another chuckle, which sounded like water gurgling down a drain.

"Does he still say nothing?"

"Absolutely nothing, sahib."

Brown stepped up closer yet, and peered into the blackness, looking straight into the eyes that glared at him, and from them down at the body of the owner of them. The Beluchi shrank away.

"Have a care, sahib! It is dangerous! This very holy--most holy--most religious man!"

"Bring that lantern back."

"He will curse you, sahib!"

"Do you hear me?"

The Beluchi came nearer again, trembling with fright. Brown snatched the lamp away from him, and pushed it forward toward the fakir, moving it up and down to get a view of the whole of him. There was nothing that he saw that would reassure or comfort or please a devil even. It was ultradevilish; both by design and accident--conceived and calculated ghastliness, peculiar to India. Brown shuddered as he looked, and it took more than the merely horrible to make him betray emotion.

"What god do you say he worships?"

"Sahib, I know not. I am a Mussulman. These Hindus worship many gods."

The fakir chuckled again, and Brown held the lantern yet nearer to him to get a better view. The fakir's skin was not oily, and for all the blanket-heat it did not glisten, so his form was barely outlined against the blackness that was all but tangible behind him.

Brown spat again, as he drew away a step. He could contrive to express more disgust and more grim determination in that one rudimentary act than even a Stamboul Softa can.

"So he's holy, is he?"

"Very, very holy, sahib!"

Again the fakir chuckled, and again Brown held his breath and pushed the lantern closer to him.

"I believe the brute understands the Queen's English!"

"He understanding all things, sahib! He knowing all things what will happen!

Mind, sahib! He may curse you!"

But Brown appeared indifferent to the danger that he ran. To the fakir's uncon-cealed discomfort, he proceeded to examine him minutely, going over him with the aid of the lantern inch by inch, from the toe-nails upward.

"Well," he commented aloud, "if the army's got an opposite, here's it! I'd give a month's pay for the privilege of washing this brute, just as a beginning!"

The man's toe-nails--for he really was a man!--were at least two inches long. They were twisted spirally, and some of them were curled back on themselves into disgusting-looking knots. What walking he had ever done had been on his heels. His feet were bent upward, and fixed upward, by a deliberately cultivated cramp.

His legs, twisted one above the other in a squatting attitude, were lean and hairy, and covered with open sores which were kept open by the swarm of insects that infested him. His loin-cloth was rotting from him. His emaciated body--pow-dered and smeared with ashes and dust and worse--was perched bolt-up-right on a flat earth dais that had once on a time been the throne of a crossroads idol. One arm, his right one, hung by his side in an almost normal attitude, and his right fingers moved incessantly like a man's who is kneading clay. But his other arm was rigid--straight up in the air above his head; set, fixed, cramped, paralyzed in that position, with the fist clenched. And through the back of the closed fist the fakir's nails were growing.

But, worse than the horror of the arm was the creature's face, with the evidence of torture on it, and fiendish delight in torture for the torture's sake. His eyes were his only organs that really lived still, and they expressed the steely hate and cruelty, the mad fanaticism, the greedy self-love--self-immolating for the sake of self--that is the thoroughgoing fakir's stock in trade. And his lips were like the graven lips of a Hindu temple god, self-satisfied, self-worshiping, contemptuous and cruel. He chuckled again, as Brown finished his inspection.

"So that crittur's holy, is he? Well, tell him that I'm set here to watch these crossroads. Tell him I'm supposed to question every one who comes, and find out what his business is, and arrest him if he can't give a proper account of himself. Say he's been here three days now, and that that's long enough for any one to find his tongue in. Tell him if I don't get an answer from him here and now I'll put him in the clink!"

"But, sahib--"

"You tell him what I say, d'you hear?"

The Beluchi made haste to translate, trembling as he spoke, and wilting visibly when the baleful eyes of the fakir rested on him for a second. The fakir answered something in a guttural undertone.

"What does he say?"

"That he will curse you, sahib!"

"Sentry!" shouted Brown.

"Sir!" came the ready answer, and the sling-swivels of a rifle clicked as the man on guard at the crossroads shouldered it. There are some men who are called "sir" without any title to it, just as there are some sergeants who receive a colonel's share of deference when out on a non-commissioned officer's command. Bill Brown was one of them.

"Come here, will you!"

There came the sound of heavy footfalls, and a thud as a rifle-butt descended to the earth again. Brown moved the lamp, and its beams fell on a rifleman who stood close beside him at attention--like a jinnee formed suddenly from empty blackness.

"Arrest this fakir. Cram him in the clink."

"Very good, sir!"

The sentry took one step forward, with his fixed bayonet at the "charge," and the fakir sat still and eyed him.

"Oh, have a care, sahib!" wailed the Beluchi. "This is very holy man!"

"Silence!" ordered Brown. "Here. Hold the lamp."

The bayonet-point pressed against the fakir's ribs, and he drew back an inch or two to get away from it. He was evidently able to feel pain when it was inflicted by any other than himself.

"Come on," growled the sentry. "Forward. Quick march. If you don't want two inches in you!"

"Don't use the point!" commanded Brown. "You might do him an injury. Treat him to a sample of the butt!"

The sentry swung his rifle round with an under-handed motion that all rifle-men used to practise in the short-range-rifle days. The fakir winced, and gabbled something in a hurry to the man who held the lamp.

"He says that he will speak, sahib!"

"Halt, then," commanded Brown. "Order arms. Tell him to hurry up!"

The Beluchi translated, and the fakir answered him, in a voice that sounded hard and distant and emotionless.

"He says that he, too, is here to watch the crossroads, sahib! He says that he will curse you if you touch him!"

"Tell him to curse away!"

"He says not unless you touch him, sahib."

"Prog him off his perch!" commanded Brown.

The rifle leaped up at the word, and its butt landed neatly on the fakir's ribs, sending him reeling backward off his balance, but not upsetting him completely. He recovered his poise with quite astonishing activity, and shuffled himself back again to the center of the dais. His eyes blazed with hate and indignation, and his breath came now in sharp gasps that sounded like escaping steam. He needed no further invitation to commence his cursing. It burst out with a rush, and paused for better effect, and burst out again in a torrent. The Beluchi hid his face between his hands.

"Now translate that!" commanded Brown, when the fakir stopped for lack of breath.

"Sahib, I dare not! Sahib--"

Brown took a threatening step toward him, and the Beluchi changed his mind. Brown's disciplining methods were a too recently encountered fact to be outdone by a fakir's promise of any kind of not-yet-met damnation.

"Sahib, he says that because your man has touched him, both you and your man shall lie within a week helpless upon an anthill, still living, while the ants run in and out among your wounds. He says that the ants shall eat your eyes, sahib, and that you shall cry for water, and there shall be no water within reach--only the sound of water just beyond you. He says that first you shall be beaten, both of you, until your backs and the soles of your feet run blood, in order that the ants may have an entrance!"

"Is he going to do all this?"

The Beluchi passed the question on, and the fakir tossed him an answer to it.

"He says, sahib, that the gods will see to it."

"So the gods obey his orders, do they. Well, they've a queer sense of duty! What else does he prophesy?"

"About your soul, sahib, and the sentry's soul."

"That's interesting! Translate!"

"He says, sahib, that for countless centuries you and your man shall inhabit the carcasses of snakes, to eat dirt and be trodden on and crushed, until you learn to have respect for very holy persons!"

"Is he going to have the ordering of that?"

"He says that the gods have already ordered it."

"It won't make much difference, then, what I do now. If that's in store for me in any case, I may as well get my money's worth before the fun begins! Tell him that unless he can give me a satisfactory reason for being here I shall treat him to a little more rifle-butt, and something else afterward that he will like even less!"

"He says," explained the Beluchi, after a moment's conversation with the fakir, "that he is here to see what the gods have prophesied. He says that India will presently be whelmed in blood!"

"Whose blood?"

"Yours and that of others. He says, did you not see the sunset?"

"What of the sunset?"

Brown looked about him and, save where the lantern cast a fitful light on the fakir and the sentry and the native servant, and threw into faint relief the shadowy, snake-like tendrils of the baobab, his eyes failed to pierce the gloom. The sunset was a memory. In that heavy, death-darkness silence it seemed almost as though there had never been a sun.

"'A blot of blood,' he says. He says the order has been given. He says that half of India shall run blood within a day, and the whole of it within a week!"

"Who gave the order?"

"He answers 'Hookum hai!'--which means 'It is an order!' Nothing more does the holy fakir say."

"To the clink with him!" commanded Brown. "I'm tired of these Old Mother Shipton babblings. That's the third useless Hindu fanatic within a week who has talked about India being drenched in blood. Let him go in to the depot under guard, and do his prophesying there! Bring him along."

The sentry's rifle-butt rose again and threatened business. The Beluchi gave a warning cry, and the fakir tumbled off his dais. Then, with the trembling Beluchi walking on ahead with the lantern, and Brown and the sentry urging from behind, the fakir jumped and squirmed and wabbled on his all but useless feet toward the guardroom. When they reached the tree where the goat had bleated, the Punjabi skin-buyer rose up, took one long look at the fakir and ran.

"Well, I'll be!" exclaimed the sentry.

"You'll be worse than that," said Brown, "if you use that language anywhere where I'm about! I'll not have it, d'you hear? Get on ahead, and open the door of the clink!"

The sentry obeyed him, and a moment later the fakir was thrust into a four-square mud-walled room, and the door was locked on him.

"Back to your post," commanded Brown. "And next time I hear you swearing, I'll treat you to a double-trick, my man! About turn. Quick march."

The sentry trudged off without daring to answer him, and Brown took a good look at the fakir through the iron bars that protected the top half of the door. Then he went off to see about his supper, of newly slaughtered goat-chops and chupatties baked in ghee. His soul revolted at the thought of it, but it was his duty to eat it and set an example to the men; and duty was the only thing that mattered in Bill Brown's scheme of things.

"Maybe it's true," he muttered, "and maybe it's all lies; there's no knowing. Maybe India's going to run blood, as these fakirs seem to think, and maybe it isn't. There'll be more blood shed than mine in that case! 'Hookum hai'--'It is orders,' heh? Well--there's more than one sort of 'Hookum hai!' I've got my orders too!"

He doubled the guard, when supper bad been eaten and the guardroom had been swept and the pots and kettle had been burnished until they shone. Then he tossed a chupatty to the imprisoned fakir, spat again from sheer disgust, lit his pipe and went and sat where he could hear the footbeats of the sentries.

"They can't help their religion," he muttered. "The poor infidels don't know no better. And they've got a right to think what they please 'about me or the Company. But I've no patience with uncleanliness! That's wrong any way you look at it. That critter can't see straight for the dirt on him, nor think straight for that matter. He's a disgrace to humanity. Priest or fakir or whatever he is, if I live to see tomorrow's sun I'll hand him over to the guard and have him washed!"

Having formed that resolution, Brown dismissed all thoughts of the fakir. His memory went back to home--the clean white cottage on the Sussex Downs, and the clean white girl who once on a time had waited for him there. For the next few hours, until the guard was changed, the only signs or sounds of life were the glowing of Brown's pipe, the steady footfalls of the sentries and occasional creakings from the hell-hot guard-room, where sleepless soldiers tossed in prickly discomfort.

II.

Bill Brown, with his twelve, had not been set to watch a lonely crossroad for the fun of it. One road was a well-made highway, and led from a walled city, where three thousand men sweated and thought of England, to another city, where five thousand armed natives drew England's pay, and wore English uniforms.

The other road was a snake-like trail, nearly as wide but not nearly so well kept. It twisted here and there amid countless swarming native villages, and was used almost exclusively by natives, whose rightful business was neither war nor peace nor the contriving of either of them. It had been a trade-road when history was being born, and the laden ox-carts creaked along it still, as they had always done and always will do until India awakes.

But there are few men in the world who attend to nothing but their rightful business, and there are even more in India than elsewhere who are prone to neglect their own affairs and stir up sedition among others. There are few fighting-men among that host. They are priests for the most part or fakirs or make-believe pedlers or confessed and shameless mendicants; and they have no liking for the trunk roads, where the tangible evidence of Might and Majesty may be seen marching in eight-hundred-man battalions. They prefer to dream along the byways, and set other people dreaming. They lead, when the crash comes, from behind.

Though the men who made the policies of the Honorable East India Company were mostly blind to the moving finger on the wall, and chose to imagine themselves secure against a rising of the millions they controlled; and though most of their military officers were blinder yet, and failed to read the temper of the native troops in their immediate command, still, there were other men who found themselves groping, at least two years before the Mutiny of '57. They were groping for something intangible and noiseless and threatening which they felt was there in a darkness, but which one could not see.

Baines was one of them--Lieutenant-General Baines, commanding at Bholat. His troops were in the center of a spider's web of roads that criss-crossed and drained a province. There were big trunk arteries, which took the flow of life from city to walled city, and a mass of winding veins in the shape of grass-grown country tracks. He could feel, if any man could, the first faint signs of fever rising, and he was placed where he could move swiftly, and cut deep in the right spot, should the knife be needed.

He was like a surgeon, though, who holds a lancet and can use it, but who lacks permission. The poison in India's system lay deep, and the fever was slow in showing itself. And meanwhile the men who had the ordering of things could see neither necessity nor excuse for so much as a parade of strength. They refused, point-blank and absolutely, to admit that there was, or, could be, any symptom of unrest.

He dared not make new posts for officers, for officers would grumble at enforced exile in the country districts, and the Government would get to hear of it, and countermand. But there were non-commissioned officers in plenty, and it was not difficult to choose the best of them--three men--and send them, with minute detachments, to three different points of vantage. Non-commissioned officers don't grumble, or if they do no one gets to hear of it, or minds. And they are just as good as officers at watching crossroads and reporting what they see and hear.

So where a little cluster of mud huts ached in the heat of a right angle where the trunk road crossed a native road some seventy miles from Bholat, Bill Brown--swordsman and sergeant and strictest of martinets, as well as sentimentalist--had been set to watch and listen and report.

There were many cleverer men in the non-commissioned ranks of Baine's command, many who knew more of the native languages, and who had more imagination. But there was none who knew better how to win the unqualified respect and the obedience of British and native alike, or who could be better counted on to obey an order, when it came, literally, promptly and in the teeth of anything.

Brown's theories on religion were a thing to marvel at, and walk singularly wide of, for he was a preacher with a pair of fists when thoroughly aroused. And his devotion to a girl in England whom no one in his regiment had ever seen, and of whom he did not even possess a likeness, was next door to being pitiable. His voice was like a raven's, with something rather less than a raven's sense of melody; he was very prone to sing, and his songs were mournful ones. He was not a social acquisition in any generally accepted sense, although his language was completely free from blasphemy or coarseness. His ideas were too cut and dried to make conversation even interesting. But his loyalty and his sense of duty were as adamant.

He had changed the double guard at the crossroads; and had posted two fresh men by the mud-walled guardroom door. He had lit his pipe for the dozenth time, and had let it go out again while he hummed a verse of a Covenanters' hymn. And he had just started up to wall over to the cell and make a cursory inspection of his prisoner, when his ears caught a distant sound that was different from any of the night sounds, though scarcely louder.

Prompt as a rifle in answer to the trigger, he threw himself down on all fours, and laid his ear to the ground. A second later, he was on his feet again.

"Guard!" he yelled. "Turn out!"

Cots squeaked and jumped, and there came a rush of hurrying feet. The eight men not on watch ran out in single file, still buttoning their uniforms, and lined up beside the two who watched the guardroom door.

"Stand easy!" commanded Brown. Then he marched off to the crossroads, finding his way in the blackness more by instinct and sense of direction than from any landmark, for even the road beneath his feet was barely visible.

"D'you mean to tell me that neither of you men can hear that sound?" he asked the sentries.

Both men listened intently, and presently one of them made out a very faint and distant noise, that did not seem to blend in with the other night-sounds.

"Might be a native drum?" he hazarded.

"No, 'tain't!" said the other. "I got it now. It's a horse galloping. Tired horse, by the sound of him, and coming this way. All right, Sergeant."

"One of you go two hundred yards along the road, and form an advance-post, so to speak. Challenge him the minute he's within ear-shot, and shoot him if he won't halt. If he halts, pass him along to Number Two. Number Two, pass him along to the guardroom, where I'll deal with him! Which of you's Number One? Number One, then--forward--quick--march!"

The sentry trudged off in one direction, and Bill Brown in another. The sentry concealed itself behind a rock that flanked the road, and Brown spent the next few minutes in making the guard "port arms," and carefully inspecting their weapons with the aid of a lantern. He had already inspected there once since supper, but he knew the effect that another inspection would be likely to produce. Nothing goes further toward making men careful and ready at the word than incessant and unexpected but quite quietly performed inspection of minutest details.

He produced the effect of setting the men on the qui vive without alarming them.

Suddenly, the farthest advanced sentry's challenge rang out.

"Frie-e-e-end!" came the answer, in nasal, high-pitched wail, but the galloping continued.

"Halt, I tell you!" A breech-bolt clicked, and then another one. They were little sounds, but they were different, and the guard could hear them plainly. The galloping horse came on.

"Cra-a-a-ack!" went the sentry's rifle, and the flash of it spurted for an instant across the road, like a sheet of lightning. And, just as lightning might, it showed an instantaneous vision of a tired gray horse, foam-flecked and furiously ridden, pounding down the road head-on. The vision was blotted by the night again before any one could see who rode the horse, or what his weapons were--if any--or form a theory as to why he rode.

But the winging bullet did what the sentry's voice had failed to do. There came a clatter of spasmodic hoof-beats, an erratic shower of sparks, a curse in clean-lipped decent Urdu; a grunt, a struggle, more sparks again, and then a thud, followed by a devoutly worded prayer that Allah, the all-wise provider of just penalties, might blast the universe.

"Stop talkin'!" said the sentry, and a black-bearded Rajput rolled free, and looked up to find a bayonet-point within three inches of his eye.

"Poggul!" snarled the Mohammedan.

"Poggul's no password!" said the sentry. "Neither to my good-nature nor to nothing else. Put up your 'ands, and get on your feet, and march! Look alive, now! Call me a fool, would yer? Wait till the sergeant's through with yer, and see!"

The Rajput chose to consider a retort beneath his dignity. He rose, and took one quick look at the horse, which was still breathing.

"Your bayonet just there," he said, "and press. So he will die quickly."

The sentry placed his bayonet-point exactly where directed, and leaned his weight above it. The horse gave a little shudder, and lay still.

"Poggul!" said the Rajput once again. And this time the sentry looked and saw cold steel within three inches of his eye!

"Your rifle!" said the Rajput. "Hand it here!"

And, to save his eyesight, the sentry complied, while the Rajput's ivory-white teeth grinned at him pleasantly.

"Now, hands to your sides! Attention! March!" the Rajput ordered, and with his own bayonet at his back the sentry had to march, whether he wanted to or not, by the route that the other chose, toward the guardroom. The Rajput seemed to know by instinct where the second sentry stood although the man's shape was quite invisible against the night. He called out, "Friend!" again as he passed him, and the sentry hearing the first sentry's footsteps, imagined that the real situation was reversed.

So, out of a pall of blackness, to the accompanying sound of rifles being brought up to the shoulder, a British sentry--feeling and looking precisely like a fool-- marched up to his own guardroom, with a man who should have been his prisoner in charge of him.

"Halt!" commanded Brown. "Who or what have you got there, Stanley?"

"Stanley is my prisoner at present!" said a voice that Brown vaguely recognized.

He stepped up closer, to make sure.

"What, you? Juggut Khan!"

"Aye, Brown sahib! Juggut Khan--with tidings, and a dead gray horse on which to bear them! If this fool could only use his bayonet as he can shoot, I think I would be dead too. His brains, though, are all behind his right eye. Tie him up, where no little child can come and make him prisoner!"

"Arrest that man!" commanded Brown, and two men detached themselves from the end of the guard, and stood him between them, behind the line.

"Here's his rifle!" smiled Juggut Khan, and Brown received it with an ill grace.

"How did you get past the other sentry?" he asked.

"Oh, easily! You English are only brave; you have no brains. Sometimes one part of the rule is broken, but the other never. You are not always brave!"

"I suppose you're angry because he killed your horse?"

"I am angry, Brown sahib, for greater happenings than that! The man conceivably was right, since I did not halt for him, and I suppose he had his orders. I am angry because the standard of rebellion is raised, and because of what it means to me!"

"Are you drunk, Juggut Khan?"

"Your honor is pleased to be humorous? No, I am not drunk. Nor have I eaten opium. I have eaten of the bread of bitterness this day, and drunk of the cup of gall. I have seen British officers--good, brave fools, some of whom I knew and loved--killed by the men they were supposed to lead. I have seen a barracks burning, and a city given over to be looted. I have seen white women--nay, sahib, steady!--I have seen them run before a howling mob, and I have seen certain of them shot by their own husbands!"

"Quietly!" ordered Brown. "Don't let the men hear!"

"One of them I slew myself, because her husband, who was wounded, sent me to her and bade me kill her. She died bravely. And certain others I have hidden where the mutineers are not likely to discover them at present. I ride now for succor--or, I rode, rather, until your expert marksman interfered with me! I now need another horse."

"You mean that the native troops have mutinied?" "I mean rather more than that, sahib. Mohammedans and Hindus are as one, and the crowd is with them. This is probably the end of the powder-train, for, from what I heard shouted by the mutineers, almost the whole of India is in revolt already!"

"Why?"

"God knows, sahib! The reason given is that the cartridges supplied are greased with the blended fat of pigs and cows, thus defiling both Hindu and Mohammedan alike. But, if you ask me, the cause lies deeper. In the meantime, the rebels have looted Jailpore and burned their barracks, and within an hour or two they will start along this road for Bholat, which they have a mind to loot likewise. My advice to you is retire at once. Get me another horse from somewhere, that I may carry warning. Then follow me as fast as you and your men can move."

"Bah!" said Brown. "They'll find General Baines to deal with them at Bholat."

"Who knows yet how many in Bholat have not risen? Are you positive that the garrison there has not already been surrounded by rebels? I am not! I would not be at all surprised to learn that General Baines is so busy defending himself that he can not move in any direction. And--does your honor mean to hold this guardroom here against five thousand?"

"I mean to obey my orders!" answered Brown.

"And your orders are?"

"My orders!"

"Would they preclude the provision of another horse for me?"

"There's a village about a mile away, down over yonder, where I think you'll find a decent horse--along that road there."

"And your honor's orders would possibly permit a certain payment for the horse?"

"Positively not!" said Brown.

"Then--'

"To seize a horse, for military use, under the spur of necessity, and after giving a receipt for it, would be in order."

"So I am to spend the night wandering around the countryside, in a vain endeavor to--"

But Brown was doing mathematics in his head. Two men to guard prisoners, two on guard at the crossroads, two at the guardroom door--six from twelve left six, and six were not enough to rape a countryside.

"Guard!" he ordered. "Release that prisoner. Now, you Stanley, let this be a lesson to you, and remember that I only set you free because I'd have been short-handed otherwise. Number One! Stand guard between the clink and the guardroom door. Keep an eye on both. The remainder--form two-deep. Right turn! By the left, quick-march! Left wheel!... Now," he said, turning to Juggut Khan, "if you'll come along I'll soon get a horse for you!"

The Rajput strode along beside him, and gave him some additional information as they went, Brown taking very good care all the time to keep out of earshot of the men and to speak to Juggut Khan in low tones. He learned, among other things, that Juggut Khan had lost every anna that he owned, and had only escaped with his life by dint of luck and swordship and most terrific riding.

"Are all of you Rajputs loyal?" asked Brown.

"I know not. I know that I myself shall stay loyal until the end!"

"Well--the end is not in doubt. There can only be one end!" commented Brown.

"Of a truth, sahib, I believe that you are right. There can only be one end. This night is not more black, this horizon is no shorter, than the outlook!"

"Then, you mean--"

"I mean, sahib, that this uprising is more serious than you--or any other Englishman--is likely to believe. I believe that the side I fight for will be the losing side."

"And yet, you stay loyal?"

"Why not?"

"All the same, Juggut Khan--I'm not emotional, or a man of many words. I don't trust Indians as a rule! I--but--here--will you shake hands?"

"Certainly, sahib!" said the Rajput. "We be two men, you and I! Why should the one be loyal and the other not?"

"When this is over," said Brown, "if it ends the way we want, and we're both alive, I'd like to call myself your friend!"

"I have always been your friend, sahib, and you mine, since the day when you bandaged up a boy and gave him your own drinking-water and carried him in to Bholat on your shoulder, twenty miles or more."

"Oh, as for that--any other man would have done the same thing. That was nothing!"

"Strange that when a white man does an honorable deed he lies about it!" said Juggut Khan. "That was not nothing, sahib, and you know it was not nothing! You know that from the heat and the exertion you were ill for more than a month afterward. And you know that there were others there, of my own people, who might have done what you did, and did not!"

"But, hang it all! Why drag up a little thing like this?"

"Because, sahib, I might have no other opportunity, and--"

"Well? And what?"

"And the Rajput boy whom you carried was my son!"

III.

The finding of a remount for Juggut Khan was not so troublesome as might have been supposed. The rumors and plans and whispered orders for the coming struggle had been passed around the countryside for months past, and every man who owned a horse had it stalled safely near him, for use when the hour should come.

There were country-ponies and Arabs and Kathiawaris and Khaubulis among which to pick, and though the average run of them was worse than merely bad, and though both best and worst were hidden away whenever possible, good horses were discoverable. Within an hour, Bill Brown; with the aid of his men, had routed out a Khaubuji stallion for Juggut Khan, one fit to carry him against time the whole of the way to Bholat.

The Rajput mounted him where Brown unearthed him, and watched the signing of a scribbled-out receipt with a cynical smile.

"If he comes to claim his money for the horse," said Juggut Khan, "I--even I, who am penniless--will pay him. Good-by, Brown sahib!" He leaned over and grasped the sergeant by the hand. "Take my advice, now. I know what is happening and what has happened. Fall back on Bholat at once. Hurry! Seize horses or even asses for your men, and ride in hotfoot. Salaam!"

He drove his right spur in, wheeled the horse and started across country in the direction of Bholat at a hand-gallop, guiding himself solely by the soldier's sixth sense of direction, and leaving the problem of possible pitfalls to the horse.

"If what he says is true," said Brown, as the clattering hoof-beats died away, "and I'm game to take my oath he wouldn't lie to me, I'd give more than a little to have him with me for the next few hours!"

The men came clustering round him now, anxious for an explanation. They had held their tongues while Juggut Khan was there, because they happened to know Brown too well to do otherwise. He would have snubbed any man who dared to question him before the Indian. But, now that the Indian was gone, curiosity could stay no longer within bounds.

"What is it, Sergeant? Anything been happening? What's the news? What's that I heard him say about rebellion? They're a rum lot, them Rajputs. D'you think he's square? Tell us, Sergeant!"

"Listen, then. Rebellion has broken out. The native barracks at Jailpore have been burned, and all the English officers are killed--or so says Juggut Khan. He's riding on, to carry the news to General Baines. He says that the mutineers are planning to come along this way some time within the next few hours!"

"What are we going to do, then?"

"That's my business! I'm in command here!"

"Yes, but, Sergeant--aren't you going back to Bholat? Aren't you going to follow him? Are you going to stay here and get cut up? We'll get caught here like rats in a trap!"

"Are you giving orders here?" asked Brown acidly. "Fall in! Come on, now! Hurry! 'Tshun--eyes right--ri'--dress. Eyes--front. Ri'--turn. By the left--quick--march! Silence, now! Left! Left! Left!"

He marched them back toward the crossroads without giving them any further opportunity to remonstrate or ask for information.

It was not until he reached the crossroads, without being challenged, that he showed any sign of being in any way disturbed.

"Sentry!" he shouted. "Sentry!"

But there was no answer.

"Halt!" he ordered, and he himself went forward to investigate. The blackness swallowed him, but the men could hear him move, and they heard him fall. They heard him muttering, too, within ten paces of them. Then they heard his order.

"Bring a light here, some one."

One man produced a piece of candle, struck a match and lit it. A moment later they had all broken order, and were standing huddled up together like a frightened flock of sheep, peering through dancing, candle-lit shadows at something horrible that Brown was handling.

"What is it, Sergeant?"

"What in hell's happened?"

"Who was that swearing?" inquired Brown, with a sudden look up across his shoulder. "You, Taylor? You again? Swearing in the presence of death? Talking of hell, with your two comrades lying dead at the crossroads, and you like to follow both o' them at any minute?"

Both of the guards lay dead. They lay quite neatly, side by side, without a sign about them to show that they had met with violence. Brown rolled one body over, though, and then the cause of death became more obvious. A stream of blood welled out of the man's back, from between the shoulder-blades--warm blood, that had not even started to coagulate.

"They've been dead about three minutes!" commented Brown, rising, and wiping his hands in the road-dust to get the blood off them. "Pick 'em up. Carefully, now! Frog-march 'em, face-downwards. That's better! Now, forward. Quick, march!"

The procession advanced toward the guardhouse in grim silence, and once again there was no challenge when there should have been. The lamp was still burning in the guardroom, for they could see it plainly as they drew nearer, but there was no noise of a sentry's footfalls, or hoarse "Halt!" and "Who comes there?"

Nor was there any sign yet of the man whom Brown had left to guard both "clink" and guardroom. Brown let them take their dead comrades into the guardroom first, then set two fresh guards at the door, and covered up the bodies with a sheet before commencing to investigate.

He started off toward the cell where he had imprisoned the fakir. He went by himself, and no one volunteered to go with him.

He had gone five yards when the second explanation met his eyes. This time there was no need to stoop down, nor to turn any body over. The sentry whom he had left to guard both cell and guardroom stood bolt upright, with his mouth and his eyes wide open; skewered to the wall of the guardhouse by an iron spike, which pierced his chest.

"A lamp and four men here!" ordered Brown, without waiting to let the horror of the sight sink in. "Take that poor chap down, and lay him in the guardroom beside the others. How? How should I know? Pull it out, or break it off--I don't care which; don't leave him there, that's all."

He walked on toward the cell-door, while they labored, and fingered gingerly around the spike, which must have been driven through the sentry's chest with a hammer.

"I thought as much!" he muttered. And, though he had not thought as much, he might have done so. "I knew that a man who could maim his own body in that way was capable of any crime in the calendar!"

The door of the cell stood open, and there was no sign of any fakir, or of any one who might have helped him go--nothing but an empty cell, with the haunting smell of the fakir still abiding in it.

Bill Brown spat, and closed the cell-door.

"I'm thinking that Juggut Khan told nothing but the truth," he muttered. "Things look right, don't they, if that's so! Obey, Obey! I'd have liked to see England just once again--I would indeed. If I could only see her just once. If I'd a letter from her, or her picture. This is a rotten, rat-in-a-hole, lonely, uncreditable way to die! I wish Juggut Khan were here. I'd have somebody to help me keep my good courage up in that case."

The lock on the cell-door was broken, so he only closed it, then started back toward the guardroom.

"Three rifles, and three ammunition pouches gone!" he muttered. "That's three weapons they've got, in any case. A hornet's nest'd be better stopping in than this place."

He overtook the men who were carrying in the nail-killed sentry, and he saw that their faces were drawn and white. So were those of the other men, who were clustered in the guardroom door.

"What next, Sergeant? Hadn't we better be quick? Why not burn the place? That'd do instead o' buryin' the dead ones, and it'd give us a light to get away by. Might serve as a beacon, too. Might fetch assistance!"

It was evident that panic had set in.

"Fall in!" commanded Brown, and his straight back took on a curve that meant straightness to the nth power.

"'Tshun! Ri'--dress! Eyes--front!"

He glared at them for just about one minute before he spoke, and during that minute each man there realized that what was coming would be quite irrevocable.

"I'm sergeant here. My orders are to hold this post until relieved. Therefore--and I hope there's no man here holds any other notion; I hope it for his own sake!--until we are relieved, we're going to hold it! Moreover, this command is going to be a real command, from now on. It's going to buck up. I'm going to put some ginger in it. There are three dead men here to be avenged, and I'm going to avenge 'em, or make you do it! And if any man imagines he's going to help himself by feeling afraid, let me assure him that the only thing he needs to fear is me! I've a right to command men--I know how--I intend to do it. And if I've got to make men first out of whey-faced cowards, why, I'm game to do it, and this is just where I begin! Now! Anybody got a word to say?"

There was grim silence.

"Good! I'll assume, then, until I'm contradicted, that you're all brave men. Into the guardroom with you!"

"Sahib! Sahib!" said a voice beside him.

"Well? What?"

It was the Beluchi interpreter who had carried the lamp for him that evening when he arrested the fakir.

"Run, sahib! It is time to run away!"

"Go on, then! Why don't you run?"

"I am afraid, sahib."

"Of what?"

"Of the men who slew the soldiers. Sahib! Remember what the fakir said. You will be pegged out on an anthill, sahib, when you have been beaten. Run, while there is yet time!"

"Did you see them kill my men?"

"Nay, sahib!"

"How was that?"

"I ran away and hid, sahib."

"How many were there?"

"Very many. The Punjabi skin-buyer brought them."

"He did, did he? Very well! Did he go off with the fakir?"

"I think he did. I did not see."

"Well, we'll suppose he did, then. And when the day breaks; we'll suppose that we can find him, and we'll go in search of him, and I wouldn't like to be that Punjabi when I do find him! Get into the guard-room, and wait in there until I give you leave to stir."

IV.

An Indian city that has yet to have its mysterie's laid bare and banished by electric light is a stage deliberately set for massacre. The bazaars run criss-crosswise; any way at all save parallel, and anyhow but straight. Between them lies always a maze of passages, and alleys, deep sided, narrow, overhung by trellised windows and loopholed walls and guarded stairways.

For every square inch where the sun can shine there are a hundred where a man could hide unseen. Through century piled on suspicious century, no designer, no architect, no builder has neglected to provide a means of secret ingress, and still more secret egress, to each new house. And the newest house is built on secret passages that hid conspirators against the kings of men who lived before the oldest house was thought of.

After the Mutiny of '57 came broader roads--so that a cannon might be trained along them.

But in '57, Jailpore was a nest of winding alley-ways and blind bat and rat holes, where weird smells and strange unlisted poisons and prophecies were born. In its midst, tight-packed in a roaring babel-din of many-colored markets, stood a stone-walled palace, built once by a Hindu king to commemorate a victory over Moslems, added to by a Moslem Nizam, to celebrate his conquest of the Hindus and added to once again by the Honorable East India Company, to make a suitable bar-racks for its native troops.

From the rat-infested slums, from the hot shadows and the mazy back-bazaars, from temples, store-houses, shops, and from the sin-steeped underworld, there screamed and surged and swept the many-graded, many-minded polyglot rebel-lion-spume. A quarter of a million underdogs had turned against their masters. A hundred factions and as many more religions, all had one common end in view--to loot. All were agreed on one thing--that the first stage of the game must be to turn

Jailpore and, after Jailpore, India, into a charnel-house.

Around and around the burning palace the mob screamed and swept uncontrolled. Moslem looted Hindu, and Hindu Moslem. Armed sepoys, with the blood of their British officers fresh-soaked on their British uniforms, and the unspent pay of "John Company" still jingling in their pockets, danced weird, wild devil-dances through the streets, clearing their way, when they saw fit, with cold steel or wanton volleys. Women screamed. Caste looted caste. Loose horses galloped madly through the streets. Here and there a pitched battle raged, where a merchant who had wealth had also courage, and apprentices and friends to help him defend his store.

And through all the din and clamor, under and above the howling and the volleys and the roar of flames, sounded the steady thumping of the sacred war-drums. The whole sky glowed red. The Indian night was scorched and smoked and lit by arson. Hell screamed with the cooking of red mutiny, and throbbed with the thunder of the sacred temple-drums. And that was only one of the hells, and a small one. India glowed red that night from end to end!

Juggut Khan, free-lance Rajput and gentleman of fortune, had ridden out of that caldron of Jailpore. His house was a heap of glowing ashes, and his goods were tossed for and distributed among a company. But his mark lay indelibly impressed upon the town. There were three European women and a child who were nowhere to be found; and there was a trail that led from somewhere near the palace to the western gate. It was a red trail.

In one spot lay a sepoy pierced through by a lance, and with half of the lance-shaft still standing upright in him. That had been bad art--sheer playing to the gallery! Juggut Khan had run him through and tried to lift him on the lance-end for a trophy. It was luck that saved the day for him that time, not swordsmanship.

But a man who has done what he had done that day may be forgiven. There lay nine other men behind him where his lance was left, and each of them lay face upward with a round red hole in his anatomy where the lance had entered.

And from the point where he had broken his lance and left it, up to where a self-appointed guard had refused at first to open the city gate for him, there was a trail that did honor to the man who taught him swordsmanship. One man lay headless, and another's head was only part of him, because the sword had split it down the middle and the two halves were still joined together at the neck.

There were men who claimed afterward that of the twenty-three who lay between his lance-shaft and the city gate, some five or six had been slain in brawls and looting forays. And Juggut Khan was never known to discuss the matter. But the fact remains that every man of them was killed by the blade or point of a cavalry-saber, and that Juggut Khan broke out of the place untouched.

And another fact worthy of record is, that underneath a stone floor, in a building that was partly powder-magazine-surrounded at every end and side by mutineers who searched for them, and very nearly stifled by the dust of decaying ages--there lay three women and a child, with a jar of water close beside them and a sack of hastily collected things to eat. They lay there in all but furnace-heat, close-huddled in the darkness, and they shuddered and sobbed and blessed Juggut Khan alternately. Below them the whispering echoes sighed mysteriously through a maze of tunnels. Around them, and around their sack of food, the rats scampered. Above them, where a ten-ton stone trapdoor lay closed over their heads, black powder stood in heaps and sacks and barrels. Closing the trapdoor had been easy. One pushed it and it fell. Not all the mutineers in Jailpore nor Juggut Khan nor any one could open it again without the secret. And no man living knew the secret. The three women and the child were safe from immediate intrusion!

Those three women and that child were not so exceptionally placed for India, of that date. Two of the women had seen their husbands slain that afternoon, before their eyes. They were mother and daughter and grandson; and the fourth was an English nurse, red-cheeked still from the kiss of English Channel breezes.

"If only Bill were here!" the nurse wailed. "I know he'd find a way out. There wasn't never nothing nowhere that beat Bill. Bill wouldn't ha' left us! Bill'd ha' took us out o' here, an' saved our lives. Bill--snnff, snnff--Bill wouldn't ha'--snnff, snnff--shoved us in a rat-hole and took hisself off!"

She had not yet lost her English point of view. She still believed that the strong right arm of an English lover could play ducks and drakes with Destiny. One-half of the world, at least, still swears that she was wrong, and her mistress and the other woman thought her despicable, ridiculous, unenlightened. It was a hardship to them, to be endured with dignity and patience, but none the less a hardship, that they should be left and should have to die with this woman of the Ranks Below to keep them company. She was an honest woman, or they would never have engaged her and paid her passage all the way to India. But she was not of their jat, and she was a fool. It happens, however, that her point of view saved England for the English, and that the other point of view had brought England to the brink of utter ruin.

"If you'd leave off talking about your truly tiresome lover, and would pray to God, Jane," said Mrs. Leslie, "the rest of us might have a chance to pray to God too! This isn't the time, let me tell you, to be thinking of carnal love-affairs. Recall your sins, one by one, and ask forgiveness for them."

In the gloom of the vault, poor Jane was quite invisible. The sound of her snuffling and sobs was the only clue to her direction. But her bridling was a thing that could be felt through the stuffy blackness, and there was a ring in her retort that gave the lie to the tears that she was shedding.

"The only sin I ask forgiveness for," she answered in a level voice, "is having let Bill come to India alone. Pray to God, is it? Go on! Pray! If Bill was here, he'd start on that stone door without no words nor argument, unless some one tried to stop him. Then there'd be an argument! And he'd get it open too. Bill's the kind that does his prayin' afterward, and God helps men like Bill!"

"Well--I'm afraid that your Bill isn't here, and can't get here. So the best thing that you can do is to pray and let us pray."

"I'll pray for Bill!" said Jane defiantly. "Bill don't know that I'm in India, and he surely doesn't know I'm here. But if he knew--Oh, God! Let him know! Tell him! He'd come so quick. He'd--snnff, snnff--he'd--why, he'd ha' been here long ago! Dear God, tell Bill I'm here, that's all!"

V.

General Baines was in a position to be envied. No soldier worthy of his salt is other than elated at the thought of war. Now for the proving of his theories. Now for the fruit of all his tireless preaching and inspection and preparing--the planned, pegged-out swoop to victory!

He knew--as few men in India knew--the length and the breadth of what was coming. And when two of his non-commissioned officers sent in word that the whole country was ablaze, he realized, as few other men did in that minute, that this was no local outbreak. The long-threatened holocaust had come, and he had to act, to smite, to strike sure and swift at the festering root of things, or Central India was lost.

But his hands were tied still. He knew. He could see. He could feel. He could hear. But he had his orders. That very morning they had been repeated to him, and with emphasis. In a letter from the Council he had been told that "slight disturbances, of a purely local character, were not without the bounds of possibility, due partly to religious unrest and partly to local causes. Under no circumstances were any extended reprisals to be undertaken until further orders, and generals commanding districts were required to keep the bulk of their commands within cantonments."

The countryside was up. All India probably was up. His own men, set by himself to watch with one definite idea, had confirmed his worst fears. And he was under orders to stay with the bulk of his command in Bholat! Corked up in cantonments, with three thousand first-class fighting-men squealing for trouble, and red rebellion running riot all around him though it might be quelled by instant action!

And then worse happened. Juggut Khan clattered in to Bholat, spurring a horse that was so spent it could barely keep its feet. It fell in a woeful heap outside the general's quarters, and Juggut Khan--all but as weary as the horse--swung himself free, staggered past the sentry at the door and rapped with his hilt on the tough teak panel. They had to give him brandy and feed him before he could summon strength enough to tell what he had seen and heard and done.

"And Brown stayed on at the crossroads?"

"Aye, General sahib! He stayed!"

The general sat back and drummed his heels together on the floor in a way that his aides had come to recognize as meaning trouble.

"You say that all of the European officers in Jailpore have been killed?"

"I did not count. I did not even know them all by mine or sight. I think, though, that all were killed. I heard men among the mutineers declare that all had been accounted for, save only three women and a child, and me. Those four I myself had hidden, and as for myself--I too was accounted for, and not without credit to the Raj for whom I fight!"

"I believe you, Juggut Khan! Did you have to cut your way out?"

The Rajput smiled.

"There was a message to deliver, sahib! What would you? Should I have waited while they arrested me?"

"Oh! You managed to evade them, did you?"

"At least I am here, sahib!"

The general chewed at his mustache, leaned his chair back against the wall and tapped at his boot with a riding-cane.

"Tell me, Juggut Khan," he said after another minute's thought, "what is your idea? Is this sporadic? Is this a local outbreak? Will this die down, if left to burn itself out?"

The Rajput laughed aloud.

"'Sporadic,'" he answered, "is a word of which I have yet to learn the meaning. If 'sporadic' means rebellion from Peshawur to Cape Cormorin--revolution, rape, massacre, arson, high treason, torture, death to every European and every half-breed and every loyal native north, south, east and west--then, yes, General sahib, 'sporadic' would be the proper word. If your Honor should mean less than that, then some other word is needed!"

"Then you confirm my own opinion. You are inclined to think that this is an organized and country-wide rebellion?"

"I know of what I speak, sahib!"

"You don't think that you are being influenced in your opinion by the fact that you have seen a massacre, and have lost everything you had?"

"Nay, sahib! This is no hour for joking, or for bearing of false tidings. I tell you, up, sahib! Boots and saddles! Strike!"

The general chewed at his mustache another minute.

"You know this province well?" he asked.

"None better than I. I have traversed every yard of it, attending to my business."

"And your business is?"

"Each to his trade, sahib. My trade is honorable."

"I have good reasons for asking, and no impertinence is meant. Be good enough to tell me. I wish to know what value I may place on your opinion."

"Sahib, I am a full sergeant of the Rajput Horse retired. I bear one medal."

"And--"

"I sell charms, sahib."

"What sort of charms?"

"All sorts. But principally charms against the evil eye, and the red sickness, and death by violence. But, also love-charms now and then, and now and then a death-charm to a man who has an enemy and lacks swordsmanship or courage. I trade with each and every man, sahib, and listen to the talk of each, and hold my tongue!"

"Strange trade for a soldier, isn't it?"

"Would you have me a robber, sahib? Or shall I sweep the streets--I, who have led a troop before now? Nay, sahib! A soldier can fight, and can do little else. When the day comes that the Raj has no more need of him--or thinks that it has no more need of him--he must either starve or become a prophet. And his own home is no place for a prophet who would turn his prophesying into silver coin!"

"Ah! Well-now, tell me! What is your opinion, without reference to what anybody else may think? You have just seen the massacre at Jailpore, and you know how many men I have here. And you know the condition of the road and the number of the mutineers. Would you, if you were in my place, strike at Jailpore immediately?"

"Nay, sahib. That I would not. I would strike north. And I would strike so swiftly that the mutineers would wonder whence I came. In Jailpore, all is over. They have done the harm, and they are in charge there. They have the powder-magazine in their possession, and the stands of arms, and the first advantage. Leave them there, then, sahib, and strike where you are not expected. In Jailpore you would be out of touch. You would have just that many more miles to march when the time comes--and it has come, sahib!--to join forces with the next command, and hit hard at the heart of things."

"And the heart of things is--"

"Delhi!"

"You display a quite amazing knowledge of the game."

"I am a soldier, sahib!"

"You would leave Jailpore, then, to its fate?"

"Jailpore has already met its fate, sahib. The barracks are afire, and the city has been given over to be looted. Reckon no more with Jailpore! Reckon only of the others. Listen, sahib! Has any message come from the next command? No? Then why? Think you that even a local outbreak could occur without some message being sent to you, and to the next division south of you? Why has no message come? Where is the next command? The next command north? Harumpore? Then why is there no news from Harumpore? I will tell you, sahib."

"You mean, I suppose, that the country is up, in between?"

"You know that it is up, sahib!"

"You think that no message could get through to me?"

"I know that it could not! Else had one already come. My advice to you, sahib, as one soldier to another and tendered with all respect, is to up and leave this Bholat. Here, of what use are you? Here you can hold a small city, until the countryside has time to rise and lay siege to you and hem you in! Outside of here, you can be a hornet-storm! They will burn Bholat behind you. Let them! Let them, too, pay the price. Swoop down on Harumpore, sahib--join there with Kendrick sahib's command. There make a fresh plan, and swoop down on some other place. But move, quickly, and keep on moving! And waste no time on places that are already lost."

"Then you would have me leave those women and that child, that you tell me of to their fate?"

"Nay, sahib! I am not of your command. I have done my duty to the Raj, and I now go about my own business."

"And that is?"

"To repay a debt that I owe the Raj, sahib!"

"Your answers are rather unnecessarily evasive, Juggut Khan. Be good enough to explain yourself!"

"I ride back to Jailpore, sahib. I would have stayed there, but it seemed right and soldierly to bring through the news first. Now, I return to do what I may to rescue those whom I hid there. I owe that to the Raj!"

"You mean that you will ride alone?"

"At least half of the distance, sahib. I had a favor to ask."

"Well?"

"Are you marching north, sahib?"

"I have not determined yet."

"Determined, sahib! This is no hour for dallying! Give orders now! Up! Strike, sahib! Listen! Should you march on Jailpore, the mutineers, who far outnumber you, will learn beforehand of your coming, and will put the place in a state of defense. It may take you weeks to fight your way in! Leave Jailpore, and those who are left in it to me, and lend me that non-commissioned officer of yours who guards the crossroads, and his twelve men. With a few, we can manage what a whole division might fail to do. And you march north, sahib, and burn and harry and slay! Strike quickly, where the trouble is yet brewing, and not where the day is lost already!"

It was case of the British power in India on one side of the scale, against three women and a child on the other; sentiment in the balance against strategy. And strategy must win, especially since this Rajput was offering his services.

"What are their names, you say?"

"Mrs. Leslie, wife of Captain Leslie; Mrs. Standish, wife of Colonel Standish and mother of Mrs. Leslie; Mrs. Leslie's child--I know not his name, he is but a child in arms--and the child's nurse."

The general still found it difficult to make up his mind.

"What proof have I of you?" he asked.

"Sahib, my honor is in question! I have a debt to pay!"

"What debt?"

"To the Raj."

"To the Raj?"

"Aye, Sahib! I have but one son, and his life was saved for me by a British soldier. A life for a life. Four lives for a life. I ride! I need, though, a fresh horse. And I ask for the loan of that sergeant, and those twelve men."

"I wonder whether a man such as you can realize exactly what it means to us to know that white women are in Jailpore, at the mercy of black mutineers? I mean, are you sufficiently aware of the extreme horror of the situation?"

"Knew you Captain Collins Sahib, of the Jailpore command?"

"Know him well."

"Knew you his memsahib?"

"She was a niece of mine."

"I slew her myself, with this sword!"

"When? Why?"

"Yesterday. Because her husband could not get to her himself, and since he and I knew each other, and he trusted me. I said to her, 'Memsahib! I have your husband's orders!' She asked me 'What orders, Juggut Khan?' I said, 'Why ask me, memsahib? Is my task easier, or yours?' She said 'Obey your orders, Juggut Khan, and accept my thanks now, since I shall be unable to thank you afterward!' And then she looked me bravely in the face, and met her death, sahib. Of a truth I know! I am to be trusted!"

"I believe you, Juggut Khan. And, incidentally, I beg your pardon for having doubted you. Have you slept?"

"Nay, Sahib. And I sleep not on this side of the crossroads!"

"I don't place Sergeant Brown under your command--you'll understand that's impossible--but, it's quite impossible for him to catch me up. He may as well cooperate with you. Wait." He paused, and wrote, then continued, "Here is a note to him, in which I order him to work with you, and to take your advice whenever possible. Go to the stables, and choose any horse you like except my first charger. Here--here is money; you may need some. Count that, will you. How much is it? Four hundred rupees? Write out a receipt for it. Now, good luck to you, Juggut Khan. And if you should get through alive--I'll pay you the compliment of admitting that you won't come through without the women, and I know that Brown won't--if you should have luck, and should happen to get through, why, look for me at Harumpore, or elsewhere to the northward of it. I start with my division in an hour."

"Salaam, sahib!" said Rajput, rising and standing at the salute.

"Salaam, Juggut Khan! Take any food, or drink, or clothing that you want. Good-by, and your good luck ride with you. I feel like a murderer, but I know I've done the best that can be done!"

VI.

Now if Sergeant Brown possessed a sweetheart, and the sweetheart lived in England, and if Brown still loved her--as has already been more than hinted at--it is not at all unreasonable to wonder why he had no likeness of her, no news of her, nothing but her memory around which to weave the woof of sentiment--at least, it's not unreasonable so to wonder in this late year of grace.

Then, though, in 1857, when a newspaper cost threepence or thereabouts, and schools were so far from being free that only the sons of gentlemen (and seldom the daughters of even gentlemen, remember) attended them, the art of reading was not so common as it now is. Writing was still more uncommon. And it has not been pretended that Brown was other than a commoner. He was a stiff-backed man, and honest. And the pride that had raised him to the rank of sergeant was even stiffer than his stock. But he came from the ranks that owned no vote, nor little else, in those days, and he owned a sweetheart of the same rank as himself, who could neither read nor write. And when people whose somewhat primitive ideas on right and wrong lead them to look on daguerreotypes as works of the devil happen too to be living more than five thousand miles apart, when one of the two can not write, nor readily afford the cost of postage, and when the other is nearly always on the move from post to post, it is not exactly to be wondered at that memory of each other was all they had to dwell upon.

A journey to India in '57 meant, to the rank and file, oblivion and worse. There were men then, of course, just as there are now, who would leave a girl behind them tied fast by a promise of futile and endless devotion; men who knew what the girls did not know--that India was all but inaccessible to any one outside of government employ, and that a common soldier's chance of sending for his girl, or of coming home again to claim her, was something in the neighborhood of one in thirty thousand.

But there were other men, like William Brown, who were a shade too honest and too stiff-chinned to buckle under to the social conditions of England in those days, and who were consequently not exactly pestered with offers of employment. And a man who could see the difference between doffing his ragged cap to a dissolute squire or parson, and saluting his better on parade, could also see the selfishness of leaving an honest girl to languish for him. Brown could not get a living in England. So he told his girl to get a better man, swung his canvas bag across his shoulder and marched away.

"What kind of a man is a better man than Bill?" she had wondered. Men like Bill seem to have a knack of judging character, and of picking girls who are as steadfast as themselves. So it is not to be wondered at that almost before her tears were dry she had set about attempting what few women of her type and time would have dreamed of. If Bill had set her free, she reasoned, Bill had no more authority over her, and she might do exactly what she chose. Bill could release, but he could not make her take another man. So, for all that the local yeomen, and local tradesmen even, haunted the little cottage on the Downs, and pestered her with their attentions, no one supplanted Bill.

Bill could tell her--and had told her--that India was no country for a white woman; that there were snakes there, and black men and tigers and even worse. But, since he had set her free, if she could manage it she was quite at liberty to brave the tigers and the snakes. And, once there, she would see whether she was free or not, and whether Bill was, either!

It took Bill Brown six years of constant honest effort to become a sergeant. It took Jane Emmett six weeks of pride-consuming and vexatious vigilance to procure for herself a job as nurse in a soldier-family. And it took her six more years of unremitting diligence, sweetened by all the attributes that seem desirable when nursing other people's children and embittered by the shame of grudging patronage, before she was considered dependable enough to be recommended for the service of a family just leaving for Bengal. Then, however, her world was a real world again!

Five months on a sailing-ship around the Cape--deep-laden, gunwales awash in a beam--on Bay-of-Biscay "snorer," hove-to for a week off Cape Agul--has, while the clumsy brigantine rolled the masts loose in her, all but dismasted in a typhoon come astray from the China Sea, fed on moldy bread, and even moldier pork, with a fretful child to nurse, and an exacting mother to be pleased! Jane Emmett laughed at it. Bill had been there before her, and had done more on his way, and worse Bengal did not frighten her. Nor did the knowledge, when she reached it, that Bill was very likely still some hundreds of miles away. She, who had come five thousand miles as the crows are said to fly and nine thousand by the map, could manage the odd hundreds. And she could wait. She had waited six long years. What was another month or two?

She had not even a notion where Bill was, beyond a vague one that he belonged to another province. For when the Honorable East India Company was muddling the affairs of India, the honors and emoluments and privileges--such as they were!-

-were reserved for the benefit of the commissioned ranks.

So a transfer to Jailpore did not mean to Jane Emmett ten extra degrees of heat, the neighborhood of jungle-fever and a brand-new breed of smells. Those disadvantages, which weighted down the souls of her employers, were completely overshadowed, so far as she was concerned, by the knowledge that she was traveling nearer by a hundred leagues or so to where her Bill was stationed. She was going west; and somewhere to the west was Bill. Anything was good--fever, and prickly heat, and smells included--that brought her any nearer him.

There would be no sense in endeavoring to analyze her sensations when the sudden outburst overwhelmed the inner-guard at Jailpore. The sight of white women being butchered, and of white men with the blood of their own women on their hands, selling their lives as dearly as the God of War would let them in a holocaust of flames, blinded her. It was probably just a splurge of fire and noise and smoke and blood in her memory, with one or two details standing out. The only real sensation that she felt--even when a tall, lean Rajput flung her across his shoulder, ran with her and dropped her down through a square hole into stifling darkness--was a longing for Bill Brown, her Bill, the one man in the world who could surely stop the butchery.

The others prayed. But she refused to pray. She felt angry--not prayerful! Had she come nine thousand miles, and sacrificed six good years of youth and youth's heritage, to be cast into a reeking dungeon and left to die there in the dark? Not if Bill should know of it! And so she changed her argument, and prayed for Bill. If only Bill knew--straight-backed, honest, stiff-chinned, uncompromising, plain Bill Brown. He would change things!

"Oh, Bill! Bill! Bill!" she sobbed. "Dear God, bring Bill to me!"

VII.

When a man knows what is out against him, and from which direction he may look to meet death, he only needs to be a very ordinary man to make at least a gallant showing. Gallery or no gallery to watch, given responsibility and trained men under hire, not one man in a thousand will fail to face death with dignity.

But Brown knew practically nothing, and understood still less, of what was happening. He had Juggut Khan's word for it that Jailpore was in flames, and that all save four of its European population had been killed. He believed that to be a probably exaggerated statement of affairs, but he did not blink the fact that he might expect to be overwhelmed almost without notice, and at any minute. That was a fact which he accepted, for the sake of argument and as a working-basis on which to build a plan of some kind--His orders were to hold that post, and he would hold it until relieved by General Baines or death. But there are several ways of holding a hot coal besides the rather obvious one of sitting on it.

It would have been a fine chance to be theatrical, had play-acting been in his line. Many and many a full-blown general has risen to authority and fame by means of absolutely useless gallery-play. He believed that he would presently be relieved by General Baines, who he felt sure would march at once on Jailpore; and had he chosen to he could have addressed the men, have set them to throwing up defenses and have made a nice theatrical redoubt that he could have held quite easily with the help of nine men for a day or two. And since the really worthwhile things go often unrewarded, but the gallery-plays never, nobody would have blamed him had he chosen some such course as that.

But Brown's idea of holding down a place was to make that place a thorn in the side of the enemy. And since he did not know who was the enemy, or where he was, nor why he was an enemy, nor when he would attack, he proposed to find out these things for himself preparatory to making the said enemy as uncomfortable as his meager resources would permit, when eked out by an honest "dogged-does-it" brain.

He buried the three men whom Fate had seemed to value at the price of a fakir's freedom. And, being a religious man, to whom religion was a fact and the rest of the universe a theory, he was able to say a full funeral service over them from memory. He said it at the grave-end, with a lantern in his hand and one man facing him across the grave--as the English used to drink when the Danes had landed, each watching for the glint of steel beyond the other's shoulder.

And, four on each side of the trench that they had dug, the remainder knelt and faced the night each way--partly from enforced piety, and partly because eight men back to back, with their bayonets outward and their butts against their knees, are an awkward proposition for an enemy. They mumbled the responses because Brown made them do it, and they kept their eyes skinned because the night seemed full of other eyes, and sounds.

"And now, you men," said Brown, changing his voice to suit the nature of his task, "you can get your sleep by fours. I don't care which four of you goes to sleep first, but there are only two watches of us left, and there are about four hours left to sleep in, by my reckoning. That's two hours' sleep for each man. And we'll keep clear of the guardroom. As I understand my orders, the important point's the cross-roads. I'm supposed to halt every one who comes, and to ask him his business. And that'd be impossible to do from the guardroom here. Let this be a lesson to you men, now. In interpretin' orders, when a point's in doubt, always look for the meaning of the orders rather than the letter of them, obeying the letter only when the meaning and the letter are the same thing. The letter of our orders says the guardroom. The meaning's clear. We're here to guard the cross-roads. We take the meaning, and let the letter hang!

"Besides! The way it seems to me, if there's any more trouble cooking in this neighborhood, it's going to cook pretty fast, and it's going to boil around that guard-room; and if we're not in the guardroom, why, that's point number one for us! Leave the guardroom lantern lighted, and bring out nothing but your cartridge-pouches and the box of ammunition. Leave everything else where it lies. Quick, now."

They obeyed him on the run, afraid to be out of his sight for a moment even, trusting him as little children trust a nurse, and ready to do anything so long as he would only keep them up and doing, and not make them stay by the scene of the murders. Brown knew their state of mind as accurately as he knew the range of their service rifles, and he knew just how he could best keep panic from them. He knew too, if not what was best to do, at least what he intended doing, and he knew how he could best get them in a state to do it.

Behind his own mind lay all the while a sense of loneliness and hopelessness. He did not entertain the thought of failure to hold the crossroads, and he was so certain that General Baines would come with his division that he could almost see the advance-guard trotting toward him down the trunk road. But there is no accounting for a soldier's moods, and something told him--something deep down inside him that he could neither name nor understand--that he was out now on the adventure of a lifetime, and that the heart-cord which had held him tight to England all these years had been cut. He felt gloomy and dispirited, but not a man of the nine who followed him had the slightest inkling of it.

He halted them outside the guardroom, and bullydamned two of them because some unimportant part of their accouterments was missing; and he "'Tshuned" them, and stood them at ease, and "'Tshuned" them again, until he had them jumping at the word. Then he marched them two abreast in and out among the huts in search of any sign of native servants. They found no sign of any one at all. Though in that black darkness it would have been quite possible for half a hundred men to lie undetected. Brown decided that the camp was empty. He thought it probable that any one concealed there would have tried his luck on somebody at least, at close range as he passed.

So he marched them back to the guard-room once again, and sent two of them in to drag out the shivering Beluchi, who had taken cover underneath a cot and refused to come out until he was dragged out by the leg. The native's terror served to pull the men together quite a little, for Tommy Atkins always does and always did behave himself with pride when what he is pleased to consider his inferiors are anywhere about. They showed that unfortunate Beluchi how white men marched into the darkness--best foot foremost; without halt or hesitation, when ghosts or murderers or unseen marksmen were close at hand.

The Beluchi let himself be dragged, trembling, between two of them. It was he who first saw something move, or heard some one breathe. For he was absolutely on edge, and had nothing to attend to but his own fear. The others had to keep both eyes and ears lifting, to please Brown the exacting. The Beluchi struggled and held back, almost breaking loose, and actually tearing his loin-cloth.

"Sahib!" he whispered hoarsely. "Sahib!"

"What is it?" demanded Brown, scarcely waiting for an answer, though. Something told him what it was that moved, and his own skin felt goose-fleshy from neck to heel.

"The fakir, sahib!"

There was a murmur through the ranks, a sibilant indrawing of the breath.

"Did I hear anybody swear?" asked Brown.

Nobody answered him. All nine men stood stock-still, leaning on their rifles, their heads craned forward and their eyes strained in the direction of the gloomy baobab.

"Form single rank!" commanded Brown.

There was no response. They stood there fixed like a row of chickens staring at a snake!

"Form single rank!"

He leaped at them, and broke the first rule of the service--as a man may when he is man enough, and the alternative would be black shame.

His fist was a hard one and heavy, and they felt the weight of it.

"Form single rank! Take one pace open order! Extend! Now, forward--by the right! Right dress, there!"

He marched in front of them, and they followed him for very shame, now that he had broken their paralysis.

"Halt! Port-arms! Charge bayonets!"

He was peering at something in the dark, something that chuckled and smelled horrible, and sat unusually still for anything that lived.

"Numbers One, Two, Three--left wheel--forward! Halt! Numbers Seven, Eight, Nine--right wheel--forward! Halt!"

They were standing now on three sides of a square. The fourth side was the trunk of the baobab. Between them and the trunk, the streaming tendrils swayed and swung, bats flitted and something still invisible sat still and chuckled.

"One pace forward--march!"

They could see now. The fakir sat and stared at them and grinned. Brown raised the lamp and let its rays fall on him. The light glinted off his eyes, and off the only other part of him that shone--the long, curved, ghastly fingernails that had grown through the palm of his upstretched hand.

"How did you get here?" demanded Brown, not afraid to speak, for fear that fright would take possession of himself as well as of his men, but quite well aware that the fakir would not answer him. Then he remembered the Beluchi.

"Ask him, you! Ask him how he came here."

The Beluchi found his tongue, and stammered out a question. The fakir chuckled, and following his chuckle let a guttural remark escape him.

"He says, sahib, that he flew!"

"Ask him, could he fly with nine fixed bayonets in him!"

There was a little laughter from the men at that sally. It takes very little in the way of humor to dispel a sense of the uncanny or mysterious.

"He answers, sahib, that you have seen what comes of striking him. He asks how many dead there be."

"Does he want me to hold him answerable for those men's lives?"

"He says he cares not, sahib! He says that he has promised what shall befall you, sahib, before a day is past--you and one other!"

"Ask him, where is the Punjabi skin-buyer?"

The fakir chuckled at that question, and let out suddenly a long, low, hollow-sounding howl, like a she-wolf's just at sundown. He was answered by another howl from near the guardroom, and every soldier faced about as though a wasp had stung him.

"Front!" commanded Brown. "Now, one of you, about turn! Keep watch that way! Is that the Punjabi?--ask him."

"He says 'Yes!' sahib. He and others!"

"Very well. Now tell him that unless he obeys my orders on the jump, word for word as I give them, I'll hang him as high as Haman by that withered arm of his, and have him beaten on the toenails with a cleaning-rod before I fill him so full of bayonet-holes that the vultures'll take him for a sponge! Say I'm a man of my word, and don't exaggerate."

The Beluchi translated.

"He says you dare not, sahib!"

"Advise him to talk sense."

"He says, sahib, 'You have had one lesson!'"

"Now it's my turn to give him one. Men! We'll have to give up that sleep I talked about. This limping dummy of a fakir thinks he's got us frightened, and we've got to teach him different. There's some reason why we're not being attacked as yet. There's something fishy going on, and this swab's at the bottom of it! We want him, too, on a charge of murder, or instigating murder, and the guardroom's the best place for him. To the guardroom with him. He'll do for a hostage anyhow. And where he is, I've a notion that the control of this treachery won't be far away! Grab him below the arms and by the legs. One of you hold a bayonet-point against his ribs. The rest, face each way on guard. Now--all together, forward to the guard-room--march!"

The fakir howled. Ululating howls replied from the surrounding night, and once a red light showed for a second and disappeared in front of them. Then the fakir howled again.

"Look, sahib! See! The guardroom!"

It was the Beluchi who saw it first--the one who was most afraid of things in general and the least afraid of Sergeant Brown. A little flame had started in the thatch.

"Halt!" ordered Brown. "Two of you hold the fakir! The remainder--volley-firing--kneeling--point-blank-range. Ready--as you were--independent firing--ready! Now, wait till you see 'em in the firelight, then blaze away all you like!"

His last words were cut off short by the sound of rifle-fire. Each rifle in turn barked out, and three rifles answered from the night.

"Let that fakir feel a bayonet-point, somebody!"

The fakir cursed between his teeth, in proof of prompt obedience by one of the men who held him.

"Tell him to order his crowd to cease fire!"

The Beluchi translated, and the fakir howled again. The flames leaped through the thatch, and in a minute more the countryside was lit for half a mile or more by the glare of the burning guardroom.

The flames betrayed more than a hundred turbaned men, who hugged the shadows.

"Keep that bayonet-point against his ribs. See? That comes o' moving instead o' sitting still! If we'd shut ourselves in the guardroom there, we'd have been merrily roasting in there now! We stole a march on them. Beauty here was sitting on his throne to see the fun. Didn't expect us. Thought we'd be all hiding under the beds, like Sidiki here! Goes to prove the worst thing that a soldier can do is to sit still when there's trouble. We're better off than ever. We're free and they won't dare do much to us as long as we've got Sacred-Smells-and-Stinks in charge. Form up round him, men, and keep your eyes skinned till morning!"

VIII.

Of course, discussing matters in the light of history, with full and intimate knowledge of everything that had a bearing on the Mutiny, there are plenty of club-armchair critics who maintain that England could not do otherwise than win in '57. They always do say that afterward of the side that won the day.

But then, with history yet to make, things looked very different, and nobody pretended that there was any certainty of anything except a victory for the mutineers. All that either side recognized as likely to reverse conditions was the notorious ability that a beaten and cornered British army has for upsetting certainties. So the rebels had more than a little argument as to what steps should be taken next, once the initial butchery and loot had taken place.

For instance, in Jailpore

More than a hundred fakirs and wandering priests and mendicants had sent in word that the province from end to end was ready, and that the British slept. But there were those in Jailpore who distrusted fakirs and religious votaries of every kind. They believed them fully capable of rousing the countryside, of working on the religious feelings of the unsophisticated rustics and setting them to murdering and plundering right and left. But they doubted their ability to judge of the army's sleepiness. These doubters were the older men, who had had experience of England's craft in war. They knew of the ability of some at least of England's generals to match guile against guile, and back up guile with swift, unexpected hammer-strokes.

There were men who claimed that what had happened in Jailpore would be repeated in Bholat and elsewhere. There was no need, these maintained, to march and join hands with other rebels. Each unit was sufficient to itself. Each city would be a British funeral pyre. Why march?

Some said, "The general at Bholat will learn of the massacre, and will learn too, that not quite all were killed. He will come hotfoot to find the four we could not find. For these British are as cobras; slay the he cobra and the she one comes to seek revenge. Slay the she one and beware! Her husband will track thee down, and strike thee. They are not ordinary folk!"

There were other factions that maintained that General Baines was strong enough, with his three thousand, to hold Bholat, unless the men of Jailpore marched, to join hands with the Bholatis--who were surely in revolt by this time. There were others who declared that he would leave Bholat and Jailpore to their fates without any doubt at all, and would march to join hands with the nearest contingent, at Harumpore.

The bolder spirits of this latter faction were for setting off at once to prevent this combination. For a little while their arguments almost prevailed.

But another faction yet, and an even more numerous one, insisted it were best to wait for news from other centers.

Why march, they argued, why strike, why run unnecessary risks, before they knew what was happening elsewhere?

"Surely," these argued, "the English will hear that four here are still unaccounted for. Some attempt will be made to find and rescue them. But if we find and slay them, and send their heads to Bholat, then will the English know that they are indeed dead. Then there will be no attempt at rescue, and we shall hold Jailpore unmolested as headquarters."

That piece of logic won the day for a while, and parties were made up to explore the place, and search in every nook and cranny for the three women. and a child who surely had not passed out through any of the gates, and who were therefore just as surely in the city. A reward was offered by the committee of rebel-leaders and, although nobody believed that the reward would actually be paid, the opportunities for looting privately while searching were so great that the search was thorough.

It failed, though, for the very simple reason that nobody suspected that the huge stone trap-door in the floor of the powder-magazine had ever been opened, or ever could be opened. The magazine had been a white man's watch. White men had kept guard over it for more than a hundred years, and the natives had forgotten that a maze of tunnels and caverns lay beneath it.

So, while bayonet-points and swords were pushed into crevices, while smoke was sent down passages and tunnels and great, loose-limbed, slobbering hounds were led on the leash and cast to find a trail, the three women and the child lay still beneath the piled-up powder, and doled out water, and biscuit in siege-time measures. They lay in pitch-darkness, in a vault where not even a sound could reach them, except the whispered echo of their own voices and the scampering of the rats. They were growing nearly blind, and nearly crazed, with the darkness and the silence and the fear.

Every second they expected to see daylight through the cracks above, as rebels levered up the door, or to hear feet and voices coming through the vaults below, for doubtless the vaults led somewhere. But for their fear of snakes and rats and unknown horrors, they would have tried to find a way through the vaults themselves. But as each movement that they made, and each word that they spoke, sent echoes reverberating through the gloom, they lay still and shuddered.

Once they heard footsteps on the stone flags overhead. But the footsteps went away again, and then all was still. Soon they lost all count of time. They were only aware of heat and discomfort and fear and utter weariness.

One woman and an infant wept. One woman prayed aloud incessantly. The third woman--the menial, the worst educated and least enlightened of the three, according to the others' notion of it--stubbornly refused to admit that there was not some human means of rescue.

"If Bill were here," she kept on grumbling, "Bill'd find a way!"

And in the darkness that surrounded her she felt that she could see Bill's face, as she remembered it--red-cheeked and clean-shaven--six years or more ago.

IX.

The blazing roof of the guardroom lit up even the crossroads for a while, and Brown and his men could see that for the present there was a good wide open space between them and the enemy. The firelight showed a tree not far from the crossroads, and since anything is cover to men who are surrounded and outnumbered, they made for that tree with one accord, and without a word from Brown.

"We've all the luck," said Brown. "There's not a detachment of any other army in the world would walk straight on to a find like this!"

He held up one frayed end of a manila rope, that was wound around the tree-trunk. Some tethered ox had rendered them that service.

"Fifty feet of good manila, and a fakir that needs hanging! Anybody see the connection?"

There was a chorus of ready laughter, and the two men who had the unenviable task of carrying the fakir picked him up and tossed him to the tree-trunk. The roof of the guardhouse was blazing fiercely, and now they had fired the other roofs. The fakir, the tree and the little bunch of men who held him prisoner were as plainly visible as though it had been daytime. A bullet pinged past Brown's ear, and buried itself in the tree-trunk with a thud.

"Let him feel that bayonet again!" said Brown.

A rifleman obeyed, and the fakir howled aloud. An answering howl from somewhere beyond the dancing shadows told that the fakir had been understood.

"And now," said Brown, paraphrasing the well-remembered wording of the drill-book, in another effort to get his men to laughing again, "when hanging a fakir by numbers--at the word one, place the noose smartly round the fakir's neck. At the word two, the right-hand man takes the bight of the rope in the hollow of his left hand, and climbs the tree, waiting on the first branch suitable for the last sound of the word three. At the last sound of the word three, he slips the rope smartly over the bough of the tree and descends smartly to the ground, landing on the balls of his feet and coming to attention. At the word four, the remainder seize the loose end of the rope, being careful to hold it in such a way that the fakir has a chance to breathe. And at the last sound of the word five, you haul all together, lifting the fakir off the ground, and keeping him so until ordered to release. Now--one!"

He had tied a noose while he was speaking, and the fakir had watched him with eyes that blazed with hate. A soldier seized the noose, and slipped it over the fakir's head.

"Two!"

The tree was an easy one to climb. "Two" and "three" were the work of not more than a minute.

"Four!" commanded Brown, and the rope drew tight across the bough. The fakir had to strain his chin upward in order to draw his breath.

"Steady, now!"

The men were lined out in single file, each with his two hands on the rope. Not half of them were really needed to lift such a wizened load as the fakir, but Brown was doing nothing without thought, and wasting not an effort. He wanted each man to be occupied, and even amused. He wanted the audience, whom he could not see, but who he knew were all around him in the shadows, to get a full view of what was happening. They might not have seen so clearly, had he allowed one-half of the men to be lookers-on.

"Steady!" he repeated. "Be sure and let him breathe, until I give the word." Then he seized the cowering Beluchi by the neck, and dragged him up close beside the fakir. "Translate, you!" he ordered. "To the crowd out yonder first. Shout to 'em, and be careful to make no mistakes."

"Speak, then, sahib! What shall I say?"

"Say this. This most sacred person here is our prisoner. He will die the moment any one attempts to rescue him."

The Beluchi translated, and repeated word for word.

"I will now talk with him, and he himself will talk with you, and thus we will come to an arrangement!'"

There was a commotion in the shadows, and somewhere in the neighborhood of fifty men appeared, keeping at a safe distance still, but evidently anxious to get nearer.

"Now talk to the fakir, and not so loudly! Ask him 'Are you a sacred person?' Ask him softly, now!"

"He says 'Yes,' sahib, 'I am sacred!'"

"Do you want to die?"

"All men must die!"

The answer made an opening for an interminable discussion, of the kind that fakirs and their kindred love. But Brown was not bent just then on dissertation. He changed his tactics.

"Do you want to die, a little slowly, before all those obedient worshipers of yours, and in such a way that they will see and understand that you can not help yourself, and therefore are a fraud?"

The Beluchi repeated the question in the guttural tongue that apparently the fakir best understood. In the fitful light cast by the burning roofs, it was evident that the fakir had been touched in the one weak spot of his armor.

There can scarcely be more than one reason why a man should torture himself and starve himself and maim and desecrate and horribly defile himself. At first sight, the reason sounds improbable, but consideration will confirm it. It is vanity, of an iron-bound kind, that makes the wandering fakir.

"Ask him again!" said Brown.

But again the fakir did not answer.

"Tell him that I'm going to let him save his face, provided he saves mine. Explain that I, too, have men who think I am something more than human!"

The Beluchi interpreted, and Brown thought that the fakir's eyes gleamed with something rather more than their ordinary baleful light. It might have been the dancing flames that lit them, but Brown thought he saw the dawn of reason.

"Say that if I let my men kill him, my men will believe me superhuman, and his men will know that he is only a man with a withered arm! But tell him this: He's got the best chance he ever had to perform a miracle, and have the whole of this province believe in him forevermore."

Again the fakir's eyes took on a keener than usual glare, as he listened to the Beluchi. He did not nod, though, and he made no other sign, beyond the involuntary evidence of understanding that his eyes betrayed.

"His men can see that noose round his neck, tell him. And his men know me, more or less, and British methods anyhow. They believe now, they're sure, they're positive that his neck's got about as much chance of escaping from that noose as a blind cow has of running from a tiger. Now then! Tell him this. Let him come the heavy fakir all he likes. Tell him to tell his gang that he's going to give an order. Let him tell them that when he says 'Hookum hai!' my men'll loose his neck straight away, and fall down flat. Only, first of all he's got to tell them that he needs us for the present. Let him say that he's got an extra-special awful death in store for us by and by, and that he's going to keep us by him until he's ready to work the miracle. Meantime, nobody's to touch us, or come near us, except to bring him and us food!"

The fakir listened, and said nothing. At a sign from Brown the rope tightened just a little. The fakir raised his chin.

"And tell him that, if he doesn't do what I say, and exactly what I say, and do it now, he's got just so long to live as it takes a man to choke his soul out!"

The fakir answered nothing.

"Just ever such a wee bit tighter, men!"

The fakir lost his balance, and had to scramble to his feet and stand there swaying on his heels, clutching at the rope above him with his one uninjured hand, and
sawing upward with his head for air. There came a murmur from the shadows, and
a dozen breech-bolts clicked. There seemed no disposition to lie idle while the holi-
est thing in a temple-ridden province dangled in mid-air.

"In case of a rush," said Brown quietly, "all but two of you let go! The remainder seize your rifles and fire independently. The two men on the rope, haul taut,
and make fast to the tree-trunk. This tree's as good a place to die as anywhere, but
he dies first! Understand?"

The fakir rolled his eyes, and tried to make some sort of signal with his free
arm.

"Just a wee shade tighter!" ordered Brown. "I'm not sure, but I think he's seeing
reason!"

The fakir gurgled. No one but a native, and he a wise one, could have recognized a meaning in the guttural gasp that he let escape him.

"He says 'All right! sahib!'" translated the Beluchi.

"Good!" said Brown. "Ease away on the rope; men! And now! You all heard
what I told him. If he says 'Hookum hai!' you all let go the rope, and fall flat. But
keep hold of your rifles!"

The fakir's voice, rose in a high-pitched, nasal wail, and from the darkness all
around them there came an answering murmur that was like the whispering of
wind through trees. By the sound, there must have been a crowd of more than a
hundred there, and either the crowd was sneaking around them to surround them
at close quarters, or else the crowd was growing.

"Keep awake, men!" cautioned Brown.

"Aye, aye, sir! All awake, sir!"

"Listen, now! And if he says one word except what I told him he might say, tip
me the wink at once."

Brown swung the Beluchi out in front of him where he could hear the fakir
better.

"I'll hang you, remember, after I've hanged him, if anything goes wrong!"

"He is saying, sahib, exactly what you said."

"He'd better! Listen now! Listen carefully! Look out for tricks!"

The fakir paused a second from his high-pitched monologue, and a murmur from the darkness answered him.

"Stand by to haul tight, you men!"

"All ready, sir!"

The rope tightened just a little--just sufficiently to keep the fakir cognizant of its position. The fakir howled out a sort of singsong dirge, which plainly had imperatives in every line of it. At each short pause for breath he added something in an undertone that made the Beluchi strain his ears.

"He says, sahib, that they understand. He says, 'Now is the time!' He says now he will order 'Hookum hai!' He says, 'Are you ready?' He says, sahib,--he says it, sahib,--not I--he says, 'Thou art a fool to stare thus! Thou and thy men are fools! Stare, instead, as men who are bewitched!'"

"Try to look like boiled owls, to oblige his Highness, men!" said Brown. "Now, that's better; watch for the word! Easy on the rope a little!"

The men did their best to pose for the part of semimesmerized victims of a superhuman power. The flame from the burning roofs was dying down already, for the thatch burned fast, and the glowing gloom was deep enough to hide indifferent acting. With their lives at stake, though, men act better than they might at other times.

The fakir spun round on his heels and, clutching with his whole hand at the rope, began to execute a sort of dance--a weird, fantastic, horrible affair of quivering limbs and rolling eyeballs, topped by a withered arm that pointed upward, and a tortured fingernail-pierced fist that nodded on a dried-out-wrist-joint.

"Hookum hai!" he screamed suddenly, waving his sound hand upward, and bringing it down suddenly with a jerk, as though by sheer force he was blasting them.

"Down with you!" ordered Brown, and all except Brown and the Beluchi tumbled over backward.

"Keep hold of your rifles!" ordered Brown.

The fakir's wailing continued for a while. With his own hand he took the noose from his neck and, now that the flames had died away to nothing but spasmodic spurts above a dull red underglow, there was no one in the watching ring who could see Brown's sword-point. Only Brown and the fakir knew that it was scratching at the skin between the fakir's shoulder-blades.

"It is done!" said the fakir presently. "Now take me back to my dais again!" And the Beluchi translated.

"I'd like to hear their trigger-springs released," suggested Brown. "This has all been a shade too slick for me. I've got my doubts yet about it's being done. Tell him to order them to uncock their rifles, so that I can hear them do it."

"He says that they are gone already!" translated the Beluchi.

"Tell him I don't believe it!" answered Brown, whose eyes were straining to pierce the darkness, which was blacker than the pit again by now.

The fakir raised his voice into a howl--a long, low, ululating howl like that he had uttered when they found him on his dais. From the distance, beyond the range of rifles, came a hundred answering howls. The fakir waited, and a minute later a hundred howls were raised again, this time from an even greater distance.

Then he spoke.

"He says that they are gone," translated the Beluchi. "He says he will go back to his dais again."

"'Tshun!" ordered Brown. "Now, men, just because we've saved our skins so far is no reason why we should neglect precautions. We're going to put this imitation angel back on his throne again, so the same two carry him that brought him here. There's no sense in giving two more men the itch, and all the other ailments the brute suffers from! Form up round him, the rest. Take open order--say two paces--and go slow. Feel your way with your fixed bayonet, and don't take a step in the dark until you're sure where it will lead you. Forward-march! One of you bring that rope along."

The weird procession crawled and crept and sidled back to where it had started from not so long before--jumping at every sound, and at every shadow that showed deeper than the coal-black night around them. It took them fifteen minutes to re-cross a hundred yards. But when they reached the earthen throne again at last, and had hoisted the fakir back in position on it, there had been no casualties, and the morale of the men in Sergeant Brown's command was as good again as the breech-mechanism of the rifles in his charge.

They were scarcely visible to him or one another in the blackness, but he sensed the change in them, and changed his own tune to fit the changed condition.

His voice had nothing in it but the abrupt military explosion when he gave his orders now--no argument, no underlying sympathy. He was no longer herding a flock of frightened children. He was ordering trained, grown men, and he knew it and they knew it. The orders ripped out, like the crack of a drover's whip.

"Fall in, now, properly! 'Tshun! Right dress! To two paces--open order--from the center--extend! Now, then! Left and right wings--last three at each end forward--right wheel--halt. That's it. 'Bout face. Now each man keep two eyes lifting till the morning. If anything shows up, or any of you hear a sound, shoot first and challenge afterward!"

They were standing so when the pale sun greeted them, in hollow square, with their backs toward the fakir, who was squatting, staring straight in front of him, on his dais, with his back turned to the tree and his withered arm still pointing up to heaven like a dead man's calling to the gods for vengeance.

A little later, Brown made each alternate man lie down and get what sleep he could just where he was, with a comrade standing over him. He himself slept so for a little while. But one of the men heard something move among the hanging tendrils of the baobab, investigated with his bayonet-point, and managed to transfix a twelve-foot python. After that there was, not so much desire for sleep. The fakir either slept with his eyes open or else dispensed with sleep. No one seemed able to determine which.

When the day grew hotter, and the utterly remorseless Indian sun bore down on them, and on the aching desolation of the plain and the burnt-out guardhouse, the fakir still sat unblinking, gazing straight out in front of him, with eyes that hated but did nothing else. He seemed to have no time nor thought nor care for anything but hate and the expression of it.

At noon, three little children came to him, and brought him water in a small brass bowl, and cooked-up vegetables wrapped in some kind of leaf. Brown let him have theirs, and bribed the frightened children to go and bring water for the men and himself. He gave them the unheard-of wealth of one rupee between them, and they went off with it--and did not come back.

Meanwhile the fakir had drunk his water, and had poured out what was left.

He had also eaten what the children had brought him, and suddenly, from vacant, implacable hatred, he woke up and began to be amused.

"Ha-ha!" he laughed at them. "Ho-ho!" And then he launched out with a string of eloquence that Brown called on the Beluchi to translate.

"Who said there would be thirst, and the sound of water! Is there a thirst? Who spoke of an anthill and of hungry ants and raw red openings in the flesh for the little ants to run in and out more easily?"

The Beluchi translated faithfully, and the men all listened.

"Tell him to hold his tongue!" growled Brown at last.

"Ha-ha! Ho-ho-ho!" laughed the fakir. "The heat grows great, and the tongues grow dry, and none bring water! Ho-ho! But I told them that I needed these for a deadlier death than any they devised! Ho-ho-ho-ho! Look at the little crows, how they wait in the branches! Ha-ha-ha-ha! See how the kites come! Where are the vultures? Wait! What speck sails in the sky there? Even the vultures come! Ho-ho-ho-ho!"

"I hear a horse, sir!" said one of the men who watched.

"I heard it more than a minute ago," said Brown.

The fakir stopped his mockery, and even he listened.

"Ask him," said Brown, "where are the men who set fire to the guardroom?"

"He says they are in the village, waiting till he sends for them!" said the Beluchi.

"Keep an eye lifting, you men," ordered Brown. "This'll be a messenger from Bholat, ten to one. Mind they don't ambush him! Watch every way at once, and shoot at anything that moves!"

"Clippety-clippety-clippety-cloppety--"

The sound of a galloping horse grew nearer; a horse hard-ridden, that was none the less sure-footed still, and going strong in spite of sun and heat. Suddenly a foam-flecked black mare swung round a bend between two banks, and the sun shone on a polished saber-hilt. A turbaned Rajput rose in his stirrups, gazed left and right and then in front of him--from the burned-out guardhouse to the baobab--drew rein to a walk and waved his hand.

"By all that's good and great and wonderful," said Brown aloud, "if here's not Juggut Khan again!"

X.

It is not easy to give any kind of real impression of India twenty-four hours after the outbreak of the mutiny. Movement was the keynote of the picture--stealthy, not-yet-quite-confident pack-movement on the one hand, concentrated here and there in blood-red eddies, and, on the other hand, swift, desperate marches in the open.

The moment that the seriousness of the outbreak had been understood, and the orders had gone out by galloper to "Get a move on!" each commanding officer strained every nerve at once to strike where a blow would have the most effect. There was no thought of anything but action, and offensive, not defensive action. Until some one at the head of things proved still to be alive, and had had time to form a plan, each divisional commander acted as he saw fit. That was all that any one was asked to do at first: to act, to strike, to plunge in headlong where the mutiny was thickest and most dangerous, to do anything, in fact; except sit still.

Even with the evidence of mutiny and treachery on every side, with red flames lighting the horizon and the stench of burning villages on every hand, the strange Anglo-Saxon quality persisted that has done more even that the fighting-quality to teach the English tongue to half the world. The native servants who had not yet run away retained their places still, unquestioned. When an Englishman has once made up his mind to trust another man, he trusts him to the hilt, whatever shade of brown or red or white his hide may be.

But, since every rule has its exceptions, there were some among the native servants, who remained ostensibly loyal to their masters, who would better have been shot or hanged at the first suggestion of an outbreak. For naturally a man who is trusted wrongly is far more dangerous than one who is held in suspicion. But it never was the slightest use endeavoring to persuade an average English officer that his own man could be anything but loyal. He may be a thief and a liar and a proved-up rogue in every other way; but as for fearing to let him sleep about the house, or fearing to let him cook his master's food, or fearing to let him carry firearms--well! Perhaps, it is conceit, or maybe just ordinary foolishness. It is not fear!

So, in a country where the art of poisoning has baffled analysts since analysts have been invented, and where blood-hungry fanatic priests, both Hindu and Mohammedan, were preaching and promising the reward of highest heaven to all who could kill an Englishman or die in the attempt, a native cook whose antecedents were obscured in mystery cooked dinner for a British general, and marched with his column to perform the same service while the general tried to trounce the cook's friends and relatives!

But General Baines felt perfectly at ease about his food. He never gave a thought to it, but ate what was brought to him, sitting his horse most likely, and chewing something as he rode among the men, and saw that they filled their bellies properly. He had made up his mind to march on Harumpore, and to take over the five-hundred-strong contingent there. Then he could swoop down on any of a dozen other points, in any one of which a blow would tell.

He was handicapped by knowing almost too much. He had watched so long, and had suspected for so long that some sort of rebellion was brewing that, now that it had come, his brain was busy with the tail-ends of a hundred scraps of plans. He was so busy wondering what might be happening to all the other men subordinate to him, who would have to be acting on their own initiative, that his own plans lacked something of directness. But there was no lack of decision, and no time was lost. The men marched, and marched their swiftest, in the dust-laden Indian heat. And he marched with them, in among them, and ate what the cook brought him, without a thought but for the best interests of the government he served.

So they buried General Baines some eighty-and-twenty miles from Harumpore, and shot the cook. And, according to the easy Indian theology, the cook was wafted off to paradise, while General Baines betook himself to hell, or was betaken. But the column, three thousand perspiring Britons strong, continued marching, loaded down with haversacks and ammunition and resolve.

It was met, long before the jackals had dug down to General Baines' remains, by the advance-guard of Colonel Kendrick's column, which was coming out of Harumpore because things were not brisk enough in that place to keep it busy. Kendrick himself was riding with the cavalry detachment that led the way southward.

"Who's in command now?" he asked, for they had told him of General Baines' death by poison.

"I am," said a gray-haired officer who rode up at that moment.

"I'm your senior, sir, by two years," answered Kendrick.

"Then you command, sir."

"Very good. Enough time's been wasted. The column can wait here until my main body reaches us. Then we'll march at once on Jailpore. This idea of leaving Jailpore to its fate is nonsense! The rebels are in strength there, and they have perpetrated an abominable outrage. There we will punish them, or else we'll all die in the attempt! If we have to raze Jailpore to the ground, and put every man in it to the sword before we find the four Europeans supposed to be left alive there, our duty is none the less obvious! Here comes my column. Tell the men to be ready to march in ten minutes."

He turned his horse, to look through the dust at the approaching column, but the man who had been superseded touched him on the sleeve.

"What's that? Better have a rest? Tired out, you say? Oh! Form them all up in hollow square, then, and I'll say a few words to them. There are other ways of reviving a leg-weary column than by letting it lie down."

Ten minutes later a dull roar rose up through a steel-shot dust-cloud, and three thousand helmets whirled upward, flashing in the sun. Three thousand weary men had given him his answer! There was no kind of handle to it; no reserve--nothing but generous and unconditional allegiance unto hunger, thirst, pain, weariness, disease or death. It takes a real commander to draw that kind of answer from a tired-out column, but it is a kind of answer, too, that makes commanders! It is not mere talk, on either side. It means that by some sixth sense a strong man and his men have discovered something that is good in each other.

XI.

"You've made good time, friend Juggut Khan!" said Brown, advancing to meet him where the men and the fakir and the interpreter would not be able to Overhear.

"Sahib, I killed one horse--the horse you looted for me--and I brought away two from Bholat. One of them carried me more than fifty miles, and then I changed to this one, leaving the other on the road. I have orders for you, sahib."

"Hand 'em over then," said Brown. "Orders first, and talk afterward, when there's time!"

The Rajput drew out a sealed envelope, and passed it to him. Brown tore it open, and read the message, scowling at the half-sheet of paper as though it were a death-sentence.

"Where's the general?"

"With his column-twenty or thirty miles away to the northward by now!"

"And he's left me, with this handful, in the lurch?"

"Nay, sahib! As I understood the orders, he has left you with a very honorable mission to fulfil!"

Brown stared hard at the half-sheet of notepaper again. Reading was not his longest suit by any means, and at that he infinitely preferred to wrestle with printed characters.

"Have you read it, Juggut Khan?" he asked.

"Nay, sahib. I can speak English, but not read it."

"Then we're near to being in the same boat, we two!" said Brown with a grin. "I'll have another try! It looks like a good-by message to me--here's the word 'good-by' written at the end above his signature."

"There were other matters, sahib. There was an order. I can not read, but I know what is in the message."

"Well?"

"You, and your twelve--"

"Nine!" corrected Brown.

"Three dead?"

Brown nodded.

"Your nine, then, sahib, and you and I are to proceed immediately to Jailpore, and to gain an entrance if we can, rescue those whom I concealed there and bring them to Harumpore, or to the northward of Harumpore, wherever we can find the column."

"Eleven men are to attempt that?"

Brown was studying out the letter word by word, and discovering to his amazement that its purport was exactly what Juggut Khan pretended.

"If there are no more than eleven of us, then yes, eleven! And, sahib, since you seem to hold at least an island here where a man may lie down unmolested, I propose to sleep for an hour or two, before proceeding. I have had no sleep since I left Jailpore."

"Nothing of the sort!" said Brown. "If we're to march on Jailpore, off we go at once! You can sleep on the road, my son! It's time we paid a visit to that village, I'm thinking. Those treacherous brutes need a lesson. I'd have been down there before, only I wanted to be in full view of the road in case anybody came looking for me from Bholat. We'll need a wagon for the fakir. You can sleep in it too."

"Sleep with a fakir? I? Allah! I am a Rajput, sahib! A sergeant of the Rajput Horse, retired!"

"I wouldn't want to sleep with him myself!" admitted Brown. "Come and look at him. You can smell him from here, but the sight of him's the real thing!"

The Rajput swaggered up beside Brown, after loosening his horse's girths and lifting the saddle for a moment.

"He's not the only one that needs a drink!" said Brown. "We're all dry as brick-dust here, except the fakir!"

"He must wait a while before he drinks. Show me the fakir. Why, Brown sahib, know you what you have there?"

"The father of all the smells, and all the dirt and all the evil eyes and evil tongues in Asia!" Brown hazarded.

"More than that, sahib! That is the nameless fakir--him whom they know as HE! Has there been no attempt made to rescue him?"

"They rescued him once, and murdered three of my men to get him. When they tried again, I put a halter round his neck and he and I arranged a sort of temporary compromise."

"And the terms of it?"

"Oh, he's supposed to have performed a miracle. He made us unslip the halter, and fall down flat, and he's supposed to be keeping us by him, by a sort of spell, so's to give us something extra-special in the line of ghastly deaths at his own convenience. That way, I was able to wait for news from Bholat--see?"

"You could have captured no more important prisoner than that, sahib, let me tell you! They believe him to be almost a god; so nearly one that the gods themselves obey his orders now and then! It was he, and no other, that told the men of Jailpore that he would make them impervious to bullets. If we have him, sahib, we have the key to Jailpore!"

"We, have certainly got him," said Brown. "You can see him, and you can smell him. I'll order one of the men to prick him with a bayonet, if you want to hear him, too! I wouldn't feel him, if I were you!"

"He must come, too, to Jailpore!"

"Of course he comes!"

"Then, sahib, let us move away from here to where there is water. There let us rest until sundown, and then march, in the cool of the evening. It will be better so. And of a truth I must sleep, or else drop dead from weariness."

"Does that message put you in command?" asked Brown, a trifle truculently.

"No, sahib! But it orders you to listen to my advice whenever possible."

"That means that you are under my orders?"

"That letter does not say so, sahib!"

"Very well, are you, or are you not?"

"We are supposed to act in concert, sahib."

"It doesn't say so in the letter! Yes, or no? Are you going to obey orders, or aren't you? In other words, are you coming with me, or do you stay behind?"

"I come with you, sahib!"

"Then you obey my orders!"

"But the letter says--"

"That I'm to take your advice whenever possible! I don't need advice just at the moment, thanks! I've got orders here to march, and I'm off at once! You can please yourself whether you come with me or not, but if you come you come on my terms."

"I go with you, sahib."

"Under my orders?"

"Yes, sahib."

"All right, Juggut Khan. Here's my hand on it. Now, we'll swoop down on that village, and take the fakir with us, with a halter round his neck for the sake of argument. We'll get two bullock-carts down there, and we'll stick him in one of them, with Sidiki the interpreter tied to him. Sidiki won't like it, but he's only a Beluchi anyway! You get in the other, and get all the sleep you can. You and I'll take turns sleeping all the way to Jailpore, so's to be fresh, both of us, and fit for anything by the time that we get there!"

"I am ready, sahib."

"You two men who carried old Stinkijink before, pick him up again!" shouted Brown. "Let him feel the bayonet if he makes a noise, but carry him gently as though you loved him. The rest--'Tshun! Form two-deep--on the center--close order, march. Ri' dress. Eyes front. Ri' turn. By the left--quick march."

The Rajput strode beside Brown, wondering wearily whether it was worth his while to offer him advice or not, and keeping his tired eyes ever moving in the direction of the distant huts.

"They have rifles, sahib?" he queried.

"Lots of 'em! Three that they took from my men, among others."

"It would not be well to march into a trap at this stage."

"As well now as later." "True, sahib! And my time has not come yet; I know it. Else had I died of weariness, as my horse did."

Brown kept rigidly to that point of view in everything he did, from that time on until he reached Jailpore. He believed himself to be engaged on a forlorn hope that was so close to being an absolute impossibility as to be almost the same thing. He had no doubt whatever in his own mind but that his own death, and the death of those with him, was a matter now of hours, or possibly of minutes. His one resolute determination was to die, and make the others die, in a manner befitting their oath of service. He had orders, and he would pass them on according to his interpretation of them. He would obey his orders, and they theirs, and the rest was no business of his or anybody's.

They put the fakir in a hut; where Juggut Khan--too weary for foraging--stood guard over him. When a crowd collected round the hut, and Juggut Khan applied the butt of a lighted cigarette to the tender skin between the fakir's shoulder-blades, the anxious fakir-worshipers were told that all was well. They were to let the white soldiers take two wagons, or three even, if they wanted them. They were to return to their houses at once, and hide, lest the devils who would shortly overwhelm the white men should make mistakes and include them, too, in the whelming. He, the fakir, intended to take the white men for a little journey along the road toward

Jailpore, where the devils who would deal with them would have no opportunity to make mistakes. And, since the natives knew that Jailpore was a rebel stronghold, and that ten white men and a native would have no chance to do the slightest damage there, they chose to believe the fakir and to obey him.

Hindus have as stubborn and unalterable a habit of obeying and believing their priests--when the fancy suits them--as white men of other religions have.

If the fakir had told them through the doorway of the hut that he intended going with the white men in the direction of Bholat, they would most surely have prevented him. But it suited them very well indeed to have the white men killed elsewhere. It was not likely, but there might be a column on its way from Bholat now; and if that column came, and found the bones of British soldiers as well as a burned-out guard-house, vengeance would be dire and prompt. Between where they were and Jailpore, the white men could not possibly escape. And at Jailpore, if not sooner, they must surely die. So they believed the fakir, and retired to the seclusion of their houses.

It was wonderful, of course, but no more wonderful than a thousand other happenings in '57. All laws of probability and general average were upset that year, when sixty thousand men held down an armed continent. Even stranger things were happening than that two bullock-carts should dawdle through a rebel-seething district in the direction of a plundered, blood-soaked rebel stronghold; stranger even than that on the foremost bullock-cart a lean and louse-infested fakir should be squatting, guarded by British soldiers, who marched on either hand; or that a Rajput, who could trace his birth from a thousand-year-long line of royal chieftains, should be sleeping in the bullock-cart behind, followed closely by a black charger with a British saddle on its back, which ate corn from the tail-board of the wagon; stranger things, even, than that a British sergeant should be marching last of all, with his stern eyes roving a little wildly but his jaw set firm and his tread as rigid and authoritative and abrupt as though he were marching to inspect accouterments.

In more than a dozen places, about a dozen men were holding a fort against an army. They were using every wile and trick and dodge that ingenuity or inspiration could provide them with, and they were mostly contriving to hold out. But there were none who did anything more daring or more unusual than to march to the attack of a city, with a hostile fakir in the van, and nothing else but their eleven selves and their rifles to assist them. There is a tremendous difference between defending when you have to, and attacking when you might retire.

XII.

There were many more causes than one that worked together to make possible the entry of Brown and his little force into Jailpore. They were brave men; they were more than brave and they held the ace of trumps, as Brown had stated, in the person of the fakir known as "He." But luck favored them as well, and but for luck they must have perished half a dozen times.

They marched the whole of the first afternoon, and met no one. They only overtook little straggling parties of rebels, making one and all for Jailpore, who bolted at the sight of them, imagining them probably to be the advance-guard of a larger force. The very idiocy of marching eleven strong through a country infested by their enemies was in their favor. Nobody could believe that there were no more than eleven of them. Even the English could not be such lunatics!

That night, they rested for a while, and then went on again. During the day following they lay in a hollow between some trees and rested, and slept by turns. They suffered agonies from the heat, and not a little from hunger, and once or twice they were hard put to it to stop the Rajput's charger from neighing when a native pony passed along the nearby road. But night came again, and with it the screen of darkness for their strange, almost defenseless caravan. Once or twice the fakir tried to shout an alarm to passing villagers, but the quick and energetic application of a cleaning-rod by Brown stopped him always in the nick of time, and they came within sight of the battlements of Jailpore without an accident.

Then, though, their problem became really serious, and it was a series of circumstances altogether out of their control and not connected with them that made their entry possible. The mutineers in Jailpore had learned that Kendrick sahib was coming down on them from the north by forced marches with thirty-five hundred men or more. They were putting the place into a state of siege, and getting ready by all means in their power to oppose him.

Little attention was being paid to small parties of arrivals from no man knew or cared where. And, in a final effort to find the four who were the lure that was bringing Kendrick down on them, the city was once more being turned upside down and inside out, and men were even being tortured who were thought to know of hiding-places.

With purely Eastern logic, the leaders of the rebels had decided that the sight of the bodies of the four, writhing in their last agony on the sun-scorched outer wall, would mightily discourage the British when they came. So no efforts were being spared and no stones left unturned to find them. The hooks on the wall were sharp and ready, so that they might be impaled without loss of time in full view of their would-be rescuers.

Almost every secret passage of the thousand odd had been explored. In the hurry to run through them and explore the next one, doors had been left open here and there that had been kept closed in some instances for centuries.

One door in particular, placed cornerwise in a buttress of the outer wall, was spotted by Juggut Khan as he circled round the city on his charger at dusk on the day following their arrival. He brought his charger back to where the others lay concealed, and then went on an exploring-expedition on foot--to discover that the outer city wall was like a sponge, a nest of honey-combed cells and passages wandering interminably in the fifty-foot-thick brick and rubble rampart.

And while he searched amid the mazy windings of the wall, Bill Brown sat in the forked top of a tree and studied out the ground-plan of the city. He was imprinting landmarks in his memory for future reference, and trying--with a brain that ached from the apparent hopelessness of the task--to figure out a plan.

He knew by now that the four he had come to rescue were hidden underneath the powder-magazine, and he could see the magazine itself. But he could think of no way of rescuing them, for the city absolutely boiled with frantic, mixed-up castes and creeds picked at random, and thrown in at random from the whole of India. A mouse could not have passed through the streets undetected! And yet, from a soldier's point of view, there were certain fascinating details to be noticed about that powder-magazine. In the first place, it had been constructed for a granary by an emperor who never heard of Joseph, but who had the same ideal plan for cornering the people's food-supply. And since labor had been unlimited, and cheap, he had gone about building the thing on the most thoroughly unpractical and most pretentious plan that he and his architects could figure out. It was big enough to hold about ten times as much grain as the province could grow in any one year of plenty. And, since that was the least practical and most ungranary-like shape, he had caused it to be built like an enormous beehive, with a tiny platform at the top.

Winding round and round the huge stone dome, and on the outside, was a six-foot-wide trail, which was the elevator. Up this, each with a sack or a basket on his head, the population was to have been induced to run in single file, dumping its hard-won corn into the granary through an opening at the top until the granary was full.

The emperor died--by poison--before he could see his cherished project put into execution, but he had been a very thorough calculator, and a builder who believed in permanency. He had foreseen that when the granary was full, and the screw-jacks were turned beneath the cost of living, there would probably be efforts made by unwashed, untutored, unenlightened mobs to rape his storehouse. So he had made the little platform at the top a veritable fortress of a place, such as a hand-ful of men could hold against a hundred thousand.

There was no known entrance to the granary above ground, except on the ground level, where a huge stone gateway frowned above a teak-and-iron door. Above that door there were galleries, and fortalices and cunningly invented battle-ments in miniature, from behind whose shelter a resolute defending-party could pour out a hundred different kinds of death on a hungry crowd. The place was naturally fire-proof and naturally cool--as far as any building can be cool in Central India. It was a first-class, ideal powder-magazine, if useless as a granary; and the last new conquerors of India had hastened to adopt it as a means of storing up the explosive medicine with which they kept their foothold.

Naturally, none but White soldiers, and a very few of the more trusted natives, had ever been allowed to go inside the powder-magazine. The secret passages be-neath it had never been intended for public convenience or information. They had been designed as a means of rushing defenders secretly into the granary, and they connected with a tunnel underneath the palace that had just been burned. They also connected with the outer wall in such a way that defenders from the ramparts might be rushed there too, if wanted in a hurry. But, since there never had been corn kept in the granary, and nobody had ever had the slightest need to force an entrance, the knowledge even of the existence of the passages had become barely a memory, and there was not a man living in Jailpore who knew exactly where they began or where they ended. There was a man outside who knew, but none inside.

The point about the powder-magazine which most appealed to Brown--next after his knowledge of its contents, mineral and human--was the fact that the little platform at its summit overlooked the city-wall, and that the side of the granary actually touched the wall on the side of the city farthest from where he sat and spied it out. Ten men on that protected platform, he thought, might suffer from the sun, but they could hold the building and command a good-sized section of the city ramparts against all comers.

He noticed too, though that seemed immaterial at the time, that one well-aimed shot from heavy ordnance might crash through the upper dome and set off the powder underneath. There was no artillery that could be brought against the place, either with the British force or with the mutineers, but the thought set him to wondering how much powder there might be stored on the huge round floor below, and what would happen should it become ignited. It was a sanguinary, in-teresting, subtle kind of thought, that suited the condition of his brain exactly! He climbed down from the tree, feeling almost good-natured.

At the bottom he met Juggut Khan, waiting for him patiently.

"What have you seen, sahib?" he asked him. "Have you formed a plan?"

"I've been wishing I was Joshua!" said Brown. "I'd like to make my men march round the city and blow trumpets, and then see the walls fall down. I can think of several things to do, if we could only get inside. But I can't think how to get there."

"I have found a way in!" said Juggut Khan. "I have cross-questioned that fakir of ours as well, with a little assistance from a cleaning-rod wielded by one of your men. He knows the way too. He says he is the only man who knows it--in which he lies, since I too have discovered it. But his knowledge may help as well."

"What's that about a cleaning-rod?" asked Brown.

"It was used on him to help him forget his vow of silence."

"When?"

"When you were up that tree, sahib!"

"Have you been giving my man orders?"

"Nay, sahib!"

"How did he come to beat the fakir, then?"

"We both arrived at the same conclusion at the same moment, and the fakir received the benefit!"

"Who held him, you?"

"Nay, sahib! God forbid! I am a clean man. I listened to his conversation. The Beluchi held him."

"Oh! Well, I like you well enough, Juggut Khan, but there are things about you that I don't like. You're too fond of doing things on your own responsibility, and you're much too fond of using oaths. Y our soul is none o' my business; you're a heathen anyhow, and no longer in the Service. But, I'll trouble you not to use those disgraceful oaths of yours in the presence of the men! Do you understand me?"

"I understand you, sahib. If my respect for all your other qualities were not so profound, I would laugh at you! As it is, if your honor should see fit to turn the bullocks loose, and tie the fakir fast between two men and follow me, it seems to me dark enough by now, and I know the way. Might I furthermore suggest that the ammunition-box would make a reasonable load for another two men?"

"Hadn't we better bring our rifles too?" asked Brown sarcastically. "Upon my honor, Juggut Khan! You're getting childish! Are your nerves upset, or what? Lead on, man! Lead on!"

"Listen. There are two ways, sahib. One way leads from the burned-out barracks to the cellar where the women lie hidden. That way is closed by debris. The other way leads from the outer wall by a very winding route to the cellar where the women are. The fakir knows that way, and I do not, though I know of it. There is a third way, though, that leads from the outer wall, where I have been exploring, straight almost, if you disregard a wind or two, to the inside of the powder-magazine. It enters the magazine through a doorway secretly contrived in an upright pillar--or so the fakir swears. Now this is my notion, sahib. If we go in by the lower way, we must come out that way, and run the risk of being caught as we emerge. That risk will be greatly enhanced when we have frightened women with us whose eyes have been blinded by the darkness. But, if we go in by the upper way, and enter the magazine itself, I can make the fakir show us how to lift the stone trapdoor

I spoke of--the one that I closed when I hid the women. Then I can ascend with him, and with say four men, while you ascend to the platform at the top with the remainder of the men, and guard our rear and our exit. From the top, you will be able to see us as we emerge, and can cover our retreat, and follow."

"That sounds like a roundabout sort of plan to me!" said Brown. "Why not go straight in by the lower route, and gather up the women, and carry 'em out, and make a bolt for it?"

"Because, sahib, we will be at the fakir's mercy."

"Nonsense! He's at our mercy."

"Think, sahib! There, he will be in his own bat's nest, so to speak. These fakirs are the only men who know the windings of all the secret passages. They are the rats of religion and intrigue. At any step he might lead us into an ambush, and we might be overwhelmed before we knew that we were attacked. If we go the other way, though, I can lead the way myself, and we need only take the fakir to show us how to open the door."

"Very well," said Brown. "Let's get a move on, though! I'm beginning to think that you're a better talker than a fighter, Juggut Khan!"

"Yes, sahib? I trust there will be no fighting!" But the Rajput smiled as he said it, and thought of a certain lance-shaft which had been broken in the streets of Jailpore.

"Lead on! Fall in behind me, men! Walk quietly, now, and remember. Hold your tongues! Each man keep his eye on me, and a finger on the trigger!"

The Beluchi and the fakir and Juggut Khan moved in the van, with two men to hold the fakir. Next marched, or rather tiptoed, Sergeant Brown, followed by the other men in single file. In that order they hastened after Juggut Khan, through the darkness, across a dried-out moat and round the corner of a huge stone buttress. There they disappeared inside the wall, and a stone swung round and closed the gap behind the last of them. There was no alarm given, and not a sign or a sound of any kind to betoken that any one had seen them. Inside the walls the city roared like a flood-fed maelstrom, and outside all was darkness and the silence of the dead.

XIII.

There was some smart work done inside the powder-magazine. To be able to appreciate it properly one would be obliged to do what they did--wander through a maze of tunnels in a city-wall, blinded by darkness, oppressed by the stored-up stuffiness and heat of ages and deafened by the stillness--then emerge unexpectedly in the lamp-lit magazine, among mutineers who sprawled, and laughed; and chewed betel-nut at their ease upon the powder-kegs.

Both sides were taken by surprise, but the mutineers had the nominal advantage, for their eyes were accustomed to the light. They had the advantage in numbers, too, by almost two to one. But they dared not fire, for fear of setting off the magazine, whereas Brown and his little force dared anything. They fully expected to die, and might as well die that way as any other. And a quick death for the women down below would be better than anything the rebels had in store for them. Brown yelled an order, and the rest was too quick, nearly, for the eye to follow.

Three rebels died with bullets in them, and the rest stampeded for the teak-and-metal door, to find it locked on them, and Brown and the Rajput standing in front of it on guard. The mutineers attacked fiercely. They flung themselves all together on the two. But they had yet to learn that they were tackling, or endeavoring to tackle, the two finest swordsmen in that part of India. And when they turned, to find more room to fight in, or to draw their breath, they had to face nine bayonets that hemmed them in, and drove them closer and even closer to the swords again. They shouted, but no sound could pierce the walls or escape through that tremendous door. Even the sound of firing merely echoed upward until it reached the dome, and then filtered out and upward through the opening above. They might as well have shouted to their friends in Bholat!

For ten minutes, perhaps, the battle surged and swayed on the stone floor first one side rushing, then the other. But man after man of the mutineers went down--appalled by the amazing swordsmanship, disheartened by the grim determination of their adversaries, bewildered to feebleness by the suddenness of the attack.

Soon there were but eight of them facing the blood-wet steel, and then Brown shouted for a fresh formation, swung his contingent into line and led them with a rush across the floor that swept the remaining mutineers off their feet.

Three more went down with steel through them, and then the rest surrendered, throwing down their arms, and begging mercy. Brown made a bundle of their arms, stowed it in a corner and made the prisoners stand together in a bunch, while he searched them thoroughly.

"If we can't get that trapdoor open now, with these to help us," he remarked, panting and wiping the dotted blood off his sword on a Hindu prisoner's trousers, "it'll be a heavier proposition than I think!"

"There's a trick to it," said Juggut Khan, panting too, for the battle had been fierce and furious while it lasted. "The fakir knows the trick. It is heavy, in any case. But, if we make him tell us, we can manage it."

There followed delay while the fakir was induced to forego the pleasure of a sulking fit. He seemed like a child, anxious to emphasize their dependence on his knowledge, and needing to be recompelled to each new thing they needed of him. He was perfectly content, though, to surrender when he felt the weight of a cleaning-rod on his anatomy, or something in the way of fire--a match or cigarette for instance--placed where he would get the most sensation from it.

Then followed more delay, while they rigged a lever of sorts, and a rope through an iron ring in the trap, and while Juggut Khan hunted for the secret catch that the fakir swore was hidden underneath a smaller stone that hinged in the middle of the floor. He found it at last, moved it and came across to lend a hand with the lever and the rope.

The fakir sat still and smiled at them. His eyes gleamed more horridly than ever, and his withered arm seemed more than ever to be calling down dire vengeance on them.

"I believe that monster is up to tricks of some kind!" swore Brown.

"He can't do anything," said Juggut Khan. "If we were all to put our weight against this, all together, we and the prisoners, sahib, we could get it open in a second."

"All together, then!" said Brown. "Come on, there! Lend a hand!"

The prisoners and Brown's men and Juggut Khan and the Beluchi bent their backs above the lever, or hauled taut on the rope, and the fakir wriggled with some secret joke.

"At the word three!" said Brown. "Then all together!"

"One!"

"Two!"

The fakir writhed delightedly. He seemed more than ever like a wickedly malicious child.

"Three!"

They strained their utmost, and the huge stone trap gave way with a sudden jerk.

"For the love of--"

They all jumped, but they were strained in the wrong position for a quick recovery, and the ten-ton rock rolled back on unseen hinges to crush them all, and rolled back and yet farther back--and then stayed! Brown had snatched a rifle, and had placed it between the rolling rock and the wall!

He stood wiping the sweat from his forehead, while the rest recovered their lost balance and walked out from behind unscathed. The rifle creaked and bent and split. Then the stone leaned farther back, reached the wall and stayed there!

"A near thing that!" said Brown. "That fakir's a bright beauty, isn't he!"

"Shall I kick him, sir?" asked one of Brown's men.

"Kick him? No! What good'd that do? What next, Juggut Khan?"

But Juggut Khan was bending down, and listening at the hole laid bare by the huge hinged trap.

"Silence!" commanded Brown.

The men held their breath, even, but not a sound came up from the darkness down below.

"Are they dead, d'you suppose?" asked Brown.

And, even as he asked it, some one in the darkness snuffled, and he heard a woman's voice that moaned.

"Snff-snff-snff! I wonder if I'm dead yet! I wouldn't be, I know, if Bill were here! He'd ha' got us out!"

"There is one of them alive!" said Juggut Khan.

"So I notice!" answered Brown, with a strange dry quaver in his voice. "Go down and bring her up, please! Take three or four men with you. It won't do to bring women and a child up here and let 'em see this awful fakir and these corpses. Take your time about bringing 'em up, while I make the prisoners carry their dead up on to the roof. I'll take the fakir up there too where he's out of mischief!"

Just as a six-foot-wide pathway ran round and round the outside of the dome, another one, scarcely more than a yard wide, ran round the inside, and formed a roadway to the top in place of a stair. It took the prisoners and Brown's men fifteen minutes of continuous effort to carry up the dead and the fakir, and lay them on the roof.

"Pitch the dead over!" ordered Brown, and the mutineers obeyed.

"I've a mind to pitch you over too!" he growled at the fakir, and the strange creature seemed to understand him, for his eyes changed from their baleful hatred to a look of fear.

The bodies slid and rolled down the rounded roof, and fell with a thud against the battlements, or else went rolling down the circular causeway that led to the street below.

Brown seemed to be garnering ideas from watching them. He gazed down at the noisy tumult of the city, watching for a while the efforts of an ill-directed crowd to put out a fire that blazed in a distant quarter of the bazaar.

There seemed to him something strangely preconcerted about much of the hurrying to and fro below him. It struck him as being far too orderly to be the mere boiling of a loot-crazed mob.

His prisoners gave the secret to him. They were leaning against the parapet on the other side--the side closest to the city-wall, and farthest from the top of the causeway--and they were chattering together excitedly in undertones. Brown walked round to where they stood, and stared where they stared. Just as they had done, he recognized what lay below him.

It was faintly outlined in the blackness, picked out here and there by lanterns, and still too far away for most civilians to name it until the sun rose and showed its detail. But Brown, the soldier, knew on the instant, and so did his men.

Suddenly and unexpectedly and sweetly, like a voice in the night that spoke of hope and strength and the rebirth of order out of chaos, a bugle gave tongue from where the lanterns swung in straight-kept lines.

"Oh, Juggut Khan! Oh, Juggut Khan!"

Bill Brown's voice boomed through the opening in the dome, and spread down the walls of the powder-magazine as though in the inside of a speaking-trumpet.

"Brown sahib?"

"The army has got here from the north! It has come down here from Harumpore! It's outside the walls now, lying on its arms, and evidently waiting to attack at daylight!"

"I, too, have news, Brown sahib! All four are living! All four lie here on the floor of the magazine, and they recover rapidly. They are all but strong enough to stand."

"Good! Then come up here, Juggut Khan!"

That winding pathway up the inside of the dome took longer to negotiate than an ordinary stairway would have done, but presently the Rajput leaned against the parapet and panted beside Brown.

"D'you see them? There they are! Now, look on this side! D'you see the preparations going on? D'you realize what the next thing's going to be? They'll come for powder for the guns, so's to have it all ready for the gun-crews when the fun begins at dawn! Listen! Here they are already!"

A thundering had started on the great teak door below--a thundering that echoed through the dome like the reverberations of an earthquake. It was punctuated by the screams of women. The prisoners changed their attitude, and eyed Brown and the Rajput with an air of truculence again.

"They'll be up this causeway in a minute, sahib! Listen. There! They've seen the dead bodies that you tossed over. Better it had been to keep them up here for a while."

"Never mind! We can hold this causeway until morning! Men! Take close order. Line up at the causeway-entrance. Kneel. Prepare for volley-firing. Now, let 'em come!"

"I am for making an immediate escape, sahib!"

"Go ahead!" said Brown, almost dreamily.

He seemed to be thinking hard on some other subject as he spoke.

"Sahib, one of the women there--she who is maid to the other two--asked me where Bill Brown might be! She swore to me that she had recognized his voice when the trapdoor opened up above her. Are you not Bill Brown?"

"Yes, I'm William Brown!"

"Her name, she says, is Emmett!"

"You don't surprise me, Juggut Khan! I thought I had recognized her voice. It seemed strangely familiar. Well--here come the rebels up the causeway. See? They're at the bottom now with lanterns! Ready, men!"

There came the answering click of breech-bolts, and a little rustling as each man eased his position, and laid his elbow on his knee.

"Can you find your way out through the way we came, Juggut Khan?"

"Of course I can!"

"Are all the women on the floor?"

"Three women and the child."

"Can you close the trap-door again?"

"Surely! It is only opening it that is difficult."

"Then close it before you go. I've got a reason! Send one of my men up here with a lantern--one of those that are burning in the magazine. I want to signal."

"Very well, sahib!"

"Then take the women, with four of my men to help them walk, and get out as quickly as you can by the way we all came in. Wait for the rest of my men when you reach the opening in the outer wall, and when they reach you allot two men to carry each woman, and run--the whole lot of you--for the army over yonder. One of the women will object. She will want to see me first. Use force, if necessary!"

"Are you, then, not coming, sahib?"

"I have another plan. Here they come! Hurry now, be off with the women! Volley-firing--ready--present!"

Pattering footsteps sounded on the causeway, and a little crowd of nearly doubled figures came up it at a run.

"Fire!"

The volley took the rebels absolutely by surprise, and no man could miss his mark at that short range. Five of the rebels fell back headlong, and the rest, who followed up the causeway, turned on their heels and ran.

"'Bout turn!" Brown shouted suddenly. "Use the steel, men! Use the steel!"

His own sword was flashing, and lunging as he spoke, and he had already checked a sudden rush by the prisoners.

They had thought the moment favorable for joining in the scrimmage from the rear.

"All right! That'll do them! I'll attend to 'em now!"

A man came running up with the lantern Brown had asked for, and Brown took it and began waving it above his head.

"They must have heard that volley!" he muttered to himself. "Ah! There's the answer!"

A red light began to dance over in the British camp, moving up and down and sidewise in sudden little jerks. Brown read the jerks, as he could never have read writing, and a moment later he answered them.

"Now, down below, the lot of you! Give me your rifle, you. I'll need it."

"Not coming, sir."

"Not yet. There's something else yet, and I can do it best. Besides, some one has got to guard the causeway still. There might be a rush again at any minute. Listen now. Obey Juggut Khan implicitly as soon as you get down. His orders are my orders. Understand? Very well, then. And you without a weapon, your job is to shut the door that you leave the magazine by tight from the outside--d'you understand me? Call up when you're all through the door, and then shut it tight!"

"But, how'll you get out, sir?"

"That's my business. One minute, though. Here they come again. Get ready to fire another volley!"

The mutineers made another and a more determined rush up the causeway, coming up it more than twenty strong, and at the double. Brown let one volley loose in the midst of them, then led his men at the charge down on them and drove them over the edge of the causeway by dint of sheer impact and cold steel. Not one of them reached the ground alive, and in the darkness it must have been impossible for the mutineers below to divine how many were the granary's defenders.

"That'll keep 'em quiet for a while, I'll wager! Now, quick, you men! Get down below, and follow Juggut Khan, and don't forget to shut the door tight on you. These prisoners here are going to follow you--they may as well go down with you for that matter. No! that won't do. They could open the door below, couldn't they? They'll have to stay up here. Got any rope? Then bind them, somebody. Bind their hands and feet. Now, off with you!"

Brown spent the next few minutes signaling with the lantern, and reading answering flashes that zig-zagged in the velvet blackness of the British lines. Then, as a voice boomed up through the granary, "All's well, sir! I'm just about to shut the door!" he fixed his eyes on the fakir, and laughed at him.

"You and I are going to turn in our accounts of how we've worked out this 'Hookum hai' business, my friend!" he told him. "You've given orders, and I've obeyed orders! We've both accounted for a death or two, and we've both accepted responsibility. We're going to know in less than five minutes from now which of us two was justified. There's one thing I know, though, without asking. There's one person, and she a woman, who'll weep for me. Will anybody weep for you, I wonder?"

A lantern waved wildly from the British camp, and Brown seized his own lantern and signaled an answer.

"See that? That's to say, you glassy-eyed horror you, that our mutual friend Juggut Khan has been seen emerging like a rat from a hole in the wall. I'll give him and his party one more minute to get clear. Then there's going to be a holocaust, my friend!"

He cocked his rifle, and examined the breech-bolt and the foresight carefully. The fakir shuddered, evidently thinking that the charge was intended for himself.

"No! It won't be that way. I know a better! I'm taking a leaf from your book and doing harm by wholesale!"

Brown leaned down into the opening of the dome, and brought the rifle to his shoulder. There was a chorus of yells from the prisoners, and a noise like a wounded horse's scream from the fakir. The rest were bound, but the fakir rose and writhed toward him on his heels, with his sound arm stretched up in an attitude of despair beside the withered one.

A chorus of bugles burst out from the British camp, and a volley ripped through the blackness.

"All right! Here goes!" said Brown. And he aimed down into the shadowy powder-magazine, and pulled the trigger.

Ten minutes later, an army three thousand and five hundred strong marched in through the gap made in the outer wall by a granary that had spread itself through--and not over--what was in its way. There were seventeen tons of powder that responded to the invitation of Brown's bullet.

XIV.

Explosions are among the few things--or the many things, whichever way you like to look at it!--that science can not undertake to harness or account for. When a gun blows up, or a powder-magazine, the shock kills whom it kills, as when a shell bursts in a dense-packed firing-line. You can not kill any man before his time comes, even if a thousand tons of solid masonry combine with you to whelm him, and go hurtling through the air with him to absolutely obvious destruction.

The fakir's time had come, and the prisoners' time had come. But Sergeant William Brown's had not.

They found him, blackened by powder, and with every stitch of clothing blown from him, clinging to a bunch of lotus-stems in a temple-pond. There was a piece of fakir in the water with him, and about a ton of broken granary, besides the remnants of a rifle and other proof that he had come belched out of a holocaust. The men who came on him had given their officer the slip, and were bent on a private looting-expedition of their own. But by the time that they had dragged him from the water, and he had looted them of wherewithal to clothe himself, their thoughts of plunder had departed from them. Brown had a way of quite monopolizing people's thoughts!

There were twenty of them, and he led them all that night, and all through the morning and the afternoon that followed. He held them together and worked them and wheeled them and coached and cheered and compelled them through the hell-tumult of the ghastliest thing there is beneath the dome of heaven--house-to-house fighting in an Eastern city. And at the end of it, when the bugles blew at last "Cease fire," and many of the men were marched away by companies to put out the conflagrations that were blazing here and there, he led them outside the city-wall, stood them at ease in their own line and saluted their commanding-officer.

"Twenty men of yours, sir. Present and correct."

"Which twenty?"

"Of Mr. Blair's half-company."

"Where's Mr. Blair?"

"Dunno, sir!"

"Since when have you had charge of them?"

"Since they broke into the city yesterday, sir."

"And you haven't lost a man?"

"Had lots of luck, sir!"

"Who are you, anyway?"

"I'm Sergeant Brown, sir."

"Of the Rifles?"

"Of the Rifles, sir."

"Were you the man who signaled to us from the magazine and blew it up and made the breach in the wall for us to enter by?"

"Yes, sir."

"Are you alive, or dead? Man or ghost?"

"I'm pretty much alive, sir, thank you!"

"D'you realize that you made the taking of Jailpore possible? That but for you we'd have been trying still to storm the walls without artillery?"

"I had the chance, sir, and I only did what any other man would ha' done under like circumstances."

"Go and tell that to the Horse Marines--or, rather, tell it to Colonel Kendrick! Go and report to him at once. Possibly he'll see it through your eyes!"

So Brown marched off to report himself, and he found Colonel Kendrick nursing a badly wounded arm before a torn and mud-stained tent.

"Who are you?" said the colonel, as Brown saluted him.

"I'm Sergeant Brown, sir."

"Not Bill Brown of the Rifles?"

"Yes, sir!"

"You lie! He was blown up on the roof of the powder-magazine! I suppose every man who's gone mad from the heat will be saying that he's Brown!"

"I'm Brown, sir! I had written orders from General Baines to enter Jailpore and rescue three women and a child."

"Where are your orders?"

"Lost 'em, sir, in the explosion."

"For a madman, you're a circumstantial liar! What happened to the women?"

The colonel sat back, and smothered an exclamation of agony as the nerves in his injured arm tortured him afresh. He had asked a question which should settle once and for all this man's pretentions, and he waited for the answer with an air of certainty. It was on his lips to call the guard to take the lunatic away.

"Juggut Khan, the Rajput, took them, with nine of my men, and brought them in to your camp last night, sir. I naturally haven't seen them since."

"Will the women know you?"

"One of them will, sir."

"Which one?"

"Jane Emmett, sir."

"Well, we'll see!"

The colonel called an orderly, and sent the orderly running for Jane Emmett. A minute later two strong arms were thrown round Bill Brown from behind, and he was all but carried off his feet.

"Oh, Bill--Bill--Bill! I knew you'd be all right! Turn round, Bill! Look at me!"

She was clinging to him in such a manner that he could not turn, but he managed to pry her hands loose, and to draw her round in front of him.

"I knew, Bill! I felt sure you'd come! And I recognized your voice the minute that the trapdoor opened and I heard it! I did, Bill! I knew you in a minute! I didn't worry then! I knew you wouldn't come and talk to me as long as there was any duty to be done. I just waited! They said you were killed in the explosion, but I knew you weren't! I knew it! I did! I knew it!"

"Face me, please!" said Colonel Kendrick. "Now, Jane Emmett, is that man Sergeant William Brown, of the Rifles?"

"Yes, sir."

"Is he the man who entered Jailpore with nine men and a Rajput, and came to your assistance?"

"Yes, sir! He's the same man who spoke in the powder-magazine;"

"Do you confirm that?" he asked Brown.

"Under favor, sir, my men must be somewhere, if they're not all killed. They'll recognize me. And there's the other lot I led all last night and all today. They'll tell you where they found me!"

"Never mind! I've decided I believe you! D'you realize that you're something of a marvel?"

"No, sir--except that I've had marvelous luck!"

"Well, I shall take great pleasure in mentioning your name in despatches. It will go direct, at first hand, to Her Majesty the Queen! There are few men, let me tell you, Sergeant Brown, who would dare what you dared in the first place. But, more than that, there are even fewer men who would leave a sweetheart in some one else's care while they blew up a powder-magazine with themselves on top of it, in order to make a breach for the army to come in by! My right hand's out of action unfortunately--you'll have to shake my left!"

The colonel rose, held his uninjured hand out and Brown shook it, since he was ordered to.

"I consider it an honor and a privilege to have shaken hands with you, Sergeant Brown!" said Colonel Kendrick.

"Thank you, sir!" said Brown, taking one step back, and then saluting. "May I join my regiment, sir?"

He joined his regiment, when he had helped to sort out the bleeding remnants of it from among the by-ways and back alleys of Jailpore. And the chaplain married him and Jane Emmett out of hand. He sent her off at once with her former mistress to the coast, and marched off with his regiment to Delphi. And at Delphi his name was once more mentioned in despatches.

When the Mutiny was over, and the country had settled down again to peace and reincarnation of a nation had begun, Brown found himself hoisted to a civil appointment that was greater and more highly paid than anything his modest soul had ever dreamed of.

He never understood the reason for it, although he did his fighting-best consistently to fill the job; and he never understood why Queen Victoria should have taken the trouble to write a letter to him in which she thanked him personally, nor why they should have singled out for praise and special notice a fellow who had merely done his duty.

Perhaps that was the reason why he was such a conspicuous success in civil life. They still talk of how Bill Brown, with Jane his wife and Juggut Khan the Rajput to advise him, was Resident Political Adviser to a Maharajah, and of how the

Maharajah loathed him, and looked sidewise at him--but obeyed. That, though, is not a war-story. It is a story of the saving of a war, and shall go on record, some day, beneath a title of its own.

FOR THE SALT HE HAD EATEN

Prologue

To the northward of Hanadra, blue in the sweltering heat-haze, lay Siroeh, walled in with sun-baked mud and listless. Through a wooden gate at one end of the village filed a string of women with their water-pots. Oxen, tethered underneath the thatched eaves or by the thirsty-looking trees, lay chewing the cud, almost too lazy to flick the flies away. Even the village goats seemed overcome with lassitude. Here and there a pariah dog sneaked in and out among the shadows or lay and licked his sores beside an offal-heap; but there seemed to be no energy in anything. The bone-dry, hot-weather wind had shriveled up verdure and ambition together.

But in the mud-walled cottages, where men were wont to doze through the long, hot days, there were murmurings and restless movement. Men lay on thong-strung beds, and talked instead of dreaming, and the women listened and said nothing--which is the reverse of custom. Hanadra was what it always had been, thatched, sun-baked lassitude; but underneath the thatch there thrummed a bee-hive atmosphere of tension.

In the center of the village, where the one main road that led from the main gate came to an abrupt end at a low mud wall, stood a house that was larger than the others and somewhat more neatly kept; there had been an effort made at sweeping the enclosure that surrounded it on all four sides, and there was even whitewash, peeling off in places but still comparatively white, smeared on the sun-cracked walls.

Here, besides murmurings and movement, there was evidence of real activity.

Tethered against the wall on one side of the house stood a row of horses, saddled and bridled and bearing evidence of having traveled through the heat; through the open doorway the sunshine glinted on a sword-hilt and amid the sound of many voices rang the jingling of a spur as some one sat cornerwise on a wooden table and struck his toe restlessly against the leg.

Another string of women started for the water-hole, with their picturesque brass jars perched at varying angles on their heads; and as each one passed the doorway of this larger house she turned and scowled. A Rajput, lean and black-bearded and swaggering, came to the door and watched them, standing proudly with his arms folded across his breast. As the last woman showed her teeth at him, he laughed aloud.

"Nay!" said a voice inside. "Have done with that! Is noticing the Hindu women fit sport for a Rajput?"

The youngster turned and faced the old, black-bearded veteran who spoke.

"If I had my way," he answered, "I would ride roughshod through this village, and fire the thatch. They fail to realize the honor that we pay them by a visit!"

"Aye, hothead! And burn thy brother's barn with what is in it! The Hindus here are many, and we are few, and there will be burnings and saberings a-plenty before a week is past, if I read the signs aright! Once before have I heard such murmurings. Once before I have seen chupatties sent from house to house at sunset--and that time blood ran red along the roadside for a month to follow! Keep thy sword sharp a while and wait the day!"

"But why," growled another deep-throated Rajput voice, "does the Sirkar wait? Why not smite first and swiftly?"

Mahommed Khan moved restlessly and ran his fingers through his beard.

"I know not!" he answered. "In the days when I was Risaldar in the Rajput Horse, and Bellairs sahib was colonel, things were different! But we conquered, and after conquest came security. The English have grown overconfident; they think that Mussulman will always war with Hindu, the one betraying the other; they will not understand that this lies deeper than jealousy--they will not listen! Six months ago I rode to Jundhra and whispered to the general sahib what I thought; but he laughed back at me. He said 'Wolf! wolf!' to me and drew me inside his bungalow and bade me eat my fill."

"Well--what matters it! This land has always been the playground of new conquerors!"

"There will be no new conquerors," growled the old Risaldar, "so long as I and mine have swords to wield for the Raj!"

"But what have the English done for thee or us?"

"This, forgetful one! They have treated us with honor, as surely no other conquerors had done! At thy age, I too measured my happiness in cattle and coin and women, but then came Bellairs sahib, and raised the Rajput Horse, and I enlisted. What came of that was better than all the wealth of Ind!"

He spread his long legs like a pair of scissors and caught a child between them and lifted him.

"Thou ruffian, thou!" he chuckled. "See how he fights! A true Rajput! Nay, beat me not. Some day thou too shalt bear a sword for England, great-grandson mine. Ai-ee! But I grow old."

"For England or the next one!"

"Nay! But for England!" said the Risaldar, setting the child down on his knee. "And thou too, hot-head. Before a week is past! Think you I called my sons and grandsons all together for the fun of it? Think you I rode here through the heat because I needed the exercise or to chatter like an ape or to stand in the doorway making faces at a Hindu woman or to watch thee do it? Here I am, and here I stay until yet more news comes!"

"Then are we to wait here? Are we to swelter in Siroeh, eating up our brother's hospitality, until thy messengers see fit to come and tell us that this scare of thine is past?"

"Nay!" said the Risaldar. "I said that I wait here! Return now to your own homes, each of you. But be in readiness. I am old, but I can ride still. I can round you up. Has any a better horse than mine? If he has, let him make exchange."

"There will be horses for the looting if this revolt of thine breaks out!"

"True! There will be horses for the looting! Well, I wait here then and, when the trouble comes, I can count on thirteen of my blood to carry swords behind me?"

"Aye, when the trouble comes!"

There was a chorus of assent, and the Risaldar arose to let his sons and grandsons file past him. He, who had beggared himself to give each one of them a start in life, felt a little chagrined that they should now refuse to exchange horses with him; but his eye glistened none the less at the sight of their stalwart frames and at the thought of what a fighting unit he could bring to serve the Raj.

"All, then, for England!" he exclaimed.

"Nay, all for thee!" said his eldest-born. "We fight on whichever side thou sayest!"

"Disloyal one!" growled the Risaldar with a scowl. But he grinned into his beard.

"Well, to your homes, then--but be ready!"

I.

The midnight jackals howled their discontent while heat-cracked India writhed in stuffy torment that was only one degree less than unendurable. Through the stillness and the blackness of the night came every now and then the high-pitched undulating wails of women, that no one answered-for, under that Tophet-lid of blackness, punctured by the low-hung, steel-white stars, men neither knew nor cared whose child had died. Life and hell-hot torture and indifference--all three were one.

There was no moon, nothing to make the inferno visible, except that here and there an oil lamp on some housetop glowed like a blood-spot against the blackness. It was a sensation, rather than sight or sound, that betrayed the neighborhood of thousands upon thousands of human beings, sprawling, writhing, twisting upon the roofs, in restless suffering.

There was no pity in the dry, black vault of heaven, nor in the bone-dry earth, nor in the hearts of men, during that hot weather of '57. Men waited for the threatened wrath to come and writhed and held their tongues. And while they waited in sullen Asiatic patience, through the restless silence and the smell--the suffocating, spice-fed, filth-begotten smell of India--there ran an undercurrent of even deeper mystery than India had ever known.

Priest-ridden Hanadra, that had seen the downfall of a hundred kings, watched through heat-wearied eyes for another whelming the blood-soaked, sudden flood that was to burst the dam of servitude and rid India of her latest horde of conquerors. But eight hundred yards from where her high brick walls lifted their age-scars in the stifling reek, gun-chains jingled in a courtyard, and, sharp-clicking on age-old flagstones, rose the ring of horses' feet.

Section Number One of a troop of Bengal Horse Artillery was waiting under arms. Sabered and grim and ready stood fifty of the finest men that England could produce, each man at his horse's head; and blacker even than the night loomed the long twelve-pounders, in tow behind their limbers. Sometimes a trace-chain jingled as a wheel-horse twitched his flank; and sometimes a man spoke in a low voice, or a horse stamped on the pavement; but they seemed like black graven images of war-gods, half-smothered in the reeking darkness. And above them, from a window that overlooked the courtyard, shone a solitary lamp that glistened here and there upon the sleek black guns and flickered on the saber-hilts, and deepened the already dead-black atmosphere of mystery.

From the room above, where the lamp shone behind gauze curtains came the sound of voices; and in the deepest, death-darkest shadow of the door below there stood a man on guard whose fingers clutched his sword-hilt and whose breath came heavily. He stood motionless, save for his heaving breast; between his fierce, black mustache and his up-brushed, two-pointed beard, his white teeth showed through parted lips. But he gave no other sign that he was not some Rajput princeling's image carved out of the night.

He was an old man, though, for all his straight back and military carriage. The night concealed his shabbiness; but it failed to hide the medals on his breast, one bronze, one silver, that told of campaigns already a generation gone. And his patience was another sign of age; a younger man of his blood and training would have been pacing to and fro instead of standing still.

He stood still even when footsteps resounded on the winding stair above and a saber-ferrule clanked from step to step. The gunners heard and stood squarely to their horses. There was a rustling and a sound of shifting feet, and, a "Whoa,--you!" to an irritated horse; but the Rajput stayed motionless until the footsteps reached the door. Then he took one step forward, faced about and saluted.

"Salaam, Bellairs sahib!" boomed his deep-throated voice, and Lieutenant Bellairs stepped back with a start into the doorway again--one hand on his sword-hilt. The Indian moved sidewise to where the lamplight from the room above could fall upon his face.

"Salaam, Bellairs sahib!" he boomed again.

Then the lieutenant recognized him.

"You, Mahommed Khan!" he exclaimed. "You old war-dog, what brought you here? Heavens, how you startled me! What good wind brought you?"

"Nay! It seems it was an ill wind, sahib!"

"What ill wind? I'm glad to see you!"

"The breath of rumor, sahib!"

"What rumor brought you?"

"Where a man's honor lies, there is he, in the hour of danger! Is all well with the Raj, sahib?"

"With the Raj? How d'you mean, Risaldar?"

Mahommed Khan pointed to the waiting guns and smiled.

"In my days, sahib," he answered, "men seldom exercised the guns at night!"

"I received orders more than three hours ago to bring my section in to Jundhra immediately--immediately--and not a word of explanation!"

"Orders, sahib? And you wait?"

"They seem to have forgotten that I'm married, and by the same token, so do you! What else could I do but wait? My wife can't ride with the section; she isn't strong enough, for one thing; and besides, there's no knowing what this order means; there might be trouble to face of some kind. I've sent into Hanadra to try to drum up an escort for her and I'm waiting here until it comes."

The Risaldar stroked at his beard reflectively.

"We of the service, sahib," he answered, "obey orders at the gallop when they come. When orders come to ride, we ride!'"

Bellairs winced at the thrust.

"That's all very fine, Risaldar. But how about my wife? What's going to happen to her, if I leave her here alone and unprotected?"

"Or to me, sahib? Is my sword-arm withered? Is my saber rusted home?"

"You, old friend! D'you mean to tell me--"

The Risaldar saluted him again.

"Will you stay here and guard her?"

"Nay, sahib! Being not so young as thou art, I know better!"

"What in Tophet do you mean, Mahommed Khan?"

"I mean, sahib,"--the Indian's voice was level and deep, but it vibrated strangely, and his eyes glowed as though war-lights were being born again behind them--"that not for nothing am I come! I heard what thy orders were and--"

"How did you hear what my orders were?"

"My half-brother came hurrying with the news, sahib. I hastened! My horse lies dead one kos from Hanadra here!"

The lieutenant laughed.

"At last, Mahommed? That poor old screw of yours? So he's dead at last, eh? So his time had come at last!"

"We be not all rich men who serve the Raj!" said the Risaldar with dignity. "Ay, sahib, his time was come! And when our time comes may thou and I, sahib, die as he did, with our harness on! What said thy orders, sahib? Haste? Then yonder lies the road, through the archway!"

"But, tell me, Risaldar, what brought you here in such a hurry?"

"A poor old screw, sahib, whose time was come--even as thou hast said!"

"Mahommed Khan, I'm sorry--very sorry, if I insulted you! I--I'm worried--I didn't stop to think. I--old friend, I--"

"It is forgotten, sahib!"

"Tell me--what are these rumors you have heard?"

"But one rumor, sahib-war! Uprising--revolution--treachery--all India waits the word to rise, sahib!"

"You mean--?"

"Mutiny among the troops, and revolution north, south, east and west!"

"Here, too, in Hanadra?"

"Here, too, in Hanadra, sahib! Here they will be among the first to rise!"

"Oh, come! I can't believe that! How was it that my orders said nothing of it then?"

"That, sahib, I know not--not having written out thy orders! I heard that thy orders came. I knew, as I have known this year past, what storm was brewing. I knew, too, that the heavenborn, thy wife, is here. I am thy servant, sahib, as I was thy father's servant--we serve one Queen; thy honor is my honor. Entrust thy memsahib to my keeping!"

"You will guard her?"

"I will bring her in to Jundhra!"

"You alone?"

"Nay, sahib! I, and my sons, and my sons' sons--thirteen men all told!"

"That is good of you, Mahommed Khan. Where are your sons?"

"Leagues from here, sahib. I must bring them. I need a horse."

"And while you are gone?"

"My half-brother, sahib--he is here for no other purpose--he will answer to me for her safety!"

"All right, Mahommed Khan, and thank you! Take my second charger, if you care to; he is a little saddle-sore, but your light weight--"

"Sahib--listen! Between here and Siroeh, where my eldest-born and his three sons live, lie seven leagues. And on from there to Lungra, where the others live, are three more leagues. I need a horse this night!"

"What need of thirteen men, Mahommed? You are sufficient by yourself, unless a rebellion breaks out. If it did, why, you and thirteen others would be swamped as surely as you alone!"

"Thy father and I, sahib, rode through the guns at Dera thirteen strong! Alone, I am an old man--not without honor, but of little use; with twelve young blades behind me, though, these Hindu rabble--"

"Do you really mean, Mahommed Khan, that you think Hanadra here will rise?"

"The moment you are gone, sahib!"

"Then, that settles it! The memsahib rides with me!"

"Nay, listen, sahib! Of a truth, thou art a hot-head as thy father was before thee! Thus will it be better. If the heavenborn, thy wife, stays behind, these rabble here will think that the section rides out to exercise, because of the great heat of the sun by day; they will watch for its return, and wait for the parking of the guns before they put torch to the mine that they have laid!"

"The mine? D'you mean they've--"

"Who knows, sahib? But I speak in metaphor. When the guns are parked again and the horses stabled and the men asleep, the rabble, being many, might dare anything!"

"You mean, you think that they--"

"I mean, sahib, that they will take no chances while they think the guns are likely to return!"

"But, if I take the memsahib with me?"

"They will know then, sahib, that the trap is open and the bird flown! Know you how fast news travels? Faster than the guns, Sahib! There will be an ambuscade, from which neither man, nor gun, nor horse, nor memsahib will escape!"

"But if you follow later, it will mean the same thing! When they see you ride off on a spent horse, with twelve swords and the memsahib--d'you mean that they won't ambuscade you?"

"They might, sahib--and again, they might not! Thirteen men and a woman ride faster than a section of artillery, and ride where the guns would jam hub-high against a tree-trunk! And thy orders, sahib--are thy orders nothing?"

"Orders! Yes, confound it! But they know I'm married. They know--"

"Sahib, listen! When the news came to me I was at Siroeh, dangling a great-grandson on my knee. There were no orders, but it seemed the Raj had need of me. I rode! Thou, sahib, hast orders. I am here to guard thy wife--my honor is thy honor--take thou the guns. Yonder lies the road!"

The grim old warrior's voice thrilled with the throb of loyalty, as he stood erect and pointed to the shadowy archway through which the road wound to the plain beyond.

"Sahib, I taught thy father how to use his sword! I nursed thee when thou wert little. Would I give three false counsel now? Ride, sahib--ride!"

Bellairs turned away and looked at his charger, a big, brown Khaubuli stallion, named for the devil and true in temper and courage to his name; two men were holding him, ten paces off.

"Such a horse I need this night, Sahib! Thy second charger can keep pace with the guns!"

Bellairs gave a sudden order, and the men led the brute back into his stable.

"Change the saddle to my second charger!" he ordered.

Then he turned to the Risaldar again, with hand outstretched.

"I'm ashamed of myself, Mahommed Khan!" he said, with a vain attempt to smile. "I should have gone an hour ago! Please take my horse Shaitan, and make such disposition for my wife's safety as you see fit. Follow as and when you can; I trust you, and I shall be grateful to you whatever happens!"

"Well spoken, Sahib! I knew thou wert a man! We who serve the Raj have neither sons, nor wives, nor sweethearts! Allah guard you, Sahib! The section waits--and the Service can not wait!"

"One moment while I tell my wife!"

"Halt, Sahib! Thou hast said good-by a thousand times! A woman's tears--are they heart-meat for a soldier when the bits are champing? Nay! See, sahib; they bring thy second charger! Mount! I will bring thy wife to Jundhra for thee! The Service waits!"

The lieutenant turned and mounted.

"Very well, Mahommed Khan!" he said. "I know you're right! Section! Prepare to mount!" he roared, and the stirrups rang in answer to him. "Mount! Good-by, Mahommed Khan! Good luck to you! Section, right! Trot, march!"

With a crash and the clattering of iron shoes on stone the guns jingled off into the darkness, were swallowed by the gaping archway and rattled out on the plain.

The Risaldar stood grimly where he was until the last hoof-beat and bump of gun-wheel had died away into the distance; then he turned and climbed the winding stairway to the room where the lamp still shone through gauzy curtains.

On a dozen roof-tops, where men lay still and muttered, brown eyes followed the movements of the section and teeth that were betel-stained grinned hideously.

From a nearby temple, tight-packed between a hundred crowded houses, came a wailing, high-pitched solo sung to Siva--the Destroyer. And as it died down to a quavering finish it was followed by a ghoulish laugh that echoed and reechoed off the age-old city-wall.

Proud as a Royal Rajput--and there is nothing else on God's green earth that is even half as proud--true to his salt, and stout of heart even if he was trembling at the knees, Mahommed Khan, two-medal man and Risaldar, knocked twice on the door of Mrs. Lellairs' room, and entered.

And away in the distance rose the red reflection of a fire ten leagues away. The Mutiny of '57 had blazed out of sullen mystery already, the sepoys were burning their barracks half-way on the road to Jundhra!

And down below, to the shadow where the Risaldar had stood, crept a giant of a man who had no military bearing. He listened once, and sneaked into the deepest black within the doorway and crouched and waited.

II.

Hanadra reeks of history, blood-soaked and mysterious. Temples piled on the site of olden temples; palaces where half-forgotten kings usurped the thrones of conquerors who came from God knows where to conquer older kings; roads built on the bones of conquered armies; houses and palaces and subterranean passages that no man living knows the end of and few even the beginning. Dark corridors and colonnades and hollow walls; roofs that have ears and peep-holes; floors that are undermined by secret stairs; trees that have swayed with the weight of rotting human skulls and have shimmered with the silken bannerets of emperors. Such is Hanadra, half-ruined, and surrounded by a wall that was age-old in the dawn of written history.

Even its environs are mysterious; outside the walls, there are carven, gloomy palaces that once re-echoed to the tinkle of stringed instruments and the love-songs of some sultan's favorite--now fallen into ruins, or rebuilt to stable horses or shelter guns and stores and men; but eloquent in all their new-smeared whitewash, or in crumbling decay, of long-since dead intrigue. No places, those, for strong men to live alone in, where night-breezes whisper through forgotten passages and dry teak planking recreaks to the memory of dead men's footsteps.

But strong men are not the only makings of an Empire, nor yet the only sufferers. Wherever the flag of England flies above a distant outpost or droops in the stagnant moisture of an Eastern swamp, there are the graves of England's women. The bones that quarreling jackals crunch among the tombstones--the peace along the clean-kept borderline--the pride of race and conquest and the cleaner pride of work well done, these are not man's only. Man does the work, but he is held to it and cheered on by the girl who loves him.

And so, above a stone-flagged courtyard, in a room that once had echoed to the laughter of a sultan's favorite, it happened that an English girl of twenty-one was pacing back and forth. Through the open curtained window she had seen her husband lead his command out through the echoing archway to the plain beyond; she had heard his boyish voice bark out the command and had listened to the rumble of the gun-wheels dying in the distance--for the last time possibly. She knew, as many an English girl has known, that she was alone, one white woman amid a swarm of sullen Aryans, and that she must follow along the road the guns had taken, served and protected by nothing more than low-caste natives.

And yet she was dry-eyed, and her chin was high; for they are a strange breed, these Anglo-Saxon women who follow the men they love to the lonely danger-zone. Ruth Bellairs could have felt no joy in her position; she had heard her husband growling his complaint at being forced to leave her, and she guessed what her danger was. Fear must have shrunk her heartbeats and loneliness have tried her courage. But there was an ayah in the room with her, a low-caste woman of the conquered race; and pride of country came to her assistance. She was firm-lipped and, to outward seeming, brave as she was beautiful.

Even when the door resounded twice to the sharp blow of a saber-hilt, and the ayah's pock-marked ebony took on a shade of gray, she stood like a queen with an army at her back and neither blanched nor trembled.

"Who is that, ayah?" she demanded.

The ayah shrank into herself and showed the whites of her eyes and grinned, as a pariah dog might show its teeth--afraid, but scenting carrion.

"Go and see!"

The ayah shuddered and collapsed, babbling incoherencies and calling on a horde of long-neglected gods to witness she was innocent. She clutched strangely at her breast and used only one hand to drag her shawl around her face. While she babbled she glanced wild-eyed around the long, low-ceilinged room. Ruth Bellairs looked down at her pityingly and went to the door herself and opened it.

"Salaam, memsahib!" boomed a deep voice from the darkness.

Ruth Bellairs started and the ayah screamed.

"Who are you? Enter--let me see you!"

A black beard and a turban and the figure of a man--and then white teeth and a saber-hilt and eyes that gleamed moved forward from the darkness.

"It is I, Mahommed Khan!" boomed the voice again, and the Risaldar stepped out into the lamplight and closed the door behind him. Then, with a courtly, long-discarded sweep of his right arm, he saluted.

"At the heavenborn's service!"

"Mahommed Khan! Thank God!"

The old man's shabbiness was very obvious as he faced her, with his back against the iron-studded door; but he stood erect as a man of thirty, and his medals and his sword-hilt and his silver scabbard-tip were bright.

"Tell me, Mahommed Khan, you have seen my husband?"

He bowed.

"You have spoken to him?"

The old man bowed again.

"He left you in my keeping, heavenborn. I am to bring you safe to Jundhra!"

She held her hand out and he took it like a cavalier, bending until he could touch her fingers with his lips.

"What is the meaning of this hurrying of the guns to Jundhra, Risaldar?"

"Who knows, memsahib! The orders of the Sirkar come, and we of the service must obey. I am thy servant and the Sirkar's!"

"You, old friend--that were servant, as you choose to call it, to my husband's father! I am a proud woman to have such friends at call!" She pointed to the ayah, recovering sulkily and rearranging the shawl about her shoulders. "That I call service, Risaldar. She cowers when a knock comes at the door! I need you, and you answer a hardly spoken prayer; what is friendship, if yours is not?"

The Risaldar bowed low again.

"I would speak with that ayah, heavenborn!" he muttered, almost into his beard. She could hardly catch the words.

"I can't get her to speak to me at all tonight, Mahommed Khan. She's terrified almost out of her life at something. But perhaps you can do better. Try. Do you want to question her alone?"

"By the heavenborn's favor, yes."

Ruth walked down the room toward the window, drew the curtain back and leaned her head out where whatever breeze there was might fan her cheek. The Risaldar strode over to where the ayah cowered by an inner doorway.

"She-Hindu-dog!" he growled at her. "Mother of whelps! Louse-ridden scavenger of sweepings! What part hast thou in all this treachery? Speak!"

The ayah shrank away from him and tried to scream, but he gripped her by the throat and shook her.

"Speak!" he growled again.

But his ten iron fingers held her in a vise-like grip and she could not have answered him if she had tried to.

"O Risaldar!" called Ruth suddenly, with her head still out of the window. He released the ayah and let her tumble as she pleased into a heap.

"Heavenborn?"

"What is that red glow on the skyline over yonder?"

"A burning, heavenborn!"

"A burning? What burning? Funeral pyres? It's very big for funeral pyres!"

"Nay, heavenborn!"

"What, then?"

She was still unfrightened, unsuspicious of the untoward. The Risaldar's arrival on the scene had quite restored her confidence and she felt content to ride with him to Jundhra on the morrow.

"Barracks, heavenborn!"

"Barracks? What barracks?"

"There is but one barracks between here and Jundhra."

"Then--then--then--what has happened, Mahommed Khan?"

"The worst has happened, heavenborn!"

He stood between her and the ayah, so that she could not see the woman huddled on the floor.

"The worst? You mean then--my--my--husband--you don't mean that my husband--"

"I mean, heavenborn that there is insurrection! All India is ablaze from end to end. These dogs here in Hanadra wait to rise because they think the section will return here in an hour or two; then they propose to burn it, men, guns and horses, like snakes in the summer grass. It is well that the section will not return! We will ride out safely before morning!"

"And, my husband--he knew--all this--before he left me here?"

"Nay! That he did not! Had I told him, he had disobeyed his orders and shamed his service; he is young yet, and a hothead! He will be far along the road to Jundhra before he knows what burns. And then he will remember that he trusts me and obey orders and press on!"

"And you knew and did not tell him!"

"Of a truth I knew!"

She stood in silence for a moment, gazing at the red glow on the skyline, and then turned to read, if she could, what was on the grim, grizzled face of Mahommed Khan.

"The ayah!" he growled. "I have yet to ask questions of the ayah. Have I permission to take her to the other room?"

She was leaning through the window again and did not answer him.

"Who's that moving in the shadow down below?" she asked him suddenly.

He leaned out beside her and gazed into the shadow. Then he called softly in a tongue she did not know and some one rose up from the shadow and answered him.

"Are we spied on, Risaldar?"

"Nay. Guarded, heavenborn! That man is my half-brother. May I take the ayah through that doorway?"

"Why not question her in here?"

The mystery and sense of danger were getting the better of her; she was thoroughly afraid now--afraid to be left alone in the room for a minute even.

"There are things she would not answer in thy presence!"

"Very well. Only, please be quick!"

He bowed. Swinging the door open, he pushed the ayah through it to the room beyond. Ruth was left alone, to watch the red glow on the skyline and try to see the outline of the watcher in the gloom below. No sound came through the heavy teak door that the Risaldar had slammed behind him, and no sound came from him who watched; but from the silence of the night outside and from dark corners of the room that she was in and from the roof and walls and floor here came little eerie noises that made her flesh creep, as though she were being stared at by eyes she could not see. She felt that she must scream, or die, unless she moved; and she was too afraid to move, and by far too proud to scream! At last she tore herself away from the window and ran to a low divan and lay on it, smothering her face among the cushions. It seemed an hour before the Risaldar came out again, and then he took her by surprise.

"Heavenborn!" he said. She looked up with a start, to find him standing close beside her.

"Mahommed Khan! You're panting! What ails you?"

"The heat, heavenborn--and I am old."

His left hand was on his saber-hilt, thrusting it toward her respectfully; she noticed that it trembled.

"Have I the heavenborn's leave to lock the ayah in that inner room?"

"Why, Risaldar?"

"The fiend had this in her possession!" He showed her a thin-bladed dagger with an ivory handle; his own hand shook as he held it out to her, and she saw that there were beads of perspiration on his wrist. "She would have killed thee!"

"Oh, nonsense! Why, she wouldn't dare!"

"She confessed before she--she confessed! Have I the heavenborn's leave?"

"If you wish it."

"And to keep the key?"

"I suppose so, if you think it wise."

He strode to the inner door and locked it and hid the key in an inside pocket of his tunic.

"And now, heavenborn," he said, "I crave your leave to bring my half-brother to the presence!"

He scarcely waited for an answer, but walked to the window, leaned out of it and whistled. A minute later he was answered by the sound of fingernails scrabbling on the outer door. He turned the key and opened it.

"Enter!" he ordered.

Barefooted and ragged, but as clean as a soldier on parade and with huge knots of muscles bulging underneath his copper skin, a Rajput entered, bowing his six feet of splendid manhood almost to the floor.

"This, heavenborn, is my half-brother, son of a low-born border-woman, whom my father chose to honor thus far! The dog is loyal!"

"Salaam!" said Ruth, with little interest.

"Salaam, memsahib!" muttered the shabby Rajput. "Does any watch?" demanded the Risaldar in Hindustanee. "Aye, one."

"And he?"

"Is he of whom I spoke."

"Where watches he?"

"There is a hidden passage leading from the archway; he peeps out through a crack, having rolled back so far the stone that seals it." He held his horny fingers about an inch apart to show the distance.

"Couldst thou approach unseen?"

The Rajput nodded.

"And there are no others there?"

"No others."

"Has thy strength left thee, or thy cunning?"

"Nay!"

"Then bring him!"

Without a word in answer the giant turned and went, and the Risaldar made fast the door behind him. Ruth sat with her face between her hands, trying not to cry or shudder, but obsessed and overpowered by a sense of terror. The mystery that surrounded her was bad enough; but this mysterious ordering and coming to and fro among her friends was worse than horrible. She knew, though, that it would be useless to question Mahommed Khan before he chose to speak. They waited there in the dimly lighted room for what seemed tike an age again; she, pale and tortured by weird imaginings; he, grim and bolt-upright like a statue of a warrior. Then sounds came from the stairs again and the Risaldar hurried to the door and opened it.

In burst the Risaldar's half-brother, breathing heavily and bearing a load nearly as big as he was.

"The pig caught my wrist within the opening!" he growled, tossing his gagged and pinioned burden on the floor. "See where he all but broke it!"

"What is thy wrist to the service of the Raj? Is he the right one?"

"Aye!" He stooped and tore a twisted loin-cloth from his victim's face, and the Risaldar walked to the lamp and brought it, to hold it above the prostrate form. Ruth left the divan and stood between the men, terrified by she knew not what fear, but drawn into the lamplight by insuperable curiosity.

"This, heavenborn," said the Risaldar, prodding at the man with his scabbard-point, "is none other than the High Priest of Kharvani's temple here, the arch-ringleader in all the treachery afoot--now hostage for thy safety!"

He turned to his half-brother. "Unbind the thing he lies with!" he commanded, and the giant unwrapped a twisted piece of linen from the High Priest's mouth.

"So the big fox peeped through the trapdoor, because he feared to trust the other foxes; and the big fox fell into the trap!" grinned the Risaldar. "Bring me that table over yonder, thou!"

The half-brother did as he was told.

"Lay it here, legs upward, on the floor.

"Now, bind him to it--an arm to a leg and a leg to a leg.

"Remove his shoes.

"Put charcoal in yon brazier. Light it. Bring it hither!"

He seized a brass tongs, chose a glowing coal and held it six inches from the High Priest's naked foot.

Ruth screamed.

"Courage, heavenborn! Have courage! This is naught to what he would have done to thee!... Now, speak, thou priest of infidels! What plans are laid and who will rise and when?"

III.

"Sergeant!"

"Sir!"

The close-cropped, pipe-clayed non-commissioned officer spurred his horse into a canter until his scabbard clattered at young Bellairs' boot. Nothing but the rattling and the jolting of the guns and ammunition-wagon was audible, except just on ahead of them the click-clack, click-click-clack of the advance-guard. To the right and left of them the shadowy forms of giant banian-trees loomed and slid past them as they had done for the past four hours, and for ten paces ahead they could see the faintly outlined shape of the trunk road that they followed. The rest was silence and a pall of blackness obscuring everything. They had ridden along a valley, but they had emerged on rising ground and there was one spot of color in the pall now, or else a hole in it.

"What d'you suppose that is burning over there?"

"I couldn't say, sir."

"How far away is it?"

"Very hard to tell on a night like this, sir. It might be ten miles away and might be twenty. By my reckoning it's on our road, though, and somewhere between here and Jundhra."

"So it seems to me; our road swings round to the right presently, doesn't it? That'll lead us right to it. That would make it Doonha more or less. D'you suppose it's at Doonha?"

"I was thinking it might be, sir. If it's Doonha, it means that the sepoy barracks and all the stores are burning--there's nothing else there that would make all that flame!"

"There are two companies of the Thirty-third there, too."

"Yes, sir, but they're under canvas; tents would blaze up, but they'd die down again in a minute. That fire's steady and growing bigger!"

"It's the sepoy barracks, then!"

"Seems so to me, sir!"

"Halt!" roared Bellairs. The advance-guard kicked up a little shower of sparks, trace-chains slacked with a jingle and the jolting ceased. Bellairs rode up to the advance-guard.

"Now, Sergeant," he ordered, "it looks as though that were the Doonha barracks burning over yonder. There's no knowing, though, what it is. Send four men on, two hundred yards ahead of you, and you and the rest keep a good two hundred yards ahead of the guns. See that the men keep on the alert, and mind that they spare their horses as much as possible. If there's going to be trouble, we may just as well be ready for it!"

"Very good, sir!"

"Go ahead, then!"

At a word from the sergeant, four men clattered off and were swallowed in the darkness. A minute later the advance-guard followed them and then, after another minute's pause, young Bellairs' voice was raised into a ringing shout again.

"Section, advance! Trot, march!"

The trace-chains tightened, and the clattering, bumping, jingling procession began again, its rear brought up by the six-horse ammunition-wagon. They rode speechless for the best part of an hour, each man's eyes on the distant conflagration that had begun now to light up the whole of the sky ahead of them. They still rode in darkness, but they seemed to be approaching the red rim of the Pit. Huge, billowing clouds of smoke, red-lit on the under side, belched upward to the blackness overhead, and a something that was scarcely sound--for it was yet too distant--warned them that it was no illusion they were riding into. The conflagration grew. It seemed to be nearly white-hot down below.

Bellairs wet his finger and held it extended upward.

"There's no wind that I can feel!" he muttered. "And yet, if that were a grass-fire, there'd be game and rats and birds and things--some of 'em would bolt this way. That's the Doonha barracks burning or I'm a black man, which the Lord forbid!"

A minute later, every man in the section pricked up his ears. There was no order given; but a sensation ran the whole length of it and a movement from easy riding to tense rigidity that could be felt by some sixth sense. Every man was listening, feeling, groping with his senses for something he could neither hear as yet nor see, but that he knew was there. And then, far-distant yet--not above, but under the jolting of the gun-wheels and the rattle of the scabbards--they could hear the clickety-clickety-clickety-click of a horse hard-ridden.

They had scarcely caught that sound, they had barely tightened up their bridle-reins, when another sound, one just as unmistakable, burst out in front of them. A ragged, ill-timed volley ripped out from somewhere near the conflagration and was answered instantly by one that was close-ripped like the fire of heavy ordnance. And then one of the advance-guard wheeled his horse and drove his spurs home rowel-deep. He came thundering back along the road with his scabbard out in the wind behind him and reined up suddenly when his horse's forefeet were abreast of the lieutenant.

"There's some one coming, sir, hard as he can gallop! He's one of our men by the sound of him. His horse is shod--and I thought I saw steel when the fire-light fell on him a minute ago!"

"Are you sure there's only one?"

"Sure, sir! You can hear him now!"

"All right! Fall in behind me!"

Bellairs felt his sword-hilt and cocked a pistol stealthily, but he gave no orders to the section. This might be a native soldier run amuck, and it might be a messenger; but in either case, friend or foe, if there was only one man he could deal with him alone.

"Halt!" roared the advance-guard suddenly. But the horse's hoof-beats never checked for a single instant.

"Halt, you! Who comes there?"

"Friend!" came the answer, in an accent that was unmistakable.

"What friend? Where are you going?"

One of the advance-guard reined his horse across the road. The others followed suit and blocked the way effectually. "Halt!" they roared in unison.

The main body of the advance came up with them.

"Who is he?" shouted the sergeant.

"We'll soon see! Here he comes!"

"Out of my way!" yelled a voice, as a foamed-flecked horse burst out of the darkness like an apparition and bore straight down on them--his head bored a little to one side, the red rims of his nostrils wide distended and his whole sense and energy, and strength concentrated on pleasing the speed-hungry Irishman who rode him. He flashed into them head-on, like a devil from the outer darkness. His head touched a man's knee--and he rose and tried to jump him! His breast crashed full into the obstruction and horse and gunner crashed down to the road.

A dozen arms reached out--twelve horses surged in a clattering melee--two hands gripped the reins and four arms seized the rider, and in a second the panting charger was brought up all-standing. The sergeant thrust his grim face closer and peered at their capture.

"Good--, if it ain't an officer!" he exclaimed. "I beg your pardon, sir!"

And at that instant the section rattled, up behind them, with Bellairs in the lead.

"Halt!" roared Bellairs. "What's this?"

"Bloody murder, arson, high treason, mutiny and death! Blood and onions, man! Don't your men know an officer when they see one? Who are you? Are you

Bellairs? Then why in God's name didn't you say so sooner? What have you waited for?

"How many hours is it since you got the message through from Jundhra? Couldn't you see the barracks burning? Who am I--I'm Captain O'Rourke, of the Thirty-third, sent to see what you're doing on the road, that's who I am! A full-fledged; able-bodied captain wasted in a crisis, just because you didn't choose to hurry! Poison take your confounded gunners, sir! Have they nothing better to engage them than holding up officers on the Queen's trunk road?"

"Supposing you tell me what's the matter?" suggested young Bellairs, prompt as are most of his breed to appear casual the moment there was cause to feel excited.

"Your gunners have taken all my breath, sir. I can't speak!"

"You shouldn't take chances with a section of artillery! They're not like infantry--they don't sleep all the time--you can't ride through them as a rule!"

"Don't sleep, don't they! Then what have you been doing on the road? And what are you standing here for? Ride, man, ride! You're wanted!"

"Get out of the way, then!" suggested Bellairs, and Captain O'Rourke legged his panting charger over to the roadside.

"Advance-guard, forward, trot!" commanded the lieutenant.

"Have you brought your wife with you?" demanded O'Rourke, peering into the jingling blackness.

"No. Of course not. Why?"

"'Of course not! Why?' says the man! Hell and hot porridge! Why, the whole of India's ablaze from end to end--the sepoys have mutinied to a man, and the rest have joined them! There's bloody murder doing--they've shot their officers--Hammond's dead and Carstairs and Welfleet and heaven knows who else. They've burned their barracks and the stores and they're trying to seize the magazine. If they get that, God help every one. They're short of ammunition as it is, but two companies of the Thirty-third can't hold out for long against that horde. You'll be in the nick of time! Hurry, man! For the love of anything you like to name, get a move on!"

IV.

"Trot, march!

"Canter!"

Bellairs was thinking of his wife, alone in Hanadra, unprotected except by a sixty-year-old Risaldar and a half-brother who was a civilian and an unknown quantity. There were cold chills running down his spine and a sickening sensation in his stomach. He rode ahead of the guns, with O'Rourke keeping pace beside him. He felt that he hated O'Rourke, hated everything, hated the Service, and the country--and the guns, that could put him into such a fiendish predicament.

O'Rourke broke silence first.

"Who is with your wife?" he demanded suddenly.

"Heaven knows! I left her under the protection of Risaldar Mahommed Khan, but he was to ride off for an escort for her."

"Not your father's old Risaldar?" asked O'Rourke.

"The same."

"Then thank God! I'd sooner trust him than I would a regiment. He'll bring her in alive or slit the throats of half Asia--maybe 'he'll do both! Come, that's off our minds! She's safer with him than she would be here. Have you lots of ammunition?"

"I brought all I had with me at Hanadra."

"Good! What you'll need tonight is grape!"

"I've lots of it. It's nearly all grape."

"Hurrah! Then we'll treat those dirty mutineers to a dose or two of pills they won't fancy! Come on, man--set the pace a little faster!"

"Why didn't my orders say anything about a mutiny or bringing in my wife?"

"Dunno! I didn't write 'em. I can guess, though. There'd be something like nine reasons. For one thing, they'd credit you with sense enough to bring her in without being told. For another, the messenger who took the note might have got captured on the way--they wouldn't want to tell the sepoys more than they could help. Then there'd be something like a hurry. They're attacked there too--can't even send us assistance. Told us to waylay you and make use of you. Maybe they forgot your wife--maybe they didn't. It's a devil of a business anyhow!"

It was difficult to talk at the speed that they were making, with their own horses breathing heavily, O'Rourke's especially; the guns thundering along behind them and the advance-guard clattering in front, and their attention distracted every other minute by the noise of volleys on ahead and the occasional staccato rattle of independent firing. The whole sky was now alight with the reflection of the burning barracks and they could see the ragged outlines of the cracking walls silhouetted against the blazing red within. One mile or less from the burning buildings they could see, too, the occasional flash of rifles where the two companies of the Thirty-third, Honorable East India Company's Light Infantry, held out against the mutineers.

"Why did they mutiny?" asked Bellairs.

"God knows! Nobody knows! Nobody knows anything! I'm thinking--"

"Thinking what?"

"Forrester-Carter is commanding. We'll settle this business pretty quickly, now you've come. Then--Steady, boy! Steady! Hold up! This poor horse of mine is just about foundered, by the feel of him. He'll reach Doonha, though. Then we'll ask Carter to make a dash on Hanadra and bring Mrs. Bellairs--maybe we'll meet her and the Risaldar half-way--who knows? The sepoys wouldn't expect that, either. The move'd puzzle 'em--it'd be a good move, to my way of thinking."

"Let's hope Carter will consent!" prayed Bellairs fervently. "Now, what's the lay of things?"

"Couldn't tell you! When I left, our men were surrounded. I had to burst through the enemy to get away. Ours are all around the magazine and the sepoys are on every side of them. You'll have to use diagonal fire unless you want to hurt some of our chaps--sweep 'em cornerwise. There's high ground over to the right there, within four hundred yards of the position. Maybe they're holding it, though--there's no knowing!"

They could hear the roar of the flames now, and could see the figures of sepoys running here and there. The rattle of musketry was incessant. They could hear howls and yells and bugle-calls blown at random by the sepoys, and once, in answer as it seemed to a more than usually savage chorus from the enemy--a chorus that was punctuated by a raging din of intermittent rifle-fire--a ringing cheer.

"They must be in a tight hole!" muttered Bellairs. "Answer that, men! All together, now! Let 'em know we're coming."

The men rose in their stirrups all together, and sent roaring through the blackness the deep-throated "Hip-hip-hur-r-a-a-a-a!" that has gladdened more than one beleaguered British force in the course of history. It is quite different from the "Hur-o-a-o-a-u-r-rh" of a forlorn hope, or the high-pitched note of pleasure that signals the end of a review. It means "Hold on, till we get there, boys!" and it carries its meaning, clear and crisp and unmistakable, in its note.

The two beleaguered companies heard it and answered promptly with another cheer.

"By gad, they must be in a hole!" remarked Bellairs.

British soldiers do not cheer like that, all together, unless there is very good reason to feel cheerless. They fight, each man according to his temperament, swearing or laughing, sobbing or singing comic songs, until the case looks grim. Then, though, the same thrill runs through the whole of them, the same fire blazes in their eyes, and the last ditch that they line has been known to be a grave for the enemy.

"Trumpeter! Sound close-order!"

The trumpet rang. The advance-guard drew rein for the section to catch up. The guns drew abreast of one another and the mounted gunners formed in a line, two deep, in front of them. The ammunition-wagon trailed like a tail behind.

"That high ground over there, I think!" suggested O'Rourke.

"Thank you, sir. Section, right! Trot, march! Canter!"

Crash went the guns and the following wagon across the roadside ditch. The tired horses came up to the collar as service-horses always will, generous to the last ounce of strength they have in them.

"Gallop!"

The limbers bumped and jolted and the short-handled whips cracked like the sound of pistol-practise. Blind, unreconnoitered, grim--like a black thunderbolt loosed into the blackness--the two guns shot along a hollow, thundered up a ridge and burst into the fire-light up above the mutineers, in the last place where any one expected them. A howl came from the road that they had left, a hundred sepoys had rushed down to block their passage the moment that their cheer had rung above the noise of battle.

"Action--front!" roared young Bellairs, and the muzzles swung round at the gallop, jerked into position by the wheeling teams.

"With case, at four hundred!"

The orders were given and obeyed almost before the guns had lost their motion. The charges had been rammed into the greedy muzzles before the horses were away, almost--and that takes but a second--the horses vanish like blown smoke when the game begins. A howl from the mutineers told that they were seen; a volley from the British infantry announced that they were yet in time; and "boom-boom!" went both guns together.

The grapeshot whined and shrieked, and the ranks of the sepoys wilted, mown down as though a scythe had swept them. Once, and once only, they gathered for a charge on the two guns; but they were met half-way up the rise by a shrieking blast of grape that ripped through them and took the heart out of them; and the grape was followed by well-aimed volleys from behind. Then they drew off to sulk and make fresh plans at a distance, and Bellairs took his section unmolested into the Thirty-third-lined rampart round the magazine.

"What kept you, sir?" demanded Colonel Forrester-Carter, nodding to him in answer to his salute and holding out his right arm while a sergeant bandaged it.

"My wife, sir--I--"

"Where is she? Didn't you bring her?"

"No, sir--I--"

"Where is she?"

"Still at Hanadra, sir--I--"

"Let the men fall in! Call the roll at once!"

"There was nothing in my orders, sir, about--" But Colonel Carter cut him short with a motion and turned his back on him.

"Much obliged, Sergeant," he said, slipping his wounded arm into an improvised sling. "How many wagons have we here?"

"Four, sir."

"And horses?"

"All shot dead except your charger, sir."

"Oh! Ask Captain Trevor to come here."

The sergeant disappeared into the shadows, and a moment later Captain Trevor came running up and saluted.

"There are seven wounded, sir, and nineteen dead," he reported.

"Better than I had hoped, Trevor! Will you set a train to that magazine, please, and blow it up the moment we are at a safe distance?"

Trevor seemed surprised, but he saluted and said nothing.

"O'Rourke! Please see about burying the dead at once. Mr. Bellairs, let me have two horses, please, and their drivers, from each gun. Sergeant! See about putting the wounded into the lightest of the wagons and harness in four gun-horses the best way you can manage."

"Very good, sir."

"Which is your best horseman, Mr. Bellairs? Is his horse comparatively fresh? I'll need him to gallop with a message. I'll dictate it to Captain O'Rourke as soon as he is ready. Let the gunner stay here close to me."

Bellairs sought out his best man and the freshest-seeming horse in wondering silence. He felt sick with anxiety, for what could one lone veteran Risaldar do to protect Mrs. Bellairs against such a horde as was in Hanadra? He looked at the barracks, which were still blazing heavenward and illuminating the whole countryside, and shuddered as he wondered whether his quarters at Hanadra were in flames yet.

"It's a good job old Carter happened to be here!" he heard one of his men mumble to another. "He's a man, that is--I'd sooner fight under him than any I know of!"

"What d'you suppose the next move is?" asked the other man.

"I'd bet on it! I'll bet you what you like that--"

But Bellairs did not hear the rest.

A bugle rang out into the night. The gunners stood by their horses. Even the sentries, posted outside the rampart to guard against alarm, stood to attention, and Colonel Carter, wincing from the pain in his right arm, walked out in front of where the men were lined up.

Captain O'Rourke walked up and saluted him.

"I've arranged to bury them in that trench we dug this evening, sir, when the trouble started. It's not very deep, but it holds them all. I've laid them in it."

"Are you sure they're all dead?"

"I've burnt their fingers with matches, sir. I don't know of any better way to make sure."

"Very well. Can you remember any of the burial service?"

"'Fraid not, sir."

"Um! That's a pity. And I'm afraid I can't spare the time. Take a firing-party, Captain O'Rourke, and give them the last honors, at all events."

A party marched away toward the trench, and several minutes later O'Rourke's voice was heard calling through the darkness, "All ready, sir!"

"Present arms!" ordered the colonel, and the gunners sat their horses with their hilts raised to their hips and the two long lines of infantry stood rigid at the general salute, while five volleys--bulleted--barked upward above the grave. They were, answered by sniping from the mutineers, who imagined that reprisals had commenced.

"Now, men!" said Colonel Carter, raising his voice until every officer and man along the line could hear him, "as you must have realized, things are very serious indeed. We are cut off from support, but now that the guns are here to help us, we could either hold out here until relieved or else fight our way into Jundhra, where I have no doubt we are very badly needed. But"--he spoke more slowly and distinctly now, with a distinct pause between each word--"there is an officer's lady alone, and practically unprotected at Hanadra. Our duty is clear. You are tired--I know it. You have had no supper, and will get none. It means forced marching for the rest of this night and a good part of tomorrow and more fighting, possibly on an empty stomach; it means the dust and the heat and the discomfort of the trunk road for all of us and danger of the worst kind instead of safety--for we shall have farther to go to reach Jundhra. But I would do the same, and you men all know it, for any soldier's wife in my command, or any English woman in India. We will march now on Hanadra. No! No demonstrations, please!"

His uplifted left hand was just in time to check a roar of answering approval.

"Didn't I tell you so?" exclaimed a gunner to the man beside him in an undertone. "Him leave a white woman to face this sort o' music? He'd fight all India first!"

Ten minutes later two companies of men marched out behind the guns, followed by a cart that bore their wounded. As they reached the trunk road they were saluted by a reverberating blast when the magazine that they had fought to hold blew skyward. They turned to cheer the explosion and then settled down to march in deadly earnest and, if need be, to fight a rear-guard action all the way.

And in the opposite direction one solitary gunner rode, hell-bent-for-leather, with a note addressed to "O. C.--Jundhra." It was short and to the point. It ran:

Have blown up magazine; Mrs. Bellairs at Hanadra;
have gone to rescue her.
(Signed) A. FORRESTER-CARTER (Col.)
per J. O'Rourke

V.

The red glow of barracks burning--an ayah from whom a dagger has been taken locked in another room--the knowledge that there are fifty thousand Aryan brothers, itching to rebel, within a stone's throw--and two lone protectors of an alien race intent on torturing a High Priest, each and every one of these is a disturbing feature. No woman, and least of all a young woman such as Ruth Bellairs, can be blamed for being nervous under the stress of such conditions or for displaying a certain amount of feminine unreasonableness.

She stood shivering for a minute and watched spellbound while Mahommed Khan held the hot coal closer and even closer to the High Priest's naked foot. The priest writhed in anticipation of the agony and turned his eyes away, and as he turned them they met Ruth's. High priests of a religion that includes sooth-saying and prophecy and bribery of gods among its rites are students of human nature, and especially of female human nature. Knowledge of it and of how it may be gulled, and when, is the first essential of their calling. Her pale face, her blue eyes strained in terror, the parted lips and the attitude of tension, these gave him an idea. Before the charcoal touched him, he screamed--screamed like a wounded horse.

"Mahommed Khan, stop! Stop this instant! I won't have it! I won't have my life, even, on those terms! D'you hear me, sir!"

"Have courage, heavenborn! There is but one way to force a Hindu priest, unless it be by cutting off his revenues--he must be hurt! This dog is unhurt as yet--see! The fire has not yet touched his foot!"

"Don't let it, Mahommed Khan! Set that iron down! This is my room. I will not have crime committed here!"

"And how long does the heavenborn think it would be her room were this evil-living pig of a priest at large, or how long before a worse crime were committed? Heavenborn, the hour is late and the charcoal dies out rapidly when it has left the fire! See. I must choose another piece!"

He rummaged in the brazier, and she screamed again.

"I will not have it, Risaldar! You must find another way."

"Memsahib! Thy husband left thee in my care. Surely it is my right to choose the way?"

"Leave me, then! I relieve you of your trust. I will not have him tortured in my room, or anywhere!"

Mahommed Khan bowed low.

"Under favor, heavenborn," he answered, "my trust is to your husband. I can be released by him, or by death, not otherwise."

"Once, and for all, Mahommed Khan, I will not have you torture him in here!"

"Memsahib, I have yet to ride for succor! At daybreak, when these Hindus learn that the guns will not come back, they will rise to a man. Even now we must find a hiding-place or--it is not good even to think what I might find on my return!"

He leaned over the priest again, but without the charcoal this time.

"Speak, thou!" he ordered, growling in Hindustanee through his savage black mustache. "I have yet to hear what price a Hindu sets on immunity from torture!"

But the priest, it seemed, had formed a new idea. He had been looking through puckered eyes at Ruth, keen, cool calculation in his glance, and in spite of the discomfort of his strained position he contrived to nod.

"Kharvani!" he muttered, half aloud.

"Aye! Call on Kharvani!" sneered the Risaldar. "Perhaps the Bride of Sivi will appear! Call louder!"

He stirred again among the charcoal with his tongs, and Ruth and the High Priest both shuddered.

"Look!" said the High Priest in Hindustanee, nodding in Ruth's direction. It was the first word that he had addressed to them. It took them by surprise, and the Risaldar and his half-brother turned and looked. Their breath left them.

Framed in the yellow lamplight, her thin, hot-weather garments draped about her like a morning mist, Ruth stood and stared straight back at them through frightened eyes. Her blue-black hair, which had become loosened in her excitement, hung in a long plait over one shoulder and gleamed in the lamp's reflection. Her skin took on a faintly golden color from the feeble light, and her face seemed stamped with fear, anxiety, pity and suffering, all at once, that strangely enhanced her beauty, silhouetted as she was against the blackness of the wall behind, she seemed to be standing in an aura, shimmering with radiated light.

"Kharvani!" said the High Priest to himself again, and the two Rajputs stood still like men dumfounded, and stared and stared and stared. They knew Kharvani's temple. Who was there in Hanadra, Christian or Mohammedan or Hindu, who did not? The show-building of the city, the ancient, gloomy, wonderful erection where bats lived in the dome and flitted round Kharvani's image, the place where every one must go who needed favors of the priests, the central hub of treason and intrigue, where every plot was hatched and every rumor had its origin--the ultimate, mazy, greedy, undisgorging goal of every bribe and every blackmail-wrung rupee!

They knew, too, as every one must know who has ever been inside the place, the amazing, awe-inspiring picture of Kharvani painted on the inner wall; of Kharvani as she was idealized in the days when priests believed in her and artists thought the labor of a lifetime well employed in painting but one picture of her--Kharvani the sorrowful, grieving for the wickedness of earth; Kharvani, Bride of Siva, ready to intercede with Siva, the Destroyer, for the helpless, foolish, purblind sons of man.

And here, before them, stood Kharvani--to the life!

"What of Kharvani?" growled Mahommed Khan.

"'A purblind fool, a sot and a Mohammedan,'" quoted the priest maliciously, "'how many be they, three or one?'"

The Risaldar's hand went to his scabbard. His sword licked out free and trembled like a tuning-fork. He flicked with his thumbnail at the blade and muttered:

"Sharp! Sharp as death itself!"

The Hindu grinned, but the blade came down slowly until the point of it rested on the bridge of his nose. His eyes squinted inward, watching it.

"Now, make thy gentle joke again!" growled the Risaldar. Ruth Bellairs checked a scream.

"No blood!" she exclaimed. "Don't hurt him, Risaldar! I'll not have you kill a man in here--or anywhere, in cold blood, for that matter! Return your sword, sir!"

The Risaldar swore into his beard. The High Priest grinned again. "I am not afraid to die!" he sneered. "Thrust with that toy of thine! Thrust home and make an end!"

"Memsahib!" said the Risaldar, "all this is foolishness and waste of time! The hour is past midnight and I must be going. Leave the room--leave me and my half-brother with this priest for five short minutes and we will coax from him the secret of some hiding-place where you may lie hid until I come!"

"But you'll hurt him!"

"Not if he speaks, and speaks the truth!"

"Promise me!"

"On those conditions--yes!"

"Where shall I go?"

The Risaldar's eyes glanced toward the door of the inner room, but he hesitated. "Nay! There is the ayah!" he muttered. "Is there no other room?"

"No, Risaldar, no other room except through that door. Besides, I would rather stay here! I am afraid of what you may do to that priest if I leave you alone with him!"

"Now a murrain on all women, black and white!" swore Mahommed Khan beneath his breath. Then he turned on the priest again, and placed one foot on his stomach.

"Speak!" he ordered. "What of Kharvani?"

"Listen, Mahommed Khan!" Ruth Bellairs laid one hand on his sleeve, and tried to draw him back. "Your ways are not my ways! You are a soldier and a gentleman, but please remember that you are of a different race! I can not let my life be saved by the torture of a human being--no, not even of a Hindu priest! Maybe it's all right and honorable according to your ideas; but, if you did it, I would never be able to look my husband in the face again! No, Risaldar! Let this priest go, or leave him here--I don't care which, but don't harm him! I am quite ready to ride with you, now, if you like. I suppose you have horses? But I would rather die than think that a man was put to the torture to save me! Life isn't worth that price!"

She spoke rapidly, urging him with every argument she knew; but the grim old Mohammedan shook his head.

"Better die here," he answered her, "than on the road! No, memsahib. With thirteen blades behind me, I could reach Jundhra, or at least make a bold attempt; but single-handed, and with you to guard, the feat is impossible. This dog of a Hindu here knows of some hiding-place. Let him speak!"

His hand went to his sword again, and his eyes flashed.

"Listen, heavenborn! I am no torturer of priests by trade! It is not my life that I would save!"

"I know that, Mahommed Khan! I respect your motive. It's the method that I can't tolerate."

The Risaldar drew his arm away from her and began to pace the room. The High Priest instantly began to speak to Ruth, whispering to her hurriedly in Hindustanee, but she was too little acquainted with the language to understand him.

"And I," said the Risaldar's half-brother suddenly, "am I of no further use?"

"I had forgotten thee!" exclaimed the Risaldar.

They spoke together quickly in their own language, drawing aside and muttering to each other. It was plain that the half-brother was making some suggestion and that the Risaldar was questioning him and cross-examining him about his plan, but neither Ruth nor the High Priest could understand a word that either of them said. At the end of two minutes or more, the Risaldar gave an order of some kind and the half-brother grunted and left the room without another word, closing the door noiselessly behind him. The Risaldar locked it again from the inside and drew the bolt.

"We have made another plan, heavenborn!" he announced mysteriously.

"Then--then--you won't hurt this priest?"

"Not yet," said the Risaldar. "He may be useful!"

"Won't you unbind him, then? Look! His wrists and ankles are all swollen."

"Let the dog swell!" he grunted.

But Ruth stuck to her point and made him loosen the bonds a little.

"A man lives and learns!" swore the Risaldar. "Such as he were cast into dungeons in my day, to feed on their own bellies until they had had enough of life!"

"The times have changed!" said Ruth.

The Risaldar looked out through the window toward the red glow on the skyline.

"Ha! Changed, have they!" he muttered. "I saw one such burning, once before!"

VI.

The most wonderful thing in history, pointing with the surest finger to the trail of destiny, has been the fact that in every tremendous crisis there have been leaders on the spot to meet it. It is not so wonderful that there should be such men, for the world keeps growing better, and it is more than likely that the men who have left their footprints in the sands of time would compare to their own disadvantage with their compeers of today. The wonderful thing is that the right men have been in the right place at the right time. Scipio met Hannibal; Philip of Spain was forced to meet Howard of Effingham and Drake; Napoleon Bonaparte, the "Man of Destiny," found Wellington and Nelson of the Nile to deal with him; and, in America, men like George Washington and Grant and Lincoln seem, in the light of history, like timed, calculated, controlling devices in an intricate machine. It was so when the Indian Mutiny broke out. The struggle was unexpected. A handful of Europeans, commissioned and enlisted in the ordinary way, with a view to trade, not statesmanship, found themselves face to face at a minute's notice with armed and vengeful millions. Succor was a question of months, not days or weeks. India was ablaze from end to end with rebel fires that had been planned in secret through silent watchful years. The British force was scattered here and there in unconnected details, and each detail was suddenly cut off from every other one by men who had been trained to fight by the British themselves and who were not afraid to die.

The suddenness with which the outbreak came was one of the chief assets of the rebels, for they were able to seize guns and military stores and ammunition at the very start of things, before the British force could concentrate. Their hour could scarcely have been better chosen. The Crimean War was barely over. Practically the whole of England's standing army was abroad and decimated by battle and disease. At home, politics had England by the throat; the income-tax was on a Napoleonic scale and men were more bent on worsting one another than on equipping armies. They had had enough of war.

India was isolated, at the rebels' mercy, so it seemed. There were no railway trains to make swift movements of troops possible. Distances were reckoned by the hundred miles--of sun-baked, thirsty dust in the hot weather, and of mud in the rainy season. There were no telegraph-wires, and the British had to cope with the mysterious, and even yet unsolved, native means of sending news--the so-called "underground route," by which news and instructions travel faster than a pigeon flies. There was never a greater certainty or a more one-sided struggle, at the start. The only question seemed to be how many days, or possibly weeks, would pass before jackals crunched the bones of every Englishman in India.

But at the British helm was Nicholson, and under him were a hundred other men whose courage and resource had been an unknown quantity until the outbreak came. Nicholson's was the guiding spirit, but it needed only his generalship to fire all the others with that grim enthusiasm that has pulled Great Britain out of so many other scrapes. Instead of wasting time in marching and countermarching to relieve the scattered posts, a swift, sudden swoop was made on Delhi, where the eggs of the rebellion had hatched.

As many of the outposts as could be reached were told to fight their own way in, and those that could not be reached were left to defend themselves until the big blow had been struck at the heart of things. If Delhi could be taken, the rebels would be paralyzed and the rescue of beleaguered details would be easier; so, although odds of one hundred or more to one are usually considered overlarge in wartime--when the hundred hold the fort and the one must storm the gate--there was no time lost in hesitation. Delhi was the goal; and from north and south and east and west the men who could march marched, and those who could not entrenched themselves, and made ready to die in the last ditch.

Some of the natives were loyal still. There were men like Risaldar Mahommed Khan, who would have died ten deaths ten times over rather than be false in one particular to the British Government. It was these men who helped to make inter-communication possible, for they could carry messages and sometimes get through unsuspected where a British soldier would have been shot before he had ridden half a mile. Their loyalty was put to the utmost test in that hour, for they can not have believed that the British force could win. They knew the extent of what was out against them and knew, too, what their fate would be in the event of capture or defeat. There would be direr, slower vengeance wreaked on them than on the alien British. But they had eaten British salt and pledged their word, and nothing short of death could free them from it. There was not a shred of self interest to actuate them; there could not have been. Their given word was law and there it ended.

There were isolated commands, like that at Jundhra, that were too far away to strike at Delhi and too large and too efficient to be shut in by the mutineers. They were centers on their own account of isolated small detachments, and each commander was given leave to act as he saw best, provided that he acted and did it quickly. He could either march to the relief of his detachments or call them in, but under no condition was he to sit still and do nothing.

So, Colonel Carter's note addressed to O. C.--Jundhra only got two-thirds of the way from Doonha. The gunner who rode with it was brought to a sudden stand-still by an advance-guard of British cavalry, and two minutes later he found himself saluting and giving up his note to the General Commanding. The rebels at Jundhra had been worsted and scattered after an eight-hour fight, and General Turner had made up his mind instantly to sweep down on Hanadra with all his force and re-lieve the British garrison at Doonha on his way.

Jundhra was a small town and unhealthy. Hanadra was a large city, the center of a province; and, from all accounts, Hanadra had not risen yet. By seizing Hanadra before the mutineers had time to barricade themselves inside it, he could paralyze the countryside, for in Hanadra were the money and provisions and, above all, the Hindu priests who, in that part of India at least, were the brains of the rebellion. So he burned Jundhra, to make it useless to the rebels, and started for Hanadra with every man and horse and gun and wagon and round of ammunition that he had.

Now news in India travels like the wind, first one way and then another. But, unlike the wind, it never whistles. Things happen and men know it and the infor-mation spreads--invisible, intangible, inaudible, but positive and, in nine cases out of ten, correct in detail. A government can no more censor it, or divert it, or stop it on the way, than it can stay the birthrate or tamper with the Great Monsoon.

First the priests knew it, then it filtered through the main bazaars and from them on through the smaller streets. By the time that General Turner had been two hours on the road with his command every man and woman and child in Hanadra knew that the rebels had been beaten back and that Hanadra was his objective. They knew, too, that the section had reached Doonha, had relieved it and started back again. And yet not a single rebel who had fought in either engagement was within twenty miles of Hanadra yet!

In the old, low-ceilinged room above the archway Mahommed Khan paced up and down and chewed at his black mustache, kicking his scabbard away from him each time he turned and glowering at the priest.

"That dog can solve this riddle!" he kept muttering. Then he would glare at Ruth impatiently and execrate the squeamishness of women. Ruth sat on the divan with her face between her hands, trying to force herself to realize the full extent of her predicament and beat back the feeling of hysteria that almost had her in its grip. The priest lay quiet. He was in a torture of discomfort on the upturned table, but he preferred not to give the Risaldar the satisfaction of knowing it. He eased his position quietly from time to time as much as his bandages would let him, but he made no complaint.

Suddenly, Ruth looked up. It had occurred to her that she was wasting time and that if she were to fight off the depression that had seized her she would be better occupied.

"Mahommed Khan," she said, "if I am to leave here on horseback, with you or with an escort, I had better collect some things that I would like to take with me. Let me in that room, please!"

"The horse will have all that it can carry, heavenborn, without a load of woman's trappings."

"My jewels? I can take them, I suppose?"

He bowed. "They are in there? I will bring them, heavenborn!"

"Nonsense! You don't know where to find them."

"The ayah--will--will show me!"

He fitted the key into the lock and turned it, but Ruth was at his side before he could pass in through the door.

"Nonsense, Risaldar! The ayah can't hurt me. You have taken her knife away, and that is my room. I will go in there alone!"

She pushed past him before he could prevent her, thrust the door back and peered in.

"Stay, heavenborn--I will explain!"

"Explain what?"

The dim light from the lamp was filtering in past them, and her eyes were slowly growing accustomed to the gloom. There was something lying on the floor, in the middle of the room, that was bulky and shapeless and unfamiliar.

"Ayah!" said Ruth. "Ayah!"

But there was no answer.

"Where is she, Risaldar?"

"She is there, heavenborn!"

"Is she asleep?"

"Aye! She sleeps deeply!"

There was, something in the Rajput's voice that was strange, that hinted at a darker meaning.

"Ayah!" she called again, afraid, though she knew not why, to enter.

"She guards the jewels, heavenborn! Wait, while I bring the lamp!"

He crossed the room, brought it and stepped with it past Ruth, straight into the room.

"See!" he said, holding the lamp up above his head. "There in her bosom are the jewels! It was there, too, that she had the knife to slay thee with! My sword is clean, yet, heavenborn! I slew her with my fingers, thus!"

He kicked the prostrate ayah, and, as the black face with the wide-open blood-shot eyes and the protruding tongue rolled sidewise and the body moved, a little heap of jewels fell upon the floor. Mahommed Khan stooped down to gather them, bending, a little painfully, on one old knee--but stopped half-way and turned. There was a thud behind him in the doorway. Ruth Bellairs had fainted, and lay as the ayah had lain when Risaldar had not yet locked her in the room.

He raised the lamp and studied her in silence for a minute, looking from her to the bound priest and back to her again.

"Now praised be Allah!" he remarked aloud, with a world of genuine relief in his voice. "Should she stay fainted for a little while, that priest--"

He stalked into the middle of the outer room. He set the lamp down on a table and looked the priest over as a butcher might survey a sheep he is about to kill.

"Now--robber of orphans--bleeder of widows' blood--dog of an idol-briber! This stands between thee and Kharvani!" He drew his sword and flicked the edges of it. "And this!" He took up the tongs again. "There is none now to plead or to forbid! Think! Show me the way out of this devil's nest, or--" He raised the tongs again.

At that minute came a quiet knock. He set the tongs down again and crossed the room and opened the door.

VII.

Mahommed Khan closed the door again behind his half-brother and turned the key, but the half-brother shot the bolt home as well before he spoke, then listened intently for a minute with his ear to the keyhole.

"Where is the priest's son?" growled the Risaldar, in the Rajput tongue.

"I have him. I have the priestling in a sack. I have him trussed and bound and gagged, so that he can neither speak nor wriggle!"

"Where?"

"Hidden safely."

"I said to bring him here!"

"I could not. Listen! That ayah--where is she?"

"Dead! What has the ayah to do with it?"

"This--she was to give a sign. She was not to slay. She had leave only to take the jewels. Her orders were either to wait until she knew by questioning that the section would not return or else, when it had returned, to wait until the memsahib and Bellairs sahib slept, and then to make a sign. They grow tired of waiting now, for there is news! At Jundhra the rebels are defeated, and at Doonha likewise."

"How know you this?"

"By listening to the priests' talk while I lay in wait to snare the priestling. Nothing is known as yet as to what the guns or garrison at Doonha do, but it is known that they of Jundhra will march on Hanadra here. They search now for their High Priest, being minded to march out of here and set an ambush on the road."

"They have time. From Jundhra to here is a long march! Until tomorrow evening or the day following they have time!"

"Aye! And they have fear also! They seek their priest--listen."

There were voices plainly audible in the courtyard down below, and two more men stood at the foot of the winding stairway whispering. By listening intently they could hear almost what they said, for the stone stairway acted like a whispering-gallery, the voices echoing up it from wall to wall.

"Why do they seek him here?"

"They have sought elsewhere and not found him; and there is talk--He claimed the memsahib as his share of the plunder. They think--"

Mahommed Khan glared at the trussed-up priest and swore a savage oath beneath his breath.

"Have they touched the stables yet?" he demanded.

"No, not yet. The loot is to be divided evenly among certain of the priests, and no man may yet lay a hand on it."

"Is there a guard there?"

"No. No one would steal what the priests claim, and the priests will not trust one another. So the horses stand in their stalls unwatched."

The voices down the stairs grew louder, and the sound of footsteps began ascending, slowly and with hesitation.

"Quick!" said the Risaldar. "Light me that brazier again!"

Charcoal lights quickly, and before the steps had reached the landing Mahommed Khan had a hot coal glowing in his tongs:

"Now speak to them!" he growled at the shuddering priest. "Order them to go back to their temple and tell them that you follow!"

The priest shut his lips tight and shook his head. With rescue so near as that, he could see no reason to obey. But the hot coal touched him, and a Hindu who may be not at all afraid to die can not stand torture.

"I speak!" he answered, writhing.

"Speak, then!" said the Risaldar, choosing a larger coal. Then, in the priest's language, which none--and least of all a Risaldar--can understand except the priests themselves, he began to shout directions, pitching his voice into a high, wailing, minor key. He was answered by another sing-song voice outside the door and he listened with a glowing coal held six inches from his eyes.

"An eye for a false move!" hissed Mahommed Khan. "Two eyes are the forfeit unless they go down the stairs again! Then my half-brother here will follow to the temple and if any watch, or stay behind, thy ears will sizzle!"

The High Priest raised his voice into a wail again, and the feet shuffled along the landing and descended.

"Put down that coal!" he pleaded. "I have done thy bidding!"

"Watch through the window!" said the Risaldar. "Then follow!"

His giant half-brother peered from behind the curtain and listened. He could hear laughter, ribald, mocking laughter, but low, and plainly not intended for the High Priest's ears.

"They go!" he growled.

"Then follow."

Once again the Risaldar was left alone with the priest and the unconscious Ruth. She was suffering from the effects of long days and nights of nerve-destroying heat, with the shock of unexpected horror super-added, and she showed no disposition to recover consciousness. The priest, though, was very far from having lost his power to think.

"You are a fool!" he sneered at the Risaldar, but the sword leaped from its scabbard at the word and he changed that line of argument. "You hold cards and know not how to play them!"

"I know along which road my honor lies! I lay no plans to murder people in their sleep."

"Honor! And what is honor? What is the interest on honor--how much per-cent?"

The Risaldar turned his back on him, but the High Priest laughed.

"'The days of the Raj are numbered!" said the priest. "The English will be slain to the last man and then where will you be? Where will be the profit on your honor?"

The Risaldar listened, for he could not help it, but he made no answer.

"Me you hold here, a prisoner. You can slay or torture. But what good will that do? The woman that you guard will fall sooner or later into Hindu hands. You can not fight against a legion. Listen! I hold the strings of wealth. With a jerk I can unloose a fortune in your lap. I need that woman there!"

"For what?" snarled the Risaldar, whirling round on him, his eyes ablaze.

"'For power! Kharvani's temple here has images and paintings and a voice that speaks--but no Kharvani!"

The Rajput turned away again and affected unconcern.

"Could Kharvani but appear, could her worshipers but see Kharvani manifest, what would a lakh, two lakhs, a crore of rupees mean to me, the High Priest of her temple? I could give thee anything! The power over all India would be in my hands! Kharvani would but appear and say thus and thus, and thus would it be done!"

The Risaldar's hand had risen to his mustache. His back was still turned on the priest, but he showed interest. His eyes wandered to where Ruth lay in a heap by the inner door and then away again.

"Who would believe it?" he growled in an undertone.

"They would all believe it! One and all! Even Mohammedans would become Hindus to worship at her shrine and beg her favors. Thou and I alone would share the secret. Listen! Loose me these bonds--my limbs ache."

Mahommed Khan turned. He stooped and cut them with his sword.

"Now I can talk," said the priest, sitting up and rubbing his ankles. "Listen. Take thou two horses and gallop off, so that the rest may think that the white woman has escaped. Then return here secretly and name thy price--and hold thy tongue!"

"And leave her in thy hands?" asked the Risaldar.

"In my keeping."

"Bah! Who would trust a Hindu priest!"

The Rajput was plainly wavering and the priest stood up, to argue with him the better.

"What need to trust me? You, sahib, will know the secret, and none other but myself will know it. Would I, think you, be fool enough to tell the rest, or, by withholding just payment from you, incite you to spread it broadcast? You and I will know it and we alone. To me the power that it will bring--to you all the wealth you ever dreamed of, and more besides!"

"No other priest would know?"

"Not one! They will think the woman escaped!"

"And she--where would you keep her?"

"In a secret place I know of, below the temple."

"Does any other know it?"

"No. Not one!"

"Listen!" said the Risaldar, stroking at his beard. "This woman never did me any wrong--but she is a woman, not a man. I owe her no fealty, and yet--I would not like to see her injured. Were I to agree to thy plan, there would needs be a third man in the secret."

"Who? Name him," said the priest, grinning his satisfaction.

"My half-brother Suliman."

"Agreed!"

"He must go with us to the hiding-place and stay there as her servant."

"Is he a silent man?"

"Silent as the dead, unless I bid him speak!"

"Then, that is agreed; he and thou and I know of this secret, and none other is to know it! Why wait? Let us remove her to the hiding-place!"

"Wait yet for Suliman. How long will I be gone, think you, on my pretended flight?"

"Nay, what think you, sahib?"

"I think many hours. There may be those that watch, or some that ride after me. I think I shall not return until long after daylight, and then there will be no suspicions. Give me a token that will admit me safely back into Hanadra--some sign that the priests will know, and a pass to show to any one that bids me halt."

The priest held out his hand. "Take off that ring of mine!" he answered. "That is the sacred ring of Kharvani--and all men know it. None will touch thee or refuse thee anything, do they have but the merest sight of it!"

The Risaldar drew off a clumsy silver ring, set with three stones--a sapphire and a ruby and an emerald, each one of which was worth a fortune by itself. He slipped it on his own finger and turned it round slowly, examining it.

"See how I trust thee," said the priest.

"More than I do thee!" muttered the Risaldar.

"I hear my brother!" growled the Risaldar after another minute. "Be ready to show the way!"

He walked across the room to Ruth, tore a covering from a divan and wrapped her in it; then he opened the outer door for his half-brother.

"Is it well?" he asked in the Rajput tongue.

"All well!" boomed the half-brother, eying the unbound priest with unconcealed surprise.

"Do any watch?"

"Not one! The priests are in the temple; all who are not priests man the walls or rush here and there making ready."

"And the priestling?"

"Is where I left him."

"Where?--I said."

"In the niche underneath the arch, where I trapped the High Priest!"

"Are the horses fed and watered?"

"Ha, sahib!"

"Good! How is the niche opened where the priestling lies?"

"There is the trunk of an elephant, carved where the largest stone of all begins to curve outward, on the side of the stone as you go outward from the courtyard."

"On which side of the archway, then?"

"On the left side, sahib. Press on the trunk downward and then pull; the stone swings outward. There are steps then--ten steps downward to the stone floor where the priestling lies."

"Good! I can find him. Now pick up the heavenborn yonder in those great arms of thine, and bear her gently! Gently, I said! So! Have a care, now, that she is not injured against the corners. My honor, aye, my honor and yours and all our duty to the Raj you bear and--and have a care of the corners?"

"Aye," answered the half-brother, stolidly, holding Ruth as though she had been a little bag of rice.

Again the Risaldar turned to the High Priest, and eyed him through eyes that glittered.

"We are ready!" he growled. "Lead on to thy hiding-place!"

VIII.

The guns rode first from Doonha, for the guns take precedence. The section ground-scouts were acting scouts for the division, two hundred yards ahead of every one. Behind the guns rode Colonel Forrester-Carter, followed by the wagon with the wounded; and last of all the two companies of the Thirty-third trudged through the stifling heat.

But, though the guns were ahead of every one, they had to suit their pace to that of the men who marched. For one thing, there might be an attack at any minute, and guns that are caught at close quarters at a distance from their escort are apt to be astonishingly helpless. They can act in unison with infantry; but alone, on bad ground, in the darkness, and with their horses nearly too tired to drag them, a leash of ten puppies in a crowd would be an easier thing to hurry with.

Young Bellairs had his men dismounted and walking by their mounts. Even the drivers led their horses, for two had been taken from each gun to drag the wounded, and the guns are calculated as a load for six, not four.

As he trudged through the blood-hot dust in clumsy riding-boots and led his charger on the left flank of the guns, Harry Bellairs fumed and fretted in a way to make no man envy him. The gloomy, ghost-like trees, that had flitted past him on the road to Doonha, crawled past him now--slowly and more slowly as his tired feet blistered in his boots. He could not mount and ride, though, for very shame, while his men were marching, and he dared not let them ride, for fear the horses might give in. He could just trudge and trudge, and hate himself and every one, and wonder.

What had the Risaldar contrived to do? Why hadn't he packed up his wife's effects the moment that his orders came and ridden off with her and the section at once, instead of waiting three hours or more for an escort for her? Why hadn't he realized at once that orders that came in a hurry that way, in the night-time, were not only urgent but ominous as well? What chance had the Risaldar--an old man, however willing he might be--to ride through a swarming countryside for thirty miles or more and bring back an escort? Why, even supposing Mohammed Khan had ridden off at once, he could scarcely be back again before the section! And what would have happened in the meantime?

Supposing the Risaldar's sons and grandsons refused to obey him? Stranger things than that had been known to happen! Suppose they were disloyal? And then--blacker though than any yet!--suppose--suppose-- Why had Mahommed Khan, the hard-bitten, wise old war-dog, advised him to leave his wife behind? Did that seem like honest advice, on second thought? Mohammedans had joined in this outbreak as well as Hindus. The sepoys at Doonha were Mohammedans! Why had Mahommed Khan seemed so anxious to send him on his way? As though an extra five minutes would have mattered! Why had he objected to a last good-by to Mrs. Bellairs?... And then--he had shown a certain knowledge of the uprising; where had he obtained it? If he were loyal, who then had told him of it? Natives who are disloyal don't brag of their plans beforehand to men who are on the other side! And if he had known of it, and was still loyal, how was it that he had not divulged his information before the outbreak came? Would a loyal man hold his tongue until the last minute? Scarcely!

He halted, pulled his horse to the middle of the road and waited for Colonel Carter to overtake him.

"Well? What is it?" asked the colonel sharply.

"Can I ride on ahead, sir? My horse is good for it and I'm in agonies of apprehension about my wife!"

"No! Certainly not! You are needed to command your section!"

"I beg your pardon, sir, but I've a sergeant who can take command. He's a first-class man and perfectly dependable."

"You could do no good, even if you did ride on," said the colonel, not unkindly.

"I'm thinking, sir, that Mahommed Khan--"

"Risaldar Mahommed Khan?"

"Yes, sir."

"Of the Rajput Horse?"

"Yes, sir. My father's Risaldar."

"You left your wife in his charge, didn't you?"

"Yes, sir, but I'm thinking that--that perhaps the Risaldar--I mean--there seem to be Mohammedans at the bottom of this business, as well as Hindus. Perhaps--"

"Bellairs! Now hear me once and for all. You thank your God that the Risaldar turned up to guard her! Thank God that your father was man enough for Mahommed Khan to love and that you are your father's son! And listen! Don't let me hear you, ever, under any circumstances, breathe a word of doubt as to that man's loyalty! D'you understand me, sir? You, a mere subaltern, a puppy just out of his 'teens, an insignificant jackanapes with two twelve-pounders in your charge, daring to impute disloyalty to Mahommed Khan!--your impudence! Remember this! That old Risaldar is the man who rode with your father through the guns at Dera! He's a pauper without a pension, for all his loyalty, but he went down the length of India to meet you, at his own expense, when you landed raw-green from England! And what d'you know of war, I'd like to know, that you didn't learn from him? Thank your God, sir, that there's some one there who'll kill your wife before she falls into the Hindus' hands!"

"But he was going to ride away, sir, to bring an escort!"

"Not before he'd made absolutely certain of her safety!" swore the colonel with conviction. "Join your section, sir!"

So Harry Bellairs joined his section and trudged along sore-footed at its side--sore-hearted, too. He wondered whether any one would ever say as much for him as Colonel Carter had chosen to say for Mahommed Khan, or whether any one would have the right to say it! He was ashamed of having left his wife behind and tortured with anxiety--and smarting from the snub--a medley of sensations that were more likely to make a man of him, if he had known it, than the whole experience of a year's campaign! But in the dust and darkness, with the blisters on his heels, and fifty men, who had overheard the colonel, looking sidewise at him, his plight was pitiable.

They trudged until the dawn began to rise, bright yellow below the drooping banian trees; only Colonel Carter and the advance-guard riding. Then, when they stopped at a stream to water horses and let them graze a bit and give the men a sorely needed rest, one of the ring of outposts loosed off his rifle and shouted an alarm. They had formed square in an instant, with the guns on one side and the men on three, and the colonel and the wounded in the middle. A thousand or more of the mutineers leaned on their rifles on the shoulder of a hill and looked them over, a thousand yards away.

"Send them an invitation!" commanded Colonel Carter, and the left-hand gun barked out an overture, killing one sepoy. The rest made off in the direction of Hanadra.

"We're likely to have a hot reception when we reach there!" said Colonel Carter cheerily. "Well, we'll rest here for thirty minutes and give them a chance to get ready for us. I'm sorry there's no breakfast, men, but the sepoys will have dinner ready by the time we get there--we'll eat theirs!"

The chorus of ready laughter had scarcely died away when a horse's hoof-beats clattered in the distance from the direction of Doonha and a native cavalryman galloped into view, low-bent above his horse's neck. The foam from his horse was spattered over him and his lance swung pointing upward from the sling. On his left side the polished scabbard rose and fell in time to his horse's movement. He was urging his weary horse to put out every ounce he had in him. He drew rein, though, when he reached a turning in the road and saw the resting division in front of him, and walked his horse forward, patting his sweat-wet neck and easing him. But as he leaned to finger with the girths an ambushed sepoy fired at him, and he rammed in his spurs again and rode like a man possessed.

"This'll be another untrustworthy Mohammedan!" said Colonel Carter in a pointed undertone, and Bellairs blushed crimson underneath the tan. "He's ridden through from Jundhra, with torture waiting for him if he happened to get caught, and no possible reward beyond his pay. Look out he doesn't spike your guns!"

The trooper rode straight up to Colonel Carter and saluted. He removed a tiny package from his cheek, where he had carried it so that he might swallow it at once in case of accident, tore the oil-silk cover from it and handed it to him without a word, saluting again and leading his horse away. Colonel Carter unfolded the half-sheet of foreign notepaper and read:

Dear Colonel Carter:
Your letter just received in which you say that you have blown
up the magazine at Doonha and are marching to Hanadra with a
view to the rescue of Mrs. Bellairs. This is in no sense
intended as a criticism of your action or of your plan, but

circumstances have made it seem advisable for me to transfer
my own headquarters to Hanadra and I am just starting. I must
ask you, please, to wait for me--at a spot as near to where
this overtakes you as can be managed. If Mrs. Bellairs, or
anybody else of ours, is in Hanadra, she--or they--are either
dead by now or else prisoners. And if they are to be rescued
by force, the larger the force employed the better. If you
were to attack with your two companies before I reached you,
you probably would be repulsed, and would, I think, endanger
the lives of any prisoners that the enemy may hold. I am
coming with my whole command as fast as possible.
Your Obedient Servant,
A. E. Turner
Genl. Officer Commanding

"Men!" said Colonel Carter, in a ringing voice that gave not the slightest indi-
cation of his feelings, "we're to wait here for a while until the whole division overtakes us. The general has vacated Jundhra. Lie down and get all the rest you can!"

The murmur from the ranks was as difficult to read as Colonel Carter's voice
had been. It might have meant pleasure at the thought of rest, or anger, or contempt, or almost anything. It was undefined and indefinable.

But there was no doubt at all as to how young Bellairs felt. He was sitting on a
trunnion, sobbing, with his head bent low between his hands.

IX.

"Come, then!" said the High Priest.

Mahommed Khan threw open the outer door and bowed sardonically. "Precedence for priests!" he sneered, tapping at his sword-hilt. "Thou goest first! Next
come I, and last Suliman with the memsahib! Thus can I reach thee with my sword,
O priest, and also protect her if need be!"

"Thou art trusting as a little child!" exclaimed the priest, passing out ahead of him.

"A priest and a liar and a thief--all three are one!" hummed the Risaldar. "Bear her gently, Suliman! Have a care, now, as you turn on the winding stairs!"

"Ha, sahib!" said the half-brother, carrying Ruth as easily as though she had been a little child.

At the foot of the stairway, in the blackness that seemed alive with phantom shadows, the High Priest paused and listened, stretching out his left hand against the wall to keep the other two behind him. From somewhere beyond the courtyard came the din of hurrying sandaled feet, scudding over cobblestones in one direction. The noise was incessant and not unlike the murmur of a rapid stream. Occasionally a voice was raised in some command or other, but the stream of sound continued, hurrying, hurrying, shuffling along to the southward.

"This way and watch a while," whispered the priest.

"I have heard rats run that way!" growled the Risaldar.

They climbed up a narrow stairway leading to a sort of battlement and peered over the top, Suliman laying Ruth Bellairs down in the darkest shadow he could find. She was beginning to recover consciousness, and apparently Mahommed Khan judged it best to take no notice of her.

Down below them they could see the city gate, wide open, with a blazing torch on either side of it, and through the gate, swarming like ants before the rains, there poured an endless stream of humans that marched--and marched--and marched; four, ten, fifteen abreast; all heights and sizes, jumbled in and out among one another, anyhow, without formation, but armed, every one of them, and all intent on marching to the southward, where Jundhra and Doonha lay. Some muttered to one another and some laughed, but the greater number marched in silence.

"That for thy English!" grinned the priest. "Can the English troops overcome that horde?"

"Hey-ee! For a troop or two of Rajputs!" sighed the Risaldar. "Or English Lancers! They would ride through that as an ax does through the brush-wood!"

"Bah!" said the priest. "All soldiers boast! There will be a houghing shortly after dawn. The days of thy English are now numbered."

"By those--there?"

"Ay, by those, there! Come!"

They climbed down the steps again, the Rajput humming to himself and smiling grimly into his mustache.

"Ay! There will be a houghing shortly after dawn!" he muttered. "Would only that I were there to see!... Where are the sepoys?" he demanded.

"I know not. How should I know, who have been thy guest these hours past? This march is none of my ordering."

The priest pressed hard on a stone knob that seemed to be part of the carving on a wall, then he leaned his weight against the wall and a huge stone swung inward, while a fetid breath of air wafted outward in their faces.

"None know this road but I!" exclaimed the priest.

"None need to!" said the Risaldar. "Pass on, snake, into thy hole. We follow."

"Steps!" said the priest, and began descending.

"Curses!" said the Risaldar, stumbling and falling down on top of him. "Have a care, Suliman! The stone is wet and slippery."

Down, down they climbed, one behind the other, Suliman grunting beneath his burden and the Risaldar keeping up a running fire of oaths. Each time that he slipped, and that was often, he cursed the priest and cautioned Suliman. But the priest only laughed, and apparently Suliman was sure-footed, for he never stumbled once. They seemed to be diving down into the bowels of the earth. They were in pitch-black darkness, for the stone had swung to behind them of its own accord. The wall on either side of them was wet with slime and the stink of decaying ages rose and almost stifled them. But the priest kept on descending, so fast that the other two had trouble to keep up with him, and he hummed to himself as though he knew the road and liked it.

"The bottom!" he called back suddenly. "From now the going is easy, until we rise again. We pass now under the city-wall."

But they could see nothing and hear nothing except their own footfalls swishing in the ooze beneath them. Even the priest's words seemed to be lost at once, as though he spoke into a blanket, for the air they breathed was thicker than a mist and just as damp. They walked on, along a level, wet, stone passage for at least five minutes, feeling their way with one band on the wall.

"Steps, now!" said the priest. "Have a care, now, for the lower ones are slippery."

Ruth was regaining consciousness. She began to move and tried once or twice to speak.

"Here, thou!" growled the Risaldar. "Thou art a younger man than I--come back here. Help with the memsahib."

The priest came back a step or two, but Suliman declined his aid, snarling vile insults at him.

"I can manage!" he growled. "Get thou behind me, Mahommed Khan, in case I slip!"

So Mahommed Khan came last, and they slipped and grunted upward, round and round a spiral staircase that was hewn out of solid rock. No light came through from anywhere to help them, but the priest climbed on, as though he were accustomed to the stair and knew the way from constant use. After five minutes of steady climbing the stone grew gradually dry. The steps became smaller, too, and deeper, and not so hard to climb. Suddenly the priest reached out his arm and pulled at something or other that hung down in the darkness. A stone in the wall rolled open. A flood of light burst in and nearly blinded them.

"We are below Kharvani's temple!" announced the priest. He led them through the opening into a four-square room hewn from the rock below the foundations of the temple some time in the dawn of history. The light that had blinded them when they first emerged proved to be nothing but the flicker of two small oil lamps that hung suspended by brass chains from the painted ceiling. The only furniture was mats spread on the cut-stone floor.

"By which way did we come?" asked the Risaldar, staring in amazement round the walls. There was not a door nor crack, nor any sign of one, except that a wooden ladder in one corner led to a trapdoor overhead, and they had certainly not entered by the ladder.

"Nay! That is a secret!" grinned the priest. "He who can may find the opening! Here can the woman and her servant stay until we need them."

"Here in this place?"

"Where else? No man but I knows of this crypt! The ladder there leads to another room, where there is yet another ladder, and that one leads out through a secret door I know of, straight into the temple. Art ready? There is need for haste!"

"Wait!" said the Risaldar.

"These soldiers!" sneered the priest. "It is wait--wait--wait with them, always!"

"Hast thou a son."

"Ay! But what of it?"

"I said 'hast,' not 'hadst'!"

"Ay. I have a son."

"Where?"

"In one of the temple-chambers overhead."

"Nay, priest! Thy son lies gagged and bound and trussed in a place I know of, and which thou dost not know!"

"Since when?"

"Since by my orders he was laid there."

"Thou art the devil! Thou liest, Rajput!"

"So? Go seek thy son!"

The priest's face had blanched beneath the olive of his skin, and he stared at Mahommed Khan through distended eyes.

"My son!" he muttered.

"Aye! Thy priestling! He stays where he is, as hostage, until my return! Also the heavenborn stays here! If, on my return, I find the heavenborn safe and sound, I will exchange her for thy son--and if not, I will tear thy son into little pieces before thy eyes, priest! Dost thou understand?"

"Thou liest! My son is overhead in the temple here!"

"Go seek him, then!"

The priest turned and scampered up the ladder with an agility that was astonishing in a man of his build and paunch.

"Hanuman should have been thy master!" jeered the Risaldar. "So run the bandar-log, the monkey-folk!"

But the priest had no time to answer him. He was half frantic with the sickening fear of a father for his only son. He returned ten minutes later, panting, and more scared than ever.

"Go, take thy white woman," he exclaimed, "and give me my son back!"

"Nay, priest! Shall I ride with her alone through that horde that are marching through the gate? I go now for an escort; in eight--ten--twelve--I know not how many hours, I will return for her, and then--thy son will be exchanged for her, or he dies thus in many pieces!"

He turned to Suliman. "Is she awake yet?" he demanded.

"Barely, but she recovers."

"Then tell her, when consciousness returns, that I have gone and will return for her. And stay here, thou, and guard her until I come."

"Ha, sahib!"

"Now, show the way!"

"But--" said the priest, "our bargain? The price that we agreed on--one lakh, was it not?"

"One lakh of devils take thee and tear thee into little pieces! Wouldst bribe a Rajput, a Risaldar? For that insult I will repay thee one day with interest, O priest! Now, show the way!"

"But how shall I be sure about my son?"

"Be sure that the priestling will starve to death or die of thirst or choke, unless I hurry! He is none too easy where he lies!"

"Go! Hurry, then!" swore the priest. "May all the gods there are, and thy Allah with them, afflict thee with all their curses--thee and thine! Up with you! Up that ladder! Run! But, if the gods will, I will meet thee again when the storm is over!"

"Inshallah!" growled Mahommed Khan.

Ten minutes later a crash and a clatter and a shower of sparks broke out in the sweltering courtyard where the guns had stood and waited. It was Shaitan, young Bellairs' Khaubuli charger, with his haunches under him, plunging across the flag-stones, through the black-dark archway, out on the plain beyond--in answer to the long, sharp-roweled spurs of the Risaldar Mahommed Khan.

X.

Dawn broke and the roofs of old Hanadra became resplendent with the varied colors of turbans and pugrees and shawls. As though the rising sun had loosed the spell, a myriad tongues, of women chiefly, rose in a babel of clamor, and the few men who had been left in. Hanadra by the night's armed exodus came all together and growled prophetically in undertones. Now was the day of days, when that part of India, at least, should cast off the English yoke.

To the temple! The cry went up before the sun was fifteen minutes high. There are a hundred temples in Hanadra, age-old all of them and carved on the outside with strange images of heathen gods in high relief, like molds turned inside out. But there is but one temple that that cry could mean--Kharvani's; and there could be but one meaning for the cry. Man, woman and child would pray Kharvani, Bride of Siva the Destroyer, to intercede with Siva and cause him to rise and smite the English. On the skyline, glinting like flashed signals in the early sun, bright English bayonets had appeared; and between them and Hanadra was a dense black mass, the whole of old Hanadra's able-bodied manhood, lined up to defend the city. Now was the time to pray. Fifty to one are by no means despicable odds, but the aid of the gods as well is better!

So the huge dome of Kharvani's temple began to echo to the sound of slippered feet and awe-struck whisperings, and the big, dim auditorium soon filled to over-flowing. No light came in from the outer world. There was nothing to illuminate the mysteries except the chain-hung grease-lamps swinging here and there from beams, and they served only to make the darkness visible. Bats flicked in and out between them and disappeared in the echoing gloom above. Censers belched out sweet-smelling, pungent clouds of sandalwood to drown the stench of hot humanity; and the huge graven image of Kharvani--serene and smiling and indifferent--stared round-eyed from the darkness.

Then a priest's voice boomed out in a solemn incantation and the whispering hushed. He chanted age-old verses, whose very meaning was forgotten in the womb of time--forgotten as the artist who had painted the picture of idealized Kharvani on the wall. Ten priests, five on either side of the tremendous idol, emerged chanting from the gloom behind, and then a gong rang, sweetly, clearly, suddenly, and the chanting ceased. Out stepped the High Priest from a niche below the image, and his voice rose in a wailing, sing-song cadence that reechoed from the dome and sent a thrill through every one who heard.

His chant had scarcely ceased when the temple door burst open and a man rushed in.

"They have begun!" he shouted. "The battle has begun!"

As though in ready confirmation of his words, the distant reverberating boom of cannon filtered through the doorway from the world of grim realities outside.

"They have twenty cannon with them! They have more guns than we have!" wailed he who brought the news. Again began the chanting that sought the aid of Siva the Destroyer. Only, there were fewer who listened to this second chant. Those who were near the doorway slipped outside and joined the watching hundreds on the roofs.

For an hour the prayers continued in the stifling gloom, priest relieving priest and chant following on chant, until the temple was half emptied of its audience. One by one, and then by twos and threes, the worshipers succumbed to human curiosity and crept stealthily outside to watch.

Another messenger ran in and shouted: "They have charged! Their cavalry have charged! They are beaten back! Their dead lie twisted on the plain!"

At the words there was a stampede from the doorway, and half of those who had remained rushed out. There were hundreds still there, though, for that great gloomy pile of Kharvani's could hold an almost countless crowd.

Within another hour the same man rushed to the door again and shouted:

"Help comes! Horsemen are coming from the north! Rajputs, riding like leaves before the wind! Even the Mussulmans are for us!"

But the chanting never ceased. No one stopped to doubt the friendship of arrivals from the north, for to that side there were no English, and England's friends would surely follow byroads to her aid. The city gates were wide open to admit wounded or messengers or friends--with a view, even, to a possible retreat--and whoever cared could ride through them unchallenged and unchecked.

Even when the crash of horses' hoofs rattled on the stone paving outside the temple there was no suspicion. No move was made to find out who it was who rode. But when the temple door reechoed to the thunder of a sword-hilt and a voice roared "Open!" there was something like a panic. The chanting stopped and the priests and the High Priest listened to the stamping on the stone pavement at the temple front.

"Open!" roared a voice again, and the thundering on the panels recommenced. Then some one drew the bolt and a horse's head--a huge Khaubuli stallion's--appeared, snorting and panting and wild-eyed.

"Farward!" roared the Risaldar Mahommed Khan, kneeling on young Bellairs' winded charger.

"Farm twos! Farward!"

Straight into the temple, two by two, behind the Risaldar, rode two fierce lines of Rajputs, overturning men and women--their drawn swords pointing this way and that--their dark eyes gleaming. Without a word to any one they rode up to the image, where the priests stood in an astonished herd.

"Fron-tt farm! Rear rank--'bout-face!" barked the Risaldar, and there was another clattering and stamping on the stone floor as the panting chargers pranced into the fresh formation, back to back.

"The memsahib!" growled Mahommed Khan. "Where is she?"

"My son!" said the High Priest. "Bring me my son!"

"A life for a life! Thy heavenborn first!"

"Nay! Show me my son first!"

The Risaldar leaped from his horse and tossed his reins to the man behind him. In a second his sword was at the High Priest's throat.

"Where is that secret stair?" he growled. "Lead on!"

The swordpoint pricked him. Two priests tried to interfere, but wilted and collapsed with fright as four fierce, black-bearded Rajputs spurred their horses forward. The swordpoint pricked still deeper.

"My son!" said the High Priest.

"A life for a life! Lead on!"

The High Priest surrendered, with a dark and cunning look, though, that hinted at something or other in reserve. He pulled at a piece of carving on the wail behind and pointed to a stair that showed behind the outswung door. Then he plucked another priest by the sleeve and whispered.

The priest passed on the whisper. A third priest turned and ran.

"That way!" said the High Priest, pointing.

"I? Nay! I go not down!" He raised his voice into an ululating howl. "O Suliman!" he bellowed. "Suliman! O!--Suliman! Bring up the heaven-born!"

A growl like the distant rumble from a bear-pit answered him. Then Ruth Bellairs' voice was heard calling up the stairway.

"Is that you, Mahommed Khan?"

"Ay, memsahib!"

"Good! I'm coming!"

She had recovered far enough to climb the ladder and the steep stone stair above it, and Suliman climbed up behind her, grumbling dreadful prophecies of what would happen to the priests now that Mohammed Khan had come.

"Is all well, Risaldar?" she asked him.

"Nay, heavenborn! All is not well yet! The general sahib from Jundhra and your husband's guns and others, making one division, are engaged with rebels eight or nine miles from here. We saw part of the battle as we rode!"

"Who wins?"

"It is doubtful, heavenborn! How could we tell from this distance?"

"Have you a horse for me?"

"Ay, heavenborn! Here! Bring up that horse, thou, and Suliman's! Ride him cross-saddle, heavenborn--there were no side-saddles in Siroeh! Nay, he is just a little frightened. He will stand--he will not throw thee! I did better than I thought, heavenborn. I come with four-and-twenty, making twenty-six with me and Suliman. An escort for a queen! So--sit him quietly. Leave the reins free. Suliman will lead him! Ho! Fronnnt! Rank--'bout-face!"

"My son!" wailed the High Priest. "Where is my son?"

"Tell him, Suliman!"

"Where I caught thee, thou idol-briber!" snarled the Risaldar's half-brother.

"Where? In that den of stinks. Gagged and bound all this while?"

"Ha! Gagged and bound and out of mischief where all priests and priests' sons ought to be!" laughed Mahommed Khan. "Farward! Farm twos Ter-r-r-ott!"

In went the spur, and the snorting, rattling, clanking cavalcade sidled and pranced out of the temple into the sunshine, with Ruth and Suliman in the midst of them.

"Gallop!" roared the Risaldar, the moment that the last horse was clear of the temple-doors. And in that instant he saw what the High Priest's whispering had meant.

Coming up the street toward them was a horde of silent, hurrying Hindus, armed with swords and spears, wearing all of them the caste-marks of the Brahman--well-fed, indignant relations of the priests, intent on avenging the defilement of Kharvani's temple.

"Canter! Fronnnt--farm--Gallop! Charge!"

Ruth found herself in the midst of a whirlwind of flashing sabers, astride of a lean-flanked Katiawari gelding that could streak like an antelope, knee to knee with a pair of bearded Rajputs, one of whom gripped her bridle-rein--thundering down a city street straight for a hundred swords that blocked her path. She set her eyes on the middle of Mahommed Khan's straight back, gripped the saddle with both hands, set her teeth and waited for the shock. Mahommed Khan's right arm rose and his sword flashed in the sunlight as he stood up in his stirrups. She shut her eyes. But there was no shock! There was the swish of whirling steel, the thunder of hoofs, the sound of bodies falling. There was a scream or two as well and a coarse-mouthed Rajput oath. But when she dared to open her eyes once more they were thundering still, headlong down the city street and Mahommed Khan was whirling his sword in mid-air to shake the blood from it.

Ahead lay the city gate and she could see another swarm of Hindus rushing from either side to close it. But "Charge!" yelled Mahommed Khan again, and they swept through the crowd, through the half-shut gate, out on the plain beyond, as a wind sweeps through the forest, leaving fallen tree-trunks in its wake.

"Halt!" roared the Risaldar, when they were safely out of range. "Are any hurt? No? Good for us that their rifles are all in the firing-line yonder!"

He sat for a minute peering underneath his hand at the distant, dark, serried mass of men and the steel-tipped lines beyond it, watching the belching cannon and the spurting flames of the close-range rifle-fire.

"See, heavenborn!" he said, pointing. "Those will be your husband's guns! See, over on the left, there. See! They fire! Those two! We can reach them if we make a circuit on the flank here!"

"But can we get through, Risaldar? Won't they see us and cut us off?"

"Heavenborn!" he answered, "men who dare ride into a city temple and snatch thee from the arms of priests dare and can do anything! Take this, heavenborn--take it as a keepsake, in case aught happens!"

He drew off the priest's ring, gave it to her and then, before she could reply:

"Canter!" he roared. The horses sprang forward in answer to the spurs and there was nothing for Ruth to do but watch the distant battle and listen to the deep breathing of the Rajputs on either hand.

XI.

There could be no retreat that day and no thought of it. Jundhra and Doonha were in ruins. The bridges were down behind them and Hanadra lay ahead. The British had to win their way into it or perish. Tired out, breakfastless, suffering from the baking heat, the long, thin British line had got--not to hold at bay but to smash and pierce--an over-whelming force of Hindus that was stiffened up and down its length by small detachments of native soldiers who had mutinied.

Numbers were against them, and even superiority of weapons was not so over-whelmingly in their favor, for those were the days of short-range rifle-fire and smoothbore artillery, and one gun was considerably like another. The mutinous sepoys had their rifles with them; there were guns from the ramparts of Hanadra that were capable of quite efficient service at close range; and practically every man in the dense-packed rebel line had a firearm of some kind. It was only in cavalry and discipline and pluck that the British force had the advantage, and the cavalry had already charged once and had been repulsed.

General Turner rode up and down the sweltering firing-line, encouraging the men when it seemed to him they needed it and giving directions to his officers. He was hidden from view oftener than not by the rolling clouds of smoke and he popped up here and there suddenly and unexpectedly. Wherever he appeared there was an immediate stiffening among the ranks, as though he carried a supply of spare enthusiasm with him and could hand it out.

Colonel Carter, commanding the right wing, turned his head for a second at the sound of a horse's feet and found the general beside him.

"Had I better have my wounded laid in a wagon, sir?" he suggested, "in case you find it necessary to fall back?"

"There will be no retreat!" said General Turner. "Leave your wounded where they are. I never saw a cannon bleed before. How's that?"

He spurred his horse over to where one of Bellairs' guns was being run forward into place again and Colonel Carter followed him. There was blood dripping from the muzzle of it.

"We're short of water, sir!" said Colonel Carter.

And as he spoke a gunner dipped his sponge into a pool of blood and rammed it home.

Bellairs was standing between his two guns, looking like the shadow of himself, worn out with lack of sleep, disheveled, wounded. There was blood dripping from his forehead and he wore his left arm in a sling made from his shirt.

"Fire!" he ordered, and the two guns barked in unison and jumped back two yards or more.

"If you'll look," said General Turner, plucking at the colonel's sleeve, "you'll see a handful of native cavalry over yonder behind the enemy--rather to the enemy's left--there between those two clouds of smoke. D'you see them?"

"They look like Sikhs or Rajputs," said the colonel.

"Yes. Don't they? I'd like you to keep an eye on them. They've come up from the rear. I caught sight of them quite a while ago and I can't quite make them out. It's strange, but I can't believe that they belong to the enemy. D'you see?--there--they've changed direction. They're riding as though they intended to come round the enemy's left flank!"

"By gad, they are! Look! The enemy are moving to cut them off!"

"I must get back to the other wing!" said General Turner. "But that looks like the making of an opportunity! Keep both eyes lifting, Carter, and advance the moment you see any confusion in the enemy's ranks."

He rode off, and Colonel Carter stared long and steadily at the approaching horsemen. He saw a dense mass of the enemy, about a thousand strong, detach itself from the left wing and move to intercept them, and he noticed that the movement made a tremendous difference to the ranks opposed to him. He stepped up to young Bellairs and touched his sleeve. Bellairs started like a man roused from a dream.

"That's your wife over there!" said Colonel Carter. "There can't be any other white woman here-abouts riding with a Rajput escort!"

Bellairs gripped the colonel's outstretched arm.

"Where?" he almost screamed. "Where? I don't see her!"

"There, man! There, where that mass of men is moving! Look! By the Lord Harry! He's charging right through the mob! That's Mahommed Khan, I'll bet a fortune! Now's our chance Bugler!"

The bugler ran to him, and he began to puff into his instrument.

"Blow the 'attention' first!"

Out rang the clear, strident notes, and the non-commissioned officers and men took notice that a movement of some kind would shortly be required of them, but the din of firing never ceased for a single instant. Then, suddenly, an answering bugle sang out from the other flank.

"Advance in echelon!" commanded Colonel Carter, and the bugler did his best to split his cheeks in a battle-rending blast.

"You remain where you are, sir!" he ordered young Bellairs. "Keep your guns served to the utmost!"

Six-and-twenty horsemen, riding full-tilt at a thousand men, may look like a trifle, but they are disconcerting. What they hit, they kill; and if they succeed in striking home, they play old Harry with formations. And Risaldar Mahommed Khan did strike home. He changed direction suddenly and, instead of using up his horses' strength in outflanking the enemy, who had marched to intercept him, and making a running target of his small command, he did the unexpected--which is the one best thing to do in war. He led his six-and-twenty at a headlong gallop straight for the middle of the crowd--it could not be called by any military name. They fired one ragged volley at him and then had no time to load before he was in the middle of them, clashing right and left and pressing forward. They gave way, right and left, before him, and a good number of them ran. Half a hundred of them were cut down as they fled toward their firing-line. At that second, just as the Risaldar and his handful burst through the mob and the mob began rushing wildly out of his way, the British bugles blared out the command to advance in echelon.

The Indians were caught between a fire and a charge that they had good reason to fear in front of them, and a disturbance on their left flank that might mean anything. As one-half of them turned wildly to face what might be coming from this unexpected quarter, the British troops came on with a roar, and at the same moment Mahommed Khan reached the rear of their firing-line and crashed headlong into it.

In a second the whole Indian line was in confusion and in another minute it was in full retreat not knowing nor even guessing what had routed it. Retreat grew into panic and panic to stampede and, five minutes after the Risaldar's appearance on the scene, half of the Indian line was rushing wildly for Hanadra and the other half was retiring sullenly in comparatively dense and decent order.

Bellairs could not see all that happened. The smoke from his own guns obscured the view, and the necessity for giving orders to his men prevented him from watching as he would have wished. But he saw the Rajputs burst out through the Indian ranks and he saw his own charger--Shaitan the unmistakable--careering across the plain toward him riderless.

"For the love of God!" he groaned, raising both fists to heaven, "has she got this far, and then been killed! Oh, what in Hades did I entrust her to an Indian for? The pig-headed, brave old fool! Why couldn't he ride round them, instead of charging through?"

As he groaned aloud, too wretched even to think of what his duty was, a galloper rode up to him.

"Bring up your guns, sir, please!" he ordered. "You're asked to hurry! Take up position on that rising ground and warm up the enemy's retreat!"

"Limber up!" shouted Bellairs, coming to himself again. Fifteen seconds later his two guns were thundering up the rise.

As he brought them to "action front" and tried to collect his thoughts to figure out the range, a finger touched his shoulder and he turned to see another artillery officer standing by him.

"I've been lent from another section," he explained: "You're wanted."

"Where?"

"Over there, where you see Colonel Carter standing. It's your wife wants you, I think!"

Bellairs did not wait for explanations. He sent for his horse and mounted and rode across the intervening space at a breakneck gallop that he could barely stop in time to save himself from knocking the colonel over. A second later he was in Ruth's arms.

"I thought you were dead when I saw Shaitan!" he said. He was nearly sobbing.

"No, Mahommed Khan rode him," she answered, and she made no pretense about not sobbing. She was crying like a child.

"Salaam, Bellairs sahib!" said a weak voice close to him. He noticed Colonel Carter bending over a prostrate figure, lifting the head up on his knee. There were three Rajputs standing between, though, and he could not see whose the figure was.

"Come over here!" said Colonel Carter, and young Bellairs obeyed him, leaving Ruth sitting on the ground where she was.

"Wouldn't you care to thank Mohammed Khan?" It was a little cruel of the colonel to put quite so much venom in his voice, for, when all is said and done: a man has almost a right to be forgetful when he has just had his young wife brought him out of the jaws of death. At least he has a good excuse for it. The sting of the reproof left him bereft of words and he stood looking down at the old Risaldar, saying nothing and feeling very much ashamed.

"Salaam, Bellairs sahib!" The voice was growing feebler. "I would have done more for thy father's son! Thou art welcome. Aie! But thy charger is a good one! Good-by! Time is short, and I would talk with the colonel sahib!"

He waved Bellairs away with a motion of his hand and the lieutenant went back to his wife again.

"He sent me away just like that, too!" she told him. "He said he had no time left to talk to women!"

Colonel Carter bent down again above the Risaldar, and listened to as much as he had time to tell of what had happened.

"But couldn't you have ridden round them, Risaldar?" he asked them.

"Nay, sahib! It was touch and go! I gave the touch! I saw as I rode how close the issue was and I saw my chance and took it! Had the memsahib been slain, she had at least died in full view of the English--and there was a battle to be won. What would you? I am a soldier--I."

"Indeed you are!" swore Colonel Carter.

"Sahib! Call my sons!"

His sons were standing near him, but the colonel called up his grandsons, who had been told to stand at a little distance off. They clustered round the Risaldar in silence, and he looked them over and counted them.

"All here?" he asked.

"All here!"

"Whose sons and grandsons are ye?"

"Thine!" came the chorus.

"This sahib says that having done my bidding and delivered her ye rode to rescue, ye are no more bound to the Raj. Ye may return to your homes if ye wish."

There was no answer.

"Ye may fight for the rebels, if ye wish! There will be a safe-permit written."

Again there was no answer.

"For whom, then, fight ye?"

"For the Raj!" The deep-throated answer rang out promptly from every one of them, and they stood with their sword-hilts thrust out toward the colonel. He rose and touched each hilt in turn.

"They are now thy servants!" said the Risaldar, laying his head back. "It is good! I go now. Give my salaams to General Turner sahib!"

"Good-by, old war-dog!" growled the colonel, in an Anglo-Saxon effort to disguise emotion. He gripped at the right hand that was stretched out on the ground beside him, but it was lifeless.

Risaldar Mahommed Khan, two-medal man and pensionless gentleman-at-large, had gone to turn in his account of how he had remembered the salt which he had eaten.

MACHASSAN AH

I.

Waist-held in the chains and soused in the fifty-foot-high spray, Joe Byng eyed his sounding lead that swung like a pendulum below him, and named it sacrilege.

"This 'ere navy ain't a navy no more," he muttered. "This 'ere's a school-gal promenade, 'and-in-'and, an' mind not to get your little trotters wet, that's what this is, so 'elp me two able seamen an' a red marine!"

From the moment that the lookout, lashed to the windlass drum up forward, had spied the little craft away to leeward and had bellowed his report of it through hollowed hands between the thunder of the waves, Joe Byng had had premonitory symptoms of uneasiness. He had felt in his bones that the navy was about to be nose-led into shame.

At the wheel, both eyes on the compass, as the sea law bids, but both ears on the more-even-than-usual-alert, Curley Crothers felt the same sensations but expressed them otherwise.

"Admiral's orders!" he muttered. "Maybe the admiral was drunk?"

The brass gongs clanged down in the bowels of H.M.S. Puncher and she gradually lost what little weigh she had, rolling her bridge ends under in the heave and hollow of a beam-on monsoon sea.

"How much does he say he wants?" asked her commander.

Joe Byng in the chains and Curley Crothers at the wheel both recognized the quarter tone instantly, and diagnosed it with deadly accuracy; every vibration of his voice and every fiber of his being expressed exasperation, though a landsman might have noticed no more than contempt for what he had seen fit to log as "half a gale."

"He says he'll take us in for fifty pounds, sir."

"Oh! Tell him to make it shillings, or else to get out of my course!"

It is not much in the way of Persian Gulf Arabic that a man picks up from textbooks but at garnering the business end of beach-born dialects--the end that gets results at least expense of time or energy--the Navy goes even the Army half a dozen better. The sublieutenant's argument, bawled from the bridge rail to the reeling little boat below, was a marvel in its own sweet way; it combined abuse and scorn with a cataclysmic blast of threat in six explosive sentences.

"He says he'll take us in for ten pounds, sir," he reported, without the vestige of a smile.

"Oh! Ask Mr. Hartley to step up on the bridge, will you?"

Two minutes later, during which the nasal howls from the boat were utterly ignored, the acting chief engineer hauled himself along the rail hand over hand to windward, ducking below the canvas guard as a more than usually big comber split against the Puncher's side and hove itself to heaven.

"It beats me how any man can keep a coat on him this weather," he remarked, and the sublieutenant noticed that the streams that ran down both his temples were not sea water. "Send for me?"

His temper, judging by his voice, would seem to be a lot worse than could be due to the pitching of the ship.

"Yes. There's a pilot overside, and our orders are to take a pilot aboard when running in, if available. There are three men bailing that boat below there, and the sea's gaining on them. They'll need rescuing within two hours. Then we'd have a pilot aboard and would have saved the government ten pounds. Point is, can you manage in the engine-room for two or three hours longer? Three more waves like that last one and the man's ours anyway!"

"He might not wait two hours," suggested Mr. Hartley. "He might get tired of looking at us, and beat back into port. Then where would be your strategy?"

"Then there wouldn't be a pilot available. I'd be justified in going in without one. Point is, can you hold out below?"

"Man," said Mr. Hartley, "you're a genius." He peered through the spray down to leeward, where the pilot's boat danced a death dance alongside, heel and toe to the Puncher's statelier swing. "Yes; there are three men bailing, and you're a genius. But no! The answer's no! The engines'll keep on turning, maybe and perhaps, until we make the shelter o' yon reef. There's no knowing what a cherry-red bearing will do. I can give ye maybe fifteen knots; maybe a leetle more for just five minutes, for steerage way and luck, and after that--"

Even crouched as he was against the canvas guard he contrived to shrug his shoulders.

"But if we go in there are you sure you can contrive to patch her up? It looks like a rotten passage, and not much of a berth beyond it."

"I could cool her down."

"Oh, if that's all you want, I can anchor outside in thirty fathoms."

Curley Crothers heard that and his whole frame stiffened; there seemed a chance yet that the Navy might not be disgraced. But it faded on the instant.

"Man, we've got to go inside and we've got to hurry! Better in there than at the bottom of the Gulf! Put her where she'll hold still for a day, or maybe two days--"

"Say a month!" suggested the commander caustically.

"Say three days for the sake of argument. Then I can put her to rights. I daren't take down a thing while she's rolling twenty-five and more, and I've got to take things down! Why, man, the engine-room is all pollution from gratings to bilge; if I loosened one more bolt than is loose a'ready her whole insides 'ud take charge and dance quadrilles until we drowned!"

"You won't try to make Bombay?"

"I'll try to give ye steam as far as the far side o' yon reef. After that I wash my hands of a' responsibility!"

"Oh, very well. Mr. White!"

The sublieutenant hauled himself in turn to windward. Curley Crothers gave the wheel a half-spoke and looked as if he had no interest in anything. Joe Byng in the chains bowed his head and groaned inwardly; his sticky, spray-washed lead seemed all-absorbing.

"Tell that black robber to hurry aboard, unless he wants me to come in without him."

The little boat had drifted fast before the wind, and the sublieutenant had to bellow through a megaphone to where the three men bailed and the ragged oars-men swung their weight against the storm. The man of ebony, who would be pilot and disgrace the Navy, balanced on a thwart with wide-spread naked toes and yelled an ululating answer. With his rags out-blown in the monsoon he looked like a sea wraith come to life. The big gongs clanged again, and the Puncher drifted rather than drove down on the smaller craft. A hand line caught the pilot precisely in the face. He grabbed it frantically, fell headlong in the sea, and was hauled aboard.

"He says he wants a tow for that boat of his," reported the sublieutenant. "Said it in English, too--seems he knows more than he pretends."

"Missed it, by gad, by just about five minutes!" said the commander aloud but to himself. "Well--the bargain's made, so it can't be helped. That boat's sinking! Throw 'em a line, quick!"

The pilot's crew displayed no overdone affection for their craft, and there was no struggle to the last to leave it. One by one--whichever could grab the line first was the first to come--they were hauled through the thundering waves and their boat was left to sink. Then, before they could adjust their unaccustomed feet to the different balance of the Puncher's heaving deck, the gongs clanged and the de-stroyer leaped ahead like a dripping sea-soused water beetle, into her utmost speed that instant.

All conscious of his new-won dignity, and utterly regardless of his boat, the pilot had found the bridge at once. He clung to the rail there and braced one naked foot against a stanchion. To him the ship's speed seemed the all-absorbing thing, for either Mr. Hartley had forgotten just how many revolutions would make fifteen knots or else he had underestimated his engine-room's capacity. The Puncher split the waves and spewed them twenty feet above her, racing head-on for the reef, and Curley Crothers was too busy at his wheel to pass the pilot the surreptitious insult he intended.

The gongs clanged presently, and the Puncher swallowed half her speed at once, giving the pilot courage.

"This exceedingly damn dangerous place, sah!" he remarked.

"No bottom at eight!" sang Joe Byng in the chains.

Three words passed between the commander and Crothers, and the Puncher hove a weed-draped underside high over the crest of a beam-on roller as she veered a dozen points, ducked her starboard rail into the trough of it, and sliced her long thin nose, sizzling and swirling, into the welter ahead. It was growing weedier and dirtier each minute.

"No bottom at eight!" chanted Joe Byng.

And at the sound of his voice the pilot hauled himself up by his leverage on the rail and found his voice again.

"This most exceedingly damn dangerous place, sah!"

But the commander was too busy acting all three L's--Log, Lead and Lookout-- his shrouded figure swaying to the heave and fall and his eyes fixed straight ahead of him on the double line of boiling foam. He had conned his course and had it charted in his head. There was no time to argue with a pilot.

"Port you-ah hel-um, sah! Port you-ah hel-um!"

"By the mark--seven!" sang Joe Byng from the chains.

"Port you-ah hel-um, sah!" yelled the pilot in an ecstasy of fright.

"Starboard a little," came the quiet command.

Curley Crothers moved his wheel and the Puncher's bow yawed twenty feet, as if Providence had pushed her.

"Gawd A'mighty!" murmured Joe Byng, gazing open-mouthed at fifty feet of jagged rock that grinned up suddenly three waves away.

The pilot braced both feet against a stanchion and tried to take the weigh off her by pulling.

"Half speed, sah! Go slow, sah! Go dead slow, sah! You'll pile up you-ah damn ship, sah! Ah tell you, sah, you'll pile her up as suah as hell, sah! 'Bout a million sharks round he-ah, sah! For the love o' God, sah--Captain, sah--"

"Oh, muzzle him, some one!" ordered the commander, and the jiggling, complaining engines danced ahead, the horrid gray beneath the pilot's ebony notwithstanding.

"By the deep--four!" warned Joe Byng in a level sing-song. The two gongs clanged like an echo to him, and the Puncher's speed was reduced at once to her point, of minimum stability. She rolled and quivered like a living thing in fear, falling on and off, nosing out a passage on her own account apparently, and seeming to be gathering all her strength for one tremendous effort.

"That's bettah, sah! That's bettah, Captain, sah! Go astern! This he-ah's the bar, sah--damn bad place, the bar, sah! Go astern, sah. Captain, sah, d'you he-ah me--go astern! Try again, 'nother place further up, sah. Captain, sah! Over that way; that way thar--that way, sah!"

He pointed through the sky-flung spray with a trembling finger and his voice was rich with doleful emphasis, but the commander held his course and carried on. There seemed neither sympathy nor understanding on that unsteadiest of ships. Curley Crothers, solemn-faced as Nemesis and looking half as compassionate, moved his wheel a trifle. Joe Byng in the chains kept up his even sing-song, expressionless, as if he were an automatic clock that did not care, but must record the truth each time his dripping pendulum touched bottom.

"And a half--three!"

White foam was boiling in among the dirty welter, and the Puncher's bow pitched suddenly as the first big bar wave lifted her; a second later her propellers chug-chug-chugged in surface spume as she kicked upward like a porpoise diving.

"Oh, lordy, lordy, lordy!" groaned the pilot. "This he-ah watah's full of sharks, an' that's the bar! You're on the bar now, Captain, sah!"

"By the mark--three!" Byng chanted steadily.

"Starboard a little more," said the commander leaning forward and shoving the pilot away to leeward at the same time. Then he shouted to the fo'castle head, where a bosun's mate and his crew had climbed and were awaiting orders in evident and most unreasonable unconcern.

"Get both anchors ready!"

"Aye, aye, sir!" came the answer, and efficiency controlled by experts proceeded at kaleidoscopic angles to defy the elements. The big steel hooks were ready in an instant.

"Stop her!" ordered the commander.

The gongs clanged out an alarm and the throbbing ceased.

"Hard astern, both engines!"

Again there was a clangor under hatches, and the suffering bearings shrieked. The Puncher dropped her stern two feet or so, and the foam boiled brown round her propellers. The shock of the reversal pitched the pilot up against the forward rail, where he clung like a drowning man.

"For the love o' God, sah! Captain; sah, we've struck! Ah told you so; Ah said--"

"And a half-three!" chanted Joe Byng.

"Stop her! Starboard engine ahead! Port engine ahead! Ease your helm! Meet her! Half speed ahead!"

The Puncher pitched and rolled, kicking at the following monsoon that thundered at her counter and tossing up the foam that seethed about her bow. She trembled from end to end, as if the pounding of the water hurt her.

"Helm amidships!" ordered the commander suddenly.

"'Midships, sir!"

"Full speed ahead, both engines!"

The Puncher leaped, as all destroyers do the second day they are loosed. She sliced through the storm straight for the coral beach beyond the bar, shaking her graceful shoulders free of the sticky spray--reeling, rolling, thugging, kicking, bucking through the welter to where quiet water waited and the ever-lasting, utterly unrighteous stink of sun-baked Arab beaches. As each tremendous breaker thundered on her stern each time she lifted to the underswell, the pilot vowed that she had struck, rolling his eyes and calling two different deities to witness that none of it was any fault of his.

"Thar's no water, sah--no water, Captain, sah--not one drop! You've piled up you-ah ship! Ah told you so; Ah said--"

"By the deep--four!"

"And a half-four!"

"By the mark--five!"

The Puncher was across the bar, gliding through muddy water on an even keel and giving the lie direct to him whose fee was ten pounds English. The pilot drew a talisman of some kind from underneath the least torn portion of his shirt, and to the commander's amazement kissed it. It is not often that a woolly headed, or any other, native of the East kisses either folk or things. But the commander was too busy at the moment to ask questions.

"Have your starboard anchor ready!" he commanded, making mental notes.

"Ready, sir!"

The glittering, wet, wind-blown beach and the little estuary slid by like a painted panorama smelling of all the evil in the world as the Puncher eased her helm a time or two seeking a comfortable berth with Joe Byng's chanted aid.

"Let go twenty fathoms!"

The pilot sighed relief as the starboard anchor splashed into the water and the cable roared after it through the hawse pipe.

"What nationality are you?" asked the commander, watching the Puncher swing and gaging distances, but sparing one eye now for his unwelcome but official guest.

"Me, sah?"

"Yes, you."

The pilot looked anywhere but at his questioner, and a picture passed before the commander's eyes--a memory, perhaps, of something he had read about at school--of Christians in Nero's day being asked what their religion was.

"Are you afraid to tell me?" he asked, softening his voice to a kinder tone as he remembered that God did not make all men Englishmen, and turning just in time to cause Crothers to withdraw his right leg.

The pilot's toes were, after all, not destined to be trodden on just then.

"No, sah, Ah'm not afraid."

"What are you, then?"

"Ah'm--"

"Well? What?"

"Ah'm English!"

"What?"

"Captain, sah, Ah'm English!"

"Oh! Are you? Um-m-m! Mr. White, give this man his ten pounds, will you? And get his receipt for it."

That appeared to end matters, so far as the commander was concerned; official dignity forbade any further interest. But it was not so very long since Mr. White was senior midshipman, and it takes a man until he is admiral of the fleet to unlearn all he knew then and forget the curiosity of those days.

"Now, I should have thought you were a Scotchman," he suggested without smiling, studying the salt-encrusted wrinkles on the ebony face. "You like whisky?"

"Yes, sah--positively, sah! Yes, Captain, sah--Ah do!"

Mr. White sent for whisky and poured out a stiff four fingers, to the awful disgust of Curley Crothers, who saw the whole transaction. The pilot consumed it so instantly that there seemed never to have been any in the glass.

"I suppose your name's Macnab--or Macphairson--which? Sign here, please."

The pilot took the proffered pen in unaccustomed fingers and made a crisscross scrawl, adorned with thirteen blots. The pen nib broke under the strain, and he handed it back with an air of confidential remonstrance.

"That thing's no mo-ah good," he volunteered.

"So I see. Now tell me your name in full, so that I can write it next to the mark. It's a wonder of a mark! Mac--what's the rest of it?"

"Hassan Ah."

"Machassan?"

"No, sah. Hassan Ah."

"And you're English?"

"Yes, sah."

"With that name?"

"Mah name makes no diffunts, sah. Ah'm English."

"Well--here's your money. Cutter away, there! Put the pilot and his crew ashore! Sorry about your boat, pilot, but it couldn't be helped."

"Makes me believe that I'm a nigger!" muttered Curley Crothers, not yet released from duty on the bridge.

"First time I ever wished I was a Dutchman!" swore Joe Byng, coiling up his sounding line.

Ten minutes later the cutter's captain swung the boat's stern in shore when he judged that he was reasonably near enough and too far in for sharks. He had his orders to put the pilot and his crew ashore, but the means had not been too exactly specified.

"Get out and swim for it, you bally Englishman!" he ordered, using a boat-hook on the nearest one to make his meaning clear.

One by one they jumped for it, the pilot going last. He plainly did not understand the point of view.

"Ah'm English!" he expostulated. "Lissen he-ah, Ah'm English! Damwell English!"

"All right; let's see you swim, English!" jeered the cutter's captain, and the pilot took the water with a splash.

"Ah su-ah am English!" he vowed, as he swam for the shore, and he stood by the sea's edge repeating his assertion with a leathery pair of lungs until the cutter had rowed out of ear-shot.

"English, is he?" said Joe Byng to Curley Crothers in the fo'castle, not twenty minutes later. "I'd show him, if I had him in here for twenty minutes!"

"That fellow's interested me," said Crothers. "He's got me thinking. I vote we investigate him."

"How?"

"Ashore, fathead."

"There'll be no shore leave."

"No? You left off being wet nurse to the dawg?" "I brush him, mornin's; if that's what you mean."

"Is he fit?"

"Fit to fight a bumboat full o' pilots!"

"Could he be sick for an hour?"

"Might be did."

"Tomorrow?"

"Morning?"

"At about two bells?"

"It could be done."

"Then do it!"

"Why?"

"Because, Joe Byng my boy, you and I want shore leave; and the pup--and he's a decent pup--must suffer for to make a 'tween-deck holiday. Get my meaning? I've a propagandrum that'll work this tide. You go and set the fuse in the pup's inside; and mind you, time it right, my son--for two bells when the old man's in the chair!"

So Joe Byng, who was something of an expert in the way and ways of dogs, departed in search of an oiler with whom he was on terms of condescension; and he returned to the fo'castle a little later with the nastiest, most awful-smelling mess that ever emanated even from the engine-room of a destroyer in the Persian Gulf (where grease and things run rancid.)

II.

Lying lazily at anchor off the reeking beach of Adra Bight, the Puncher looked peaceful and complacent--which is altogether opposite to what she and her commander were, or had been, for a month. The ship hummed her shut-in discontent, as a hive does when the bees propose to swarm, and her commander--who never, be it noted, went to windward of the one word "damn"--used that one word very frequently.

He sat "abaft the mainmast" at a table that was splotched already with abundant perspiration, and the acting engineer who stood in front of him shifted from foot to foot in attitudes expressive of increasing agony of mind. It grew obvious at last that there was a limit to Mr. Hartley's store of courteous deference.

There had been news, red hot but wrong, of dhows loaded to the water-line with guns and ammunition somewhere up the Gulf. India, ever fretful for her tribes beyond the border, had borrowed Applewaite and his destroyer by instant cablegram, and jealously held records had been broken while the Puncher quartered those indecent seas and heated up her bearings. It was almost too much to have to come back empty-handed. It was quite too much to have to run for shelter under the lee of Adra's uninviting coral reef. And to be told by an acting engineer that he would have to stay a week was utterly beyond the scope of polite conversation.

"Why a week?" asked Commander Applewaite, with eyebrows raised to the nth power of incredulity.

"Why a week?" asked Mr. Hartley, breaking down the barrier of self-restraint at last. "I'll tell you why. Because, although the guts of her are so much scrap-iron, you've a crew of engineers who could build machinery of hell-slag--build it, mind--and could get steam out o' the Sahara, where there isn't any water at all.

"Because--conditional upon the act o' God and your permission--I'm willing to perform a miracle. Because the whole engine-room complement is dancing mad for shore leave, and there'll be none this side o' Bombay; and because, in consequence o' that, creation would be a mild name for what's about to happen under gratings until the shafts revolve again. Man, I wish ye'd take one peep at her bearings, though ye wouldn't understand.

"Because you're lucky; any other engineer in all the navies o' the world would take a month to tinker with her, even if he didn't have to send to Bombay for a tow. Because--"

"That'll do!" said Applewaite, his mind wandering already in search of suitable employment for the crew. "Get the repairs done as soon as possible; we stay here until you have finished what is necessary."

It looked like an evil moment for asking favors, but it was the time laid down in Regulations when such things as favors may be had; and it was the moment Curley Crothers had picked out for asking for shore leave.

"Come 'ere, Scamp. Come along, Scamp. Come along 'ere--good boy!" he coaxed, dragging by a short chain in his wake the sorriest-looking bull terrier that ever acted mascot in the British or any other navy. Courteous and huge and cap in hand, his weather-beaten face smiling respectfully above a snow-white uniform, he took his stand before the little table. His outward bearing was one of certainty, but his shrewd, slightly puckered eyes alternately conned the expression of his commander's face and watched the dog.

The lee, scuppers were the goal of the dog's immediate ambition, for he was a well-brought-up dog and such of the decencies as were not his by instinct he had learned by painful and repeated acquisition. But at the moment Curley Crothers showed a wondrous disregard for etiquette.

"He's very sick, sir," he asserted, tugging a little at the chain in the hope of producing instant proof of his contention. But the dog was gamiest of the game, and swallowed hurriedly.

"Well? I'm not a vet. What about it?"

"The whole ship's crew 'ud be sorry, sir, if 'e was to lose 'is number. He's the best mascot this ship ever had, by all accounts."

"He hasn't brought us much luck this run!" smiled Applewaite, remembering a long list of "previous convictions" and wondering what Crothers might be up to next.

"No, sir? We're still a-top o' the water, sir."

"Oh! He gets the credit for that, eh? But for him, I suppose we'd have piled up on the reef yesterday?"

"Saving your presence, sir."

Curley Crothers made a gesture expressive of a world of compliment and praise, but he kept one eye steadily on the dog; he seemed to imply that but for the presence of the dog on board the commander might have forgotten his seamanship.

"Well? What do you suggest?"

"Seeing the poor dog's sick, sir, and you and all of us so fond of him, and all he needs is exercise, I thought perhaps as 'ow you'd order me an' Byng, sir, to take 'im for a run ashore. There'd be jackals and pi-dogs for 'im to chase. A bit o' sport 'ud set 'im up in a jiffy. He's languishing--that's what's the matter with him."

There were almost tears in his voice as he tugged at the chain surreptitiously, in a vain effort to produce the cataclysm that was overdue. But for all his efforts to appear affected, his eyes were smiling. So were his commander's.

"Why Byng?" he asked.

"Byng cleans him, sir. He knows Byng."

"Then, why you?"

"Why; he knows me too, sir, and between the two of us, we'd manage him proper. S'posin' he was to get huntin' on his own and one of us was tired out chasin' him, t'other could run and catch him. If there was only one of us, he couldn't."

"I see. Well? One of the other men might take him on the chain. A good-conduct man, for instance."

Crothers tugged at the chain, and the unhappy dog drew away toward the scuppers with all his remaining strength.

"He's cussed about the chain, sir--apt to drag on it and try to chaw it through. Besides, sir, when a dawg's sick, he's like a man--same as me an' you; he likes to 'ave 'is partic'lar pals with 'im. Now, that dawg's fond o' me an' Byng.'

"I see. But supposing exercise isn't what he wants after all? Suppose he needs a long rest and lots of sleep? How about that?"

The argument had reached a crisis, and Curley realized it. Joking or not, when the commander of a ship takes too long in reaching a decision he generally does not reach a favorable one. The leash was tugged again, this time with some severity. The martyred Scamp was drawn on his protesting haunches close to the official table, that the commander might have a better view of his distress. And then the expected happened--voluminously.

Curley stood with an expression of wooden-headed, abject innocence on his big, broad face, and looked straight in front of him.

"He certainly is sick, sir," he remarked.

"Sick. Good heavens! The dog's turning himself inside out! That's the last time a thing like this happens; he's the last dog I ever take on a cruise. Take him away at once! Bosun--call some one to wipe up that disgusting mess!"

"Take him ashore, did you say, sir?"

"Take him out of this! Take him anywhere you like! Yes, take him ashore and lose him--feed him to the sharks--give him to the Arabs--take him away, that's all!"

"Me and Byng, sir?"

"Yes, you and Byng! Did you hear me tell you to take him away?"

"Very good, sir; thank you!"

Curley Crothers saluted without the vestige of a smile, and hurried off before the dog could show too early signs of recovering health and strength or the commander could change his mind.

"Come on, Scamp," he whispered. "That was nothing but a temporary disaccommodation to your tummy, doglums; we'll soon have you to rights again."

He dived into the fo'castle with the dog behind him, and there were those who noticed that the terrier's whip-like tail no longer hugged his stomach, but was waving to the world at large.

And thirty minutes later, as the Puncher's launch put off with Curley and Joe Byng comfortably seated in the stern, it was obvious to any one who cared to look that Scamp was the happiest and healthiest terrier in Asia.

"Now, I wonder what they did to him," mused the Puncher's commander, watching from beneath his awning. "Those two men live up to the name they brought aboard! I believe they'd find means and a good excuse for walking to windward of a First Sea Lord!"

III.

Now an Arab would as soon allow a dog to lick his face as he would think of eating pork in public with his women folk; so the bearded, hook-nosed believers in the Prophet who looked down from the rock wall that lines one side of Adra knew what to think of Curley and his friend Joe Byng long before either of them realized that they were being watched.

Arrayed from head to ankles in spotless white, their black boots looking blacker by comparison, they proceeded in the general direction of the distant village, with the order and decorum of sea lords descending on a dockyard for inspection purposes. The trackless sand proved hot and sharp; the dog proved in poor condition from the voyage and the morning's incidental martyrdom, and Byng was generous-hearted. He picked up the dog and carried him; and Scamp displayed his gratitude in customary canine way.

The comments of the watching Arabs would not fit into any story in the world, and it is quite as well that Crothers and Joe Byng did not hear them and could not have translated them, for in the other case trouble would have started even sooner than it did. As it was, they tumbled and maneuvered over unresisting sand through almost tangible stench to where a gap in the ragged wall did duty as a gate. As they came nearer, a banner with the star and crescent was displayed from the wall-top, but no other sign was given that their coming was observed.

It was not until they had debouched (as Crothers termed it) to their half-right front and had taken to a narrow one-man track that ran below the wall that any over attention was paid them. Suddenly a hook-nosed Asiatic gentleman emerged through the once-was gateway--a picture of a Bible shepherd but for the long-barreled gun he carried instead of crook--a brown shadow against brown masonry. He challenged them in Arabic, and Curley Crothers answered him in Queen Victoria's English that all was well.

"Everything in the garden's lovely!" he asserted, in a deep-sea sing-song. "How's yourself?"

The man repeated whatever he had said before, this time with a gesture of impatience.

"Friend!" roared Byng and Curley both together. And the bull terrier took the joint yell for a war cry, or a bunting call, or possibly the herald's overture that summons bull pups to Valhalla. He was bred right and British Navy trained and his was not to reason why. He waited for no second invitation, but lit out from Byng's arms like a streak--a whip-tail, snow-white streak--for where the Arab's hard lean legs shone shiny-brown below his fluttering brown raiment.

"Come back, there!" yelled both keepers in excited unison, but they called too late.

Each grabbed for the chain too late. Their heads and shoulders cannoned and they fell together on the hot, dirty sand while Scamp and the Arab made each other's intimate acquaintance in a whirl of ripping cloth and legs and teeth and blasphemy.

That in itself was bad enough, and good enough excuse if such were wanted for war between the Shadow of God Upon Earth and England's distant Queen; but there was worse to follow.

One does not laugh, between certain parallels, unless the ultimate degree of insult is intended. And Curley Crothers and Joe Byng did laugh. They held their ribs and laughed until their muscles ached and their strong men's strength oozed out of them.

They were laughing when they grabbed the dog at last and pulled him off. They laughed as they set the Arab on his feet and gave him back his gun; and they laughed at him with Christian and mannerly good grace when he spat at them in awful frenzy until the spittle matted in his beard. And, being gentlemen after a fashion quite their own, they smilingly apologized.

Arabia lies in the middle of the zone where laughter is not wisdom. And a smile lies midway in the measure of a laugh. A laugh might be unintentional. A smile must be deliberate. And the Arab's spittle was run dry. Creed, custom, law of tooth for tooth and the thought of half a hundred co-religionists all watching him from crannies in the wall combined to make him shoot, since further means of showing malice were denied him; and he raised the long butt to his shoulder with meaning that was unmistakable.

And so, with sorrow that the East should be so lacking in good fellowship, but with the ready instinct of men who have been trained for war, they closed with him from two directions, swiftly, bull-dog-wise, and took his gun away. And how could even an able seaman help the dog's taking a share in the game again?

So far, nobody had done anything intended to be wrong--least of all the dog. The Arab was defending institutions; Crothers and Joe Byng were bent on holiday, and full of kind regards for anything that lived; and the dog was living dogfully up to well-bred-terrier tradition. It was as if two harmless chemicals had met and blended into nitroglycerin.

Deprived of his gun, the Arab drew a knife; and no British sailor lives who does not understand the quick-loosed answer to the glint of steel. Fist and boot both landed on the Arab quicker than his own thought served the knife, and the weight of quick concussions jarred him into all but coma. This time Byng caught the dog in time and held him back, leaving Curley Crothers to finish matters by making the long knife prize of war. Once more he helped the Arab on his feet, smiling hugely and gentling the iron sinews with huge paws that could have wrenched them all apart if need be.

"Take my advice, cully, and weigh quick!" he counseled, looking the Arab over and making sure the unfortunate had not been too much hurt. "Run for shelter where you can cool your bearings! Run off to the mosque and pray, to make up for all that cussing. Go and be good! And next time you meets us, be friendly--see?"

The Arab was too apoplectically angry to comply, but Crothers took him by both shoulders and shoved him; and finding himself shot forward out of reach, seeing safety ahead and its possible corollary of awful vengeance, he suddenly achieved discretion and scampered through the gap in the wall.

"'E's gone to fetch his pals. Look out, mate!" warned Joe Byng.

"Not 'im!" vowed Crothers. "'E's 'ad enough, that's all! We've seen the last of 'im!"

And the most amazing thing of all was that Crothers believed just what he said--Curley Crothers, to whom Red Sea and Persian Gulf ports were as an open book, and to whom the Arab customs and religion and reprehensible tendencies were currently supposed to be first-reader knowledge. It was he who had proved there were no harems--he who coined the Navy adage, "Search an Arab first, and sit on him, before you come to terms!"

Yet here he was, advising Byng to disregard a looted Arab's spittle! There is no accounting, ever, for the ways of shore-leave sailor-men.

"Come on, Joe," he said. "Lead 'the dawg--he can walk now--and let's see what Adra looks like."

IV.

All might have been well, and both seamen might have reached the Puncher again with dignity and grace, had they not entered Adra, past the only jail in that part of Arabia. And an Arab jail being rarer and one percent more evil than any other evil thing there is, the two of them quite naturally paused to make its closest possible acquaintance.

"Look out for vermin!" cautioned Curley, standing on tiptoe to peer in through the close-spaced iron bars.

They forgot the dog. The jail, for the moment, challenged all their waking senses, the olfactory by no means least.

"Can you see anything?" asked Byng.

Before Crothers could answer him, a snarl, then a yap, then a quick, determined growl gave warning of the terrier's interest in something else than fleas.

He had been scratching himself peacefully a moment earlier; now, like a bower anchor taking charge, he ripped the chain through Byng's hand and was off--chin, back and tail in one straight, striving line--in full chase of a pariah.

The yellow cur yapped its agony of fear; the nearest hundred and odd mangy monsters of the gutter took up the chorus; within five seconds of the start there was the Puncher's mascot racing after one abominable scavenger, and after him in just as hot pursuit there raced the whole street-cleaning force of Adra--tongues out, eyes blazing, and their mean thin barks all working overtime.

"Good-by, Scamp!" groaned Byng, estimating rapidly.

"Not yet it ain't!" said Crothers, grabbing Byng's arm and nearly tearing out the muscles.

It was a crude way of rousing Byng's latent speed, both of thought and movement, but it worked. Before Joe could swear, even, Crothers was off like the wind, with Joe after him, using the string of oaths he had meant for Crothers on the sand that gave under him and made him stumble at every other stride.

Adra turned out, as a colony of prairie dogs might from planless burrows; only these had more venom in their bite than prairie dogs and came from structural in-stead of natural, from flea-bepeppered instead of grass-grown dirt. Man, woman and child--the grown men armed, the women veiled in dirt-brown, some of them, and some (mostly the better-looking) unveiled and unashamed, the little children most-ly naked and colored with all the human hues there are--raced, yelling, through a swarm of flies in hot pursuit. Never since Shem's great-grandson gat the Arab race was there a procession like it.

Behind its mud-and-Masonry decrepit wall that guards only the seaward side, Adra straggles quite a distance desertward; and there are winding streets enough to hide an army in, provided that the army did not mind the fleas. Scamp, view-halloaing his utmost, led that most amazing hunt a quite considerable circuit before other men and dogs, arriving from a dozen different directions, set a limit to his unobstructed movement.

He knew what he was after, but they did not; they had come to see. For a mo-ment they seemed to think that Scamp was the object of the chase, and a dozen guns of a dozen different kinds and dates were aimed at him.

And then, as consciousness dawns on a man recovering from chloroform, there swept over their lethargic Eastern brains the simultaneous idea that Curley Croth-ers and Joe Byng were the real quarry; and--again like men recovering from chloro-form--they did not quite know what to do. Should they slay, there was the Puncher to be reckoned with; and the Puncher's port quick-firers could be seen command-ing Adra by any man who cared to climb the wall.

Besides, an Arab's hospitality is proverbial. He very seldom kills a visitor on sight.

On the other hand a man, and particularly a British sailor, who runs has reason, as a rule. Therefore these two men were evidently guilty. Therefore they must not escape. In five seconds the affair had changed from a spectacular amusement, with Adra's population in the role of super-heated audience, to a hunt of Crothers and Joe Byng.

Within ten seconds each of the sailors lay with his face pressed hard into the sand and at least a dozen Arabs sitting on him. Scamp--utterly forgotten now by all except the sailors--still behind the one stray pariah and ahead of all the rest but beginning to appreciate the fact that he was hunted, and beginning to feel spent-- raced on, took three sharp turns in close succession, and was gathered all unwilling in the arms of an enormous black man who snatched him from the very teeth of the following pack and dispersed them, howling, by means of well-directed kicks.

"Ah seed you yesterday, Ah did," said his deliverer in English; and, recalling principle, the terrier bit at him--only to find himself muzzled by a horny, huge fist that caressed even while it rendered impotent.

"Ah'm fond of little dogs! Ah'm English!"

Scamp understood nothing of the conversation, but with canine instinct real- ized that he was safe; and after that he was satisfied to lie and pant. With five red inches of tongue hanging out, and no sign whatever of his white-uniformed guard- ians to trouble him, a black man's arms were as good as any other place; he did not waste half a thought on Byng and Crothers.

But Byng, three turnings back, spat filthy sand out of his mouth the moment an Arab deemed it safe to leave off sitting on his head, looked wildly around for Crothers, and bellowed--

"Where's the pup?"

Crothers, spitting out sand, too, twenty yards behind where the swifter Byng had fallen, called back:

"Dunno. Whistle him!"

Byng tried to whistle, and the Arabs mistook the effort for a signal. In an in- stant both men were face-downward again, struggling for breath and clawing at the dirt. Then worse befell. The gentleman whose brown anatomy had suffered from the seamen's feet and fists just previous to their invasion of the town limped up with his eye teeth showing and his flapping cotton raiment still unmended where the dog had torn it. Any other wrath, however awful, could be nothing but the shadow of his state of mind; and since he knew the more vindictive portions of the Koran all by heart, and was quoting as he came, there was little need of words to illustrate further his attitude.

He seemed to be a person of authority. An Arab town or village is a democracy in which each free man has his say; not even a sheik can overrule the vote of a majority, and this man was no sheik. But rage and self-assertion will generally exercise a certain weight in tribal councils, and the crowd in this case was too doubtful of the facts to have any settled notions of its own.

"To the jail with them!" the new arrival almost shrieked, and about a dozen in the crowd took up the cry--

"To jail with them!"

"Infidels! Worshipers of dogs! Wine-drinkers! Eaters of pig flesh! Dogs and the sons of dogs--what mothers gave them birth? Are your hands, True-believers, fit bonds for them? To the jail! To the jail that Abdul Hamid caused his men to build for such as these!"

He stooped and looked deliberately to make sure that Crothers could not break away, then came closer and spat on him, saving half his spittle with impartial fore-thought for the struggling Byng, who looked up in time to see what was in store for him. Being spat on is even less exhilarating than it sounds or looks, and Byng waxed speechless after passing through a many-worded stage of blasphemy.

Crothers, the larger of the two and by six brawny inches more phlegmatic, bode his time in silence, so that neither of them spoke a word while they were hustled and cuffed along the street between the unbaked brick hovels. It was not until the reinforced iron door of Adra's one stone building slammed on them that either of them said a word.

Then--

"I'm not a mean man," protested Crothers.

"No?" said Byng, monosyllabic for a start.

"No," repeated Crothers, "I am not, Joe Byng. But--and I says it solemn; I says it with one 'and above my 'ed, and I'd take my affidavy on it in a court o' law, if it's the last word I ever does say an' it's my dying oath--so 'elp me Solomon and all 'is glory; I'm a Dutchman if I wouldn't like to 'ave a come-back at that Arab."

Byng lay full length on his stomach, and buried his face in his arms. He was still too full of wrath for words.

"I'd kick his mother, if I couldn't land on him," mused Crothers. And then he busied himself about conning his new bearings. It was a four-walled jail--one-doored, one-windowed, iron-barred--ill-smelling, verminous, too hot for words and too suggestive of the opposite of home, sweet home to call forth humor, even from a seaman.

"They'll come an' rescue us," moaned Byng. "They'll quarantine the pair of us for being lousy, and they'll turn the perishing salt-water hose on us. We're due for the brig for Gawd knows 'ow long; our reppitation's gone; we've been spat on by a--by a Arab, and we 'aven't hit 'im back; an' we've lost the pup. We've gone an' lost the pup! Gawd! There ain't no more good in nothin'!"

Which shows no more than that Joe Byng in his sorrow overlooked a circumstance or two. For instance, there were rings in the floor that Crothers eyed with keen curiosity. They were anchored in the solid blocks of stone.

"It's better than it might be, mate!" he argued optimistically. "They might 'ave gone and chained us up to those!"

V.

Arabia has some peculiarities, not all of them discreditable, which she does not share with any other country. There is, for instance, the kind custom that dictates the setting free of slaves when they have rendered seven years' good service.

That rule (and it is rather rule than law) tends to eliminate all class and color prejudice. Provided that a man will bow to Mecca three times daily and refrain from pork and wine, he may wear whatever skin God gave him and yet mingle with the best. He may even marry whom he will and can afford; and he may be whatever his ability, ambition, and audacity dictate.

And Hassan Ah had never been a slave, so he had even less to overcome than might have been the case. He stalked Adra socially uncondemned where once he had caught fish, groomed camels, and done other irritating jobs. His old fish-catching days had given him an intimate acquaintance with the reef, and his small-boat seamanship, born of hard pulling in the trough of beam-on-seas, was well suited to the local type of craft.

So nobody questioned his right to the title of harbor pilot. And if certain perquisites went with an otherwise barren office, that was to be expected. Who worked for nothing, or for the empty honor of it, in Arabia?

Nobody can pass the reef at night in shallow-draft lateen-sail boats without having him on board; and though he was never ostensibly paid for his services, it was understood that he performed pilot service in return for certain other opportunities that sometimes came his way. When things happened on the high sea that were not discussed in public, it was understood that Hassan Ah could have discussed them as thoroughly as anybody if he chose.

On the whole, then, and within limits that were only more or less definable, he was something of a personality. Men listened to him when he raised his voice in argument, and as one who could grant favors on occasion his words had weight.

The sun was very nearly in its zenith, beating down on dry Arabia between racing black clouds, when he had finished talking to the local council in the ramshackle old council-house, skin and mat curtained, that faced the sheik's where the main street broadened for a hundred filthy yards into a market-place. All through his argument he had held a pure-white bull terrier between his knees as proof that he knew whereof he spoke.

"Can any of you hold him without being bitten?" he demanded. And they did not seem to care to try.

"I know the ways of these men!" he asserted, drawing extravagant expressions of contentment from the dog in proof of it.

So the others in the stuffy council place gave the dog a wide berth and no privilege, but conceded him the right to hold the beast, if he wanted to, without personal defilement. And since the way of the world is that a man who has won the first of his contentions can win all the rest with half the ease, he persuaded them with a hurricane of black man's rhetoric to do what Arabs consider almost wicked.

Unbelievers who are prisoners should die, beyond all question.

"As the dregs of oil shall the fruit of the tree of Al Zakkum boil in the bellies of the damned!" the sheik quoted. "They should be hurried, therefore, to the punishment that waits!"

But Hassen Ah outargued him.

"Then they will land men from the ship, who will search our houses," he asserted. "Is there a majority in the council who would like to be searched by unbelievers?"

"Then bind them, and take them to their ship, and tell a tale of much drunkenness and wrong-doing. Ask an indemnity, and show the proofs, which will be easy to arrange."

"They, too, will tell their tale!" said Hassan Ah in perfect Arabic.

Unlike the more enlightened peoples of the West, Arabs do not encourage the mutilation of their mother-tongue; they teach it as carefully as they talk it, and this negro spoke like an Arab of the blood.

"There are certain damages they have received--some bruises on the face and tears in the clothing that does not belong to them but their government," he continued. "They would lay all the blame on us, and would breathe in the face of an appointed man, in proof that they were not drunk. And who could get other drink than coffee or water here? And who would believe the rest of our story, having found that part to be a lie? There would be a landing, and a search for proof, and much unpleasantness. Besides--"

If he had intended to add further arguments, the sheik saw fit to nip them in the bud; for there were some men in the council-room who did not know as much as Hassan Ah. Any free man may speak in council in Arabia.

"What is thy way, then?" he asked.

The woolly headed pilot laughed aloud, taking care to make it evident that he was laughing at the prisoners; to laugh at a sheik or a sheik's bewilderment would be too dangerous.

"I would send them to the ship well satisfied," he answered.

"With money?" asked the sheik.

"With whose money?" asked Hassan Ah.

"With thine?" shot back the sheik.

"In the name of Allah, no!"

The black man laughed again, and rose to lean against the wall behind him, gathering the dog up in his arms.

"If it is the order of the council," he asserted, "I will send them back satisfied, with a tale to tell that will bring about no landing. Also, I will give the council much amusement."

"But will other sailors land afterward, seeking similar amusement?" asked the sheik.

"No! There will be an order that none land!"

The sheik took a vote on it. Heads nodded solemnly all around the room as his eyes sought each half-veiled face in turn. His own face was almost altogether shielded by the brown linen head-dress, for men of his race like to reach a judgment unobserved. They were all nods that answered him, and he saw fit to keep his own opinion to himself.

"Thou seest? These others are all with thee. Have it thine own way, Hassan Ah. Unlock thou the riddle and on thy head be the answer! Thou hast our leave to go."

So Hassan Ah set out undaunted for the jail, with a terrier in tow behind him and a huge smile on his broad-beamed face. And behind him a murmur rose that:

"It was well. He brought the warship in, instead of leaving it outside or--as any wise man would have done--wrecking it on the outer reef, where it could have been plundered at discretion. Let him send the sailors back again and bear the consequences!"

And within a minute of the pilot's arrival at the window of the jail (through which he peered for two minutes before speaking) the whole of Adra's council, followed by the city's children in a noisy horde, proceeded in a cluster after him and took up position, each as he saw fit, at different vantage points.

Then Hassan Ah shook a loose bar of the window until it rattled, and so called attention to himself. Crothers and Joe Byng raced for the window neck and neck, and reached it simultaneously.

"You two men want you-ah dog?" asked Hassan Ah, and the chained dog leaped up at the window as both men swore at once.

"You pass him in here! Come on, you black-faced cornerman! There'll be a cutter's crew ashore pretty soon to rescue us, and if you don't hand that dog over before they get here you'll get the worst whipping you ever had in all your black life!"

"They'll feed you to the dog when they're through with you!" vowed Byng.

"Come on, MacHassan!" ordered Crothers. "Get the key and pass the dog in. That'll settle your account. T hen you's free. You needn't be 'fraid."

"Ah'm English," said the pilot of the day before, with an enormous grin that showed a pound or two of yellow ivory. "Ah'm not afraid; Ah can lick you; Ah can fight same as you men. Ah'm English!"

"Fight? You Irish Chink! Which of us two do you want to fight?" asked the outraged Byng. "Come on in here! I'll fight you!"

But to Byng's amazement Hassan Ah pointed to Crothers, who was heavier by forty pounds or more and taller by at least half a head.

"Ah choose him!" he grinned; and Curley Crothers clenched both fists in absolute but quite unterrified amazement.

"Come on, then," he answered. "Open the door." Then, as an afterthought--"I'll fight you for the dog."

"Ah don't want to kill that little man," said Hassan Ah. "But Ah'll give you the dog, win or lose, if you'll fight me. You fight fair? You fight English?"

"Well, I'm damned!" said Crothers. "I fight Queensberry rules. That suit you?"

"Oh-ah, yes! Keensby rules, that's it. All right-o!"

Hassan Ah produced his key and turned it in the creaking lock. He was stripping himself even before the two sailors were out in the sun, and by the time that Crothers and Joe Byng had realized that there was an audience of something like a thousand, including children, he was standing posed like a gladiator, with the straight-down tropic sun streaming off his ebony hide. As Crothers, not quite sure even yet that the whole affair was not a joke, began to doff his blouse it dawned on him that if the thing were true it would not be a picnic.

"Do you mean this?" he asked.

"Ah shohly do. Are you afraid o' me?"

That, of course, settled matters. The thing was not a joke, and Englishman or nigger--black, green, white, or gray--the plot must be licked forthwith and in accordance with the rules.

Crothers spat into his hands, while Joe Byng folded up his blouse and knelt on it. He eyed his antagonist for at least a minute, summing him up and ignoring none of the woolly-headed one's physical advantages in weight and strength, in height and reach, in being used to the climate and the glare, the odds were all with Hassan Ah. Then he sized up the moral odds; and though a biased audience might be at first supposed to weigh against him too, the sight of all those Arabs waiting to see him beaten roused his fighting dander.

"Do you represent the bloke that spat on us two men?" asked Crothers.

"Ah represent maself! Ah'm English! Ah fight English, and Ah'll prove it!"

"Aw, wade into him!" advised Joe Byng. "London Prize Rules--no time called until a man's down. Go on, Curley--lead!"

"Do you agree?" asked Crothers.

"Suttainly!" The black man seemed disposed to agree to anything so long as he could get what he was after.

"Then here goes!" said Crothers; and he stepped in and led for the honor of the British Navy.

Oh! It was a fight! Crothers knew what he was up against the instant that his left fist slid along an ebony forearm and his nose collided with what seemed like an iron club. Steamship pilot this man might not be, but fighting man he very surely was. He hit straight and guarded high. He was no untutored savage. He had the hardest to acquire of all the Christian arts at his fingers' (or rather his fists') ends, and the heavyweight champion of Gosport took a double reef in his fighting tactics while he sparred for time in which to recover from the shock of that first blow. The claret was streaming down his face and he was dizzy.

"Oh, wade into him, mate!" urged Joe.

It is always easier to see what should be done than to do it. The sand was not slipping and giving under Joe Byng's feet, nor were his fists and wrists aching from contact with hard ebony. To him the thing seemed easy, and he was as anxious to get into the fight himself as was the terrier that strained at his chain. But Crothers, who had won a hundred fights at least in cleaner climes, fought canny and tried to make the black man tire himself with wasted effort.

And the Arabs sat in silence, like a row of vultures waiting for the end. Even the little children held their clamor and subsided into motionless calm. There was not a movement along the roofs or the wall, or in the rings of those who squatted. Arabia was spellbound, watching something she had never seen before and trying to puzzle out the wherefore of it. There were knives and guns available, yet these men fought without weapons. The white contender had a friend, but the friend did not join in. Why? Had Allah struck all three men mad? They sat still to see the end, having no doubt but that it would prove to be a judgment.

Curley Crothers was the first to close a round. He put an end to round one at the end of three minutes by missing with a heavy right swing, ducking to avoid terrific punishment, slipping in the yielding sand and falling.

"Back with you!" yelled Joe Byng, afraid that the pilot would take liberties and ready to jump in and stop him if need be. But he wasted his excitement.

"Ah told you Ah'm English!" said the pilot, stepping back and letting Crothers find his corner.

Curley was glad enough of a rest on Joe Byng's knee, and too intent on getting back his wind to listen over carefully to Joe's advice. When Joe called "Time" he stepped in readily again; and this time it was Hassan Ah who suffered from surprise.

Curley had been getting out of practise on board ship; he had needed waking up, and round one had done it for him. Round two and the six that followed it were exhibitions of the "noble art" that men in any of the larger cities of the world would have paid out a fortune to have seen.

There was racial prejudice, and service pride, as well as the usual decent man's desire to win to make a real mill of what might have been nothing out of ordinary; and there were the quite considerable odds against him that--after the first repulse--usually make men like Crothers do their utmost.

Even the Arabs lost their stoicism while round two was under way. Byng yelled, and the terrier yelped, but the Arabs only shifted their position. That, though, was proof enough of their excitement; they actually sighed in unison when Hassan Ah thrust his ungainly chin in the way of a crushing right-hand smash, and laid his broad back on the sand.

After that it was slug-and-come-again with both of them, each getting wilder as round succeeded round, but neither man obtaining much advantage. Twice it was Crothers who went down; then he discovered a soft spot in Hassan's ribs, and after that he kept the black man busy on the desperate defensive.

There was no doubt of the end, then, barring accidents. Even Hassan Ah could not have doubted it; but he did his black man's uttermost to put it off, and he fought as gamely as anybody ever fought since prize-ring rules were drafted. He did not foul, or take undue advantage once.

It was a plain, right-handed, battering-ram punch to the neck that ended things, and Hassan Ah lay coughing on the sand with bulging eyes while Joe Byng tended Curley's hurts.

"Hasn't the nigger got any pals?" asked Crothers; and then it occurred to Byng that the most hurt man was surely most in need of mending. Both he and Crothers bent over him, then, and they soon had him on his feet again.

"Ah told you Ah'm English!" were the first words he succeeded in spluttering through swollen lips.

"Now, what d'you mean by that exactly?" asked Joe Byng, his attitude toward him almost entirely changed. A man who loses gamely is entitled to respect if not to friendship.

Hassan Ah searched in the tattered shirt that he had laid aside, and pulled out a folded piece of paper after a lot of fumbling. He opened it gingerly, and holding one corner of it displayed the rest with evident intention not to allow it out of his grasp.

"That says Ah'm English!" he explained.

"Oh!" said Crothers, rubbing an injured eye in order to see it better. "Can you read, you black heathen?"

"No," said the pilot. "That says Ah'm English, but Ah can't read!"

"Well, MacHassan," said Curley Crothers, reading the document a second time. "Black or white, you fight like a gentleman. I'm proud to have licked you. Good-by, and good luck! Here's my hand!"

They shook hands, and the seamen started shoreward with the terrier in tow.

"Did you read the paper?" asked Crothers. "It was dated Aden--non-coms' mess of some regiment or other. 'This is to certify that this regiment taught Hassan Ah to use his fists, and that he has since licked every single mother's son of us!' Pity I didn't see that first, eh?"

"Oh, I dunno," said Joe Byng, who had not had to do the fighting. "You licked the savage, anyway."

Hassan Ah was right. There was no more shore leave granted. Crothers and Joe Byng were punished with extra duty and "confined to ship" for coming back with the marks of fighting on them; and the Puncher gave no further signs of life until, some three I days later, her long-suffering engines turned again and she departed through the channel that had brought her in.

Then the sheik and three others and a certain Hassan Ah went down at midnight to the jail and lifted with the aid of long poles passed through the rings in them the largest floor stones of that vermin-infested building. But the vermin did not trouble them. What they were after and what they lifted out was the cases of guns and cartridges the Puncher had contrived to miss.

www.bookjungle.com *email: sales@bookjungle.com fax: 630-214-0564 mail: Book Jungle PO Box 2226 Champaign, IL 61825*

The Codes Of Hammurabi And Moses
W. W. Davies

QTY

The discovery of the Hammurabi Code is one of the greatest achievements of archaeology, and is of paramount interest, not only to the student of the Bible, but also to all those interested in ancient history...

Religion **ISBN:** *1-59462-338-4*   **Pages:132**
MSRP $12.95

The Theory of Moral Sentiments
Adam Smith

QTY

This work from 1749. contains original theories of conscience amd moral judgment and it is the foundation for systemof morals.

Philosophy **ISBN:** *1-59462-777-0*   **Pages:536**
MSRP $19.95

Jessica's First Prayer
Hesba Stretton

QTY

In a screened and secluded corner of one of the many railway-bridges which span the streets of London there could be seen a few years ago, from five o'clock every morning until half past eight, a tidily set-out coffee-stall, consisting of a trestle and board, upon which stood two large tin cans, with a small fire of charcoal burning under each so as to keep the coffee boiling during the early hours of the morning when the work-people were thronging into the city on their way to their daily toil...

Pages:84

Childrens **ISBN:** *1-59462-373-2*   **MSRP $9.95**

My Life and Work
Henry Ford

QTY

Henry Ford revolutionized the world with his implementation of mass production for the Model T automobile. Gain valuable business insight into his life and work with his own auto-biography... "We have only started on our development of our country we have not as yet, with all our talk of wonderful progress, done more than scratch the surface. The progress has been wonderful enough but..."

Pages:300

Biographies/ **ISBN:** *1-59462-198-5*   **MSRP $21.95**

The Art of Cross-Examination
Francis Wellman

QTY

I presume it is the experience of every author, after his first book is published upon an important subject, to be almost overwhelmed with a wealth of ideas and illustrations which could readily have been included in his book, and which to his own mind, at least, seem to make a second edition inevitable. Such certainly was the case with me; and when the first edition had reached its sixth impression in five months, I rejoiced to learn that it seemed to my publishers that the book had met with a sufficiently favorable reception to justify a second and considerably enlarged edition. ..

Pages:412

Reference   **ISBN:** *1-59462-647-2*   *MSRP $19.95*

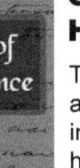

On the Duty of Civil Disobedience
Henry David Thoreau

QTY

Thoreau wrote his famous essay, On the Duty of Civil Disobedience, as a protest against an unjust but popular war and the immoral but popular institution of slave-owning. He did more than write—he declined to pay his taxes, and was hauled off to gaol in consequence. Who can say how much this refusal of his hastened the end of the war and of slavery ?

Law   **ISBN:** *1-59462-747-9*   **Pages:48**

MSRP $7.45

Dream Psychology Psychoanalysis for Beginners
Sigmund Freud

QTY

Sigmund Freud, born Sigismund Schlomo Freud (May 6, 1856 - September 23, 1939), was a Jewish-Austrian neurologist and psychiatrist who co-founded the psychoanalytic school of psychology. Freud is best known for his theories of the unconscious mind, especially involving the mechanism of repression; his redefinition of sexual desire as mobile and directed towards a wide variety of objects; and his therapeutic techniques, especially his understanding of transference in the therapeutic relationship and the presumed value of dreams as sources of insight into unconscious desires.

Pages:196

Psychology   **ISBN:** *1-59462-905-6*   *MSRP $15.45*

The Miracle of Right Thought
Orison Swett Marden

QTY

Believe with all of your heart that you will do what you were made to do. When the mind has once formed the habit of holding cheerful, happy, prosperous pictures, it will not be easy to form the opposite habit. It does not matter how improbable or how far away this realization may see, or how dark the prospects may be, if we visualize them as best we can, as vividly as possible, hold tenaciously to them and vigorously struggle to attain them, they will gradually become actualized, realized in the life. But a desire, a longing without endeavor, a yearning abandoned or held indifferently will vanish without realization.

Pages:360

Self Help   **ISBN:** *1-59462-644-8*   *MSRP $25.45*

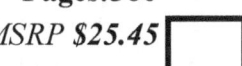

www.bookjungle.com *email: sales@bookjungle.com fax: 630-214-0564 mail: Book Jungle PO Box 2226 Champaign, IL 61825*

QTY

The Rosicrucian Cosmo-Conception Mystic Christianity *by Max Heindel*   ISBN: *1-59462-188-8*   **$38.95**
The Rosicrucian Cosmo-conception is not dogmatic, neither does it appeal to any other authority than the reason of the student. It is: not controversial, but is: sent forth in the, hope that it may help to clear...   New Age/Religion Pages 646

Abandonment To Divine Providence *by Jean-Pierre de Caussade*   ISBN: *1-59462-228-0*   **$25.95**
"The Rev. Jean Pierre de Caussade was one of the most remarkable spiritual writers of the Society of Jesus in France in the 18th Century. His death took place at Toulouse in 1751. His works have gone through many editions and have been republished...   Inspirational/Religion Pages 400

Mental Chemistry *by Charles Haanel*   ISBN: *1-59462-192-6*   **$23.95**
Mental Chemistry allows the change of material conditions by combining and appropriately utilizing the power of the mind. Much like applied chemistry creates something new and unique out of careful combinations of chemicals the mastery of mental chemistry...   New Age Pages 354

The Letters of Robert Browning and Elizabeth Barret Barrett 1845-1846 vol II   ISBN: *1-59462-193-4*   **$35.95**
by Robert Browning and Elizabeth Barrett   Biographies Pages 596

Gleanings In Genesis (volume I) *by Arthur W. Pink*   ISBN: *1-59462-130-6*   **$27.45**
Appropriately has Genesis been termed "the seed plot of the Bible" for in it we have, in germ form, almost all of the great doctrines which are afterwards fully developed in the books of Scripture which follow...   Religion/Inspirational Pages 420

The Master Key *by L. W. de Laurence*   ISBN: *1-59462-001-6*   **$30.95**
In no branch of human knowledge has there been a more lively increase of the spirit of research during the past few years than in the study of Psychology, Concentration and Mental Discipline. The requests for authentic lessons in Thought Control, Mental Discipline and...   New Age/Business Pages 422

The Lesser Key Of Solomon Goetia *by L. W. de Laurence*   ISBN: *1-59462-092-X*   **$9.95**
This translation of the first book of the "Lernegton" which is now for the first time made accessible to students of Talismanic Magic was done, after careful collation and edition, from numerous Ancient Manuscripts in Hebrew, Latin, and French...   New Age/Occult Pages 92

Rubaiyat Of Omar Khayyam *by Edward Fitzgerald*   ISBN:*1-59462-332-5*   **$13.95**
Edward Fitzgerald, whom the world has already learned, in spite of his own efforts to remain within the shadow of anonymity, to look upon as one of the rarest poets of the century, was born at Bredfield, in Suffolk, on the 31st of March, 1809. He was the third son of John Purcell...   Music Pages 172

Ancient Law *by Henry Maine*   ISBN: *1-59462-128-4*   **$29.95**
The chief object of the following pages is to indicate some of the earliest ideas of mankind, as they are reflected in Ancient Law, and to point out the relation of those ideas to modern thought.   Religion/History Pages 452

Far-Away Stories *by William J. Locke*   ISBN: *1-59462-129-2*   **$19.45**
"Good wine needs no bush, but a collection of mixed vintages does. And this book is just such a collection. Some of the stories I do not want to remain buried for ever in the museum files of dead magazine-numbers an author's not unpardonable vanity..."   Fiction Pages 272

Life of David Crockett *by David Crockett*   ISBN: *1-59462-250-7*   **$27.45**
"Colonel David Crockett was one of the most remarkable men of the times in which he lived. Born in humble life, but gifted with a strong will, an indomitable courage, and unremitting perseverance...   Biographies/New Age Pages 424

Lip-Reading *by Edward Nitchie*   ISBN: *1-59462-206-X*   **$25.95**
Edward B. Nitchie, founder of the New York School for the Hard of Hearing, now the Nitchie School of Lip-Reading, Inc, wrote "LIP-READING Principles and Practice". The development and perfecting of this meritorious work on lip-reading was an undertaking...   How-to Pages 400

A Handbook of Suggestive Therapeutics, Applied Hypnotism, Psychic Science   ISBN: *1-59462-214-0*   **$24.95**
by Henry Munro   Health/New Age/Health/Self-help Pages 376

A Doll's House: and Two Other Plays *by Henrik Ibsen*   ISBN: *1-59462-112-8*   **$19.95**
Henrik Ibsen created this classic when in revolutionary 1848 Rome. Introducing some striking concepts in playwriting for the realist genre, this play has been studied the world over.   Fiction/Classics/Plays 308

The Light of Asia *by sir Edwin Arnold*   ISBN: *1-59462-204-3*   **$13.95**
In this poetic masterpiece, Edwin Arnold describes the life and teachings of Buddha. The man who was to become known as Buddha to the world was born as Prince Gautama of India but he rejected the worldly riches and abandoned the reigns of power when...   Religion/History/Biographies Pages 170

The Complete Works of Guy de Maupassant *by Guy de Maupassant*   ISBN: *1-59462-157-8*   **$16.95**
"For days and days, nights and nights, I had dreamed of that first kiss which was to consecrate our engagement, and I knew not on what spot I should put my lips..."   Fiction/Classics Pages 240

The Art of Cross-Examination *by Francis L. Wellman*   ISBN: *1-59462-309-0*   **$26.95**
Written by a renowned trial lawyer, Wellman imparts his experience and uses case studies to explain how to use psychology to extract desired information through questioning.   How-to/Science/Reference Pages 408

Answered or Unanswered? *by Louisa Vaughan*   ISBN: *1-59462-248-5*   **$10.95**
Miracles of Faith in China   Religion Pages 112

The Edinburgh Lectures on Mental Science (1909) *by Thomas*   ISBN: *1-59462-008-3*   **$11.95**
This book contains the substance of a course of lectures recently given by the writer in the Queen Street Hall, Edinburgh. Its purpose is to indicate the Natural Principles governing the relation between Mental Action and Material Conditions...   New Age/Psychology Pages 148

Ayesha *by H. Rider Haggard*   ISBN: *1-59462-301-5*   **$24.95**
Verily and indeed it is the unexpected that happens! Probably if there was one person upon the earth from whom the Editor of this, and of a certain previous history, did not expect to hear again...   Classics Pages 380

Ayala's Angel *by Anthony Trollope*   ISBN: *1-59462-352-X*   **$29.95**
The two girls were both pretty, but Lucy who was twenty-one who supposed to be simple and comparatively unattractive, whereas Ayala was credited, as her Bombwhat romantic name might show, with poetic charm and a taste for romance. Ayala when her father died was nineteen...   Fiction Pages 484

The American Commonwealth *by James Bryce*   ISBN: *1-59462-286-8*   **$34.45**
An interpretation of American democratic political theory. It examines political mechanics and society from the perspective of Scotsman James Bryce   Politics Pages 572

Stories of the Pilgrims *by Margaret P. Pumphrey*   ISBN: *1-59462-116-0*   **$17.95**
This book explores pilgrims religious oppression in England as well as their escape to Holland and eventual crossing to America on the Mayflower, and their early days in New England...   History Pages 268

QTY

The Fasting Cure *by Sinclair Upton*　　　　　　　　ISBN: *1-59462-222-1*　**$13.95**
In the Cosmopolitan Magazine for May, 1910, and in the Contemporary Review (London) for April, 1910, I published an article dealing with my experiences in fasting. I have written a great many magazine articles, but never one which attracted so much attention... New Age/Self Help/Health Pages 164

Hebrew Astrology *by Sepharial*　　　　　　　　　ISBN: *1-59462-308-2*　**$13.45**
In these days of advanced thinking it is a matter of common observation that we have left many of the old landmarks behind and that we are now pressing forward to greater heights and to a wider horizon than that which represented the mind-content of our progenitors... Astrology Pages 144

Thought Vibration or The Law of Attraction in the Thought World　　ISBN: *1-59462-127-6*　**$12.95**

by William Walker Atkinson　　　　　　　　　　　　Psychology/Religion Pages 144

Optimism *by Helen Keller*　　　　　　　　　　ISBN: *1-59462-108-X*　**$15.95**
Helen Keller was blind, deaf, and mute since 19 months old, yet famously learned how to overcome these handicaps, communicate with the world, and spread her lectures promoting optimism. An inspiring read for everyone... Biographies/Inspirational Pages 84

Sara Crewe *by Frances Burnett*　　　　　　　　ISBN: *1-59462-360-0*　**$9.45**
In the first place, Miss Minchin lived in London. Her home was a large, dull, tall one, in a large, dull square, where all the houses were alike, and all the sparrows were alike, and where all the door-knockers made the same heavy sound... Childrens/Classic Pages 88

The Autobiography of Benjamin Franklin *by Benjamin Franklin*　　ISBN: *1-59462-135-7*　**$24.95**
The Autobiography of Benjamin Franklin has probably been more extensively read than any other American historical work, and no other book of its kind has had such ups and downs of fortune. Franklin lived for many years in England, where he was agent... Biographies/History Pages 332

Name	
Email	
Telephone	
Address	
City, State ZIP	

☐ **Credit Card**　　　　　☐ **Check / Money Order**

Credit Card Number	
Expiration Date	
Signature	

Please Mail to:　Book Jungle
PO Box 2226
Champaign, IL 61825
or Fax to:　　　630-214-0564

ORDERING INFORMATION

web*: www.bookjungle.com*
email*: sales@bookjungle.com*
fax*: 630-214-0564*
mail*: Book Jungle PO Box 2226 Champaign, IL 61825*
or PayPal *to sales@bookjungle.com*

Please contact us for bulk discounts

DIRECT-ORDER TERMS

**20% Discount if You Order
Two or More Books**
Free Domestic Shipping!
Accepted: Master Card, Visa,
Discover, American Express